STRANGER AND STRAN

Georgiana knew nothing of the man she found on the brink of death from a bullet wound. And she knew even less the more she saw of him.

Was he a traveling drawing master, as his pens and brushes, sketchpad, and portable easel suggested? Or was he a blackguard on the run from the law, as so many other clues indicated?

Was he of humble birth, as he declared? Or of the bluest of blood, as his arrogance proclaimed?

And above all, was he a man she could trust with her heart—this stranger who toyed with the truth and could so easily make her a plaything . . . ?

Carol Proctor was born and raised in Harlingen, Texas. She attended the College of William and Mary in Virginia, where she received her B.A. in English with a minor in European History. She obtained her Master's degree in Scriptwriting from the University of Texas in Austin. After working in broadcasting in various parts of Texas, she married and now has a young son. Her favorite pastimes include gardening, fishing, and music.

THE
DRAWING MASTER'S
DILEMMA

by Carol Proctor

A SIGNET BOOK

SIGNET
Published by the Penguin Group
Penguin Books USA Inc., 375 Hudson Street,
New York, New York, 10014, U.S.A.
Penguin Books Ltd, 27 Wrights Lane, London W8 5TZ, England
Penguin Books Australia Ltd, Ringwood, Victoria, Australia
Penguin Books Canada Ltd, 2801 John Street,
Markham, Ontario, Canada L3R 1B4
Penguin Books (N.Z.) Ltd, 182-190 Wairau Road,
Auckland 10, New Zealand

Penguin Books Ltd, Registered Offices:
Harmondsworth, Middlesex, England

First published by Signet, an imprint of Penguin Books USA Inc.

First Printing, July, 1990

10 9 8 7 6 5 4 3 2 1

BOOKS ARE AVAILABLE AT QUANTITY DISCOUNTS WHEN USED TO PROMOTE
PRODUCTS OR SERVICES. FOR INFORMATION PLEASE WRITE TO PREMIUM
MARKETING DIVISION, PENGUIN BOOKS USA INC., 375 HUDSON STREET.
NEW YORK. NEW YORK 10014.

To Laura Parker
For advice, encouragement, and inspiration

Deo Optimo Maximo

AUTHOR'S NOTE

Georgiana's discovery is based on an actual find in Oxfordshire during this period. The jawbone, thought at the time to be mammalian, actually took some years to be identified correctly since no one in England at this point had ever heard of a dinosaur.

1

"*Dash* it, Aubrey, but you've become quite dull." The young man glanced over at his companion as he spoke, but not with any real expectation of receiving a reply. Since none was forthcoming, he merely heaved a little sigh and slumped deeper into the damask-covered wing chair. His Hessian-booted leg, draped so casually over the chair arm, ceased its idle clockwise rotations and then leisurely began to circle in the opposite direction. He stared glumly about him at the debris that cluttered the darkened room. Papers were flung on the floor randomly, the furniture had been tipped about so as to destroy any semblance of order, and a half-eaten dinner from the day before reposed unappetisingly on the table beside him. His lip curled in disgust. Indeed, it was hard to imagine what could have persuaded a young gentleman, attentive to fashion and fastidious in his dress, to remain indoors in such unwholesome surroundings on a beautiful spring day. He might have been riding in the park instead, doing his best to cause a flutter among a few female hearts or passing the afternoon exchanging pleasantries and wine with acquaintances at his club. He might have used the day to investigate the latest horses to arrive at Tattersall's or driven out of town to see a mill. He even might have spent the time more profitably with his tailor, bootmaker, glovemaker, or hatter. In short, there were a thousand things he might have and would rather have been doing.

Part of the answer to this riddle lay in the patiently resigned expression on his stolid, handsome face. It was apparent that William Darley was one of those persons who might be said to have been born into middle age. He was clearly a person capable of putting duty before personal considerations. A less obvious but equally powerful influence upon him was the sincere affection he felt for the gangly, odd-looking individual in the other corner of the room.

There could be no greater contrast than that between these two men. Whereas Darley was attired in a scrupulously correct tailcoat of dark-blue superfine, impeccable cravat, and tasteful biscuit-colored pantaloons, the other wore simple trousers and a shirt open at the throat. Topped by an ancient dressing gown, this ensemble was daubed liberally with paint, creating an effect eccentric in the extreme. In like manner, there was little in either their physiques or physiognomies that suggested the relationship between the two. Darley was as stockily built as his cousin was lanky. His handsome, regular features were not echoed in his cousin's face, which was thin and mobile, with a prominent, beaked nose. In contrast to Darley's carefully arranged curls of burnished gold, a muddy blond shock of hair fell carelessly across the other's forehead. The only features that saved him from plainness were the arresting brown eyes. They sparkled with humor, and the charm they habitually exuded had been enough to make many a female forget that their possessor was not a handsome man. Of late, that deviltry had been missing from those eyes, and it was this fact that had brought his cousin to him with an ill-disguised concern.

Lord Aubrey Tarrant, the Viscount Herne, made one last stroke upon the canvas with his brush and stepped back with a little sigh. After a moment's pause, he turned and seemed to notice his visitor for the first time.

"William, good Lord! How long have you been here?" he inquired, reaching for a rag and wiping his hands on it.

Darley straightened up in the chair painfully. "Only a few hours, I should imagine."

The viscount glanced at the clock on the mantelpiece. "What, it is afternoon already?" He stripped off his dressing gown and replaced it with a slightly more respectable one. "I'll ring for some tea, or perhaps sherry might be better . . ." He glanced about him, noting the disarray as if for the first time. "I'll have it brought to the library."

As the viscount was making his wishes known to a servant, Darley rose from his chair and walked over to examine the painting. Unconsciously, he made a wry face.

"Do you dislike it?" the viscount asked, with mock innocence.

Darley made a hapless gesture. "Why must you paint it like that, so gray and dismal?" he asked. "The sun is out; it's a beautiful day."

A twinkle shone for a moment in the viscount's eye. "Well, I suppose I must be thankful that you're not Hazlitt," he remarked. He linked his arm through his cousin's and led him to the library. "But tell me, William, what are you doing here? Not that I'm not delighted to see you, of course, but I should have thought you'd be at the club this afternoon or—"

"Actually, I thought that I might persuade you to give up this hermitlike existence and come down to the club with me," said Darley, settling down into his chair. "You know that none of us has seen you for weeks."

"That's not quite fair," said the viscount reproachfully as he seated himself. "You know I only returned from Dorset last week."

"It was three weeks ago," William said firmly.

The viscount looked puzzled. "Could it have been?"

Their debate was interrupted by the arrival of a tray containing a roast joint, a cold meat pie, cheese, and a loaf of bread.

The viscount looked suspiciously at his servant. "I thought all I asked for was sherry."

"Yes, my lord," replied the footman with equanimity as he set the tray down. "But Mrs. Johnson thought as how you hadn't eaten since last night, you might be hungry."

"Well," said the viscount grudgingly, "I suppose I am—a bit."

"Very good, my lord," said the footman, bowing impassively. "Is there anything else that you require?"

The viscount gave a quick shake of the head, and the footman prepared to exit, pausing for a moment at the door. "By the way, my lord—"

"Yes?"

"Mrs. Johnson wished me to inform you that she will have a currant tart ready presently, if you should wish it."

"Very good."

The viscount looked up to see blue eyes fixed candidly upon

him. He flushed slightly. "You know it's hard to pay attention to meals when I am painting."

William frowned, but made no reply. The viscount gestured at the tray and for a moment conversation was suspended as the two young men attacked the food.

Darley was not a man to be deterred from his purpose for long, however. As soon as he had blunted the edge of his appetite, he put his fork down and regarded the viscount with a serious expression.

"Actually, Aubrey, I *had* hoped to persuade you to accompany me to the club today."

The viscount, busy with his dinner, waved a careless hand.

Darley felt free to continue. "Your absence has been noted. Why, Fitzwilliam was asking me just yesterday what had become of you. You know he still loves to talk about the bet he had with you." A little smile lit Darley's face. "You remember, when you bribed the farmer to trade places with you . . ." Darley was beginning to chuckle at the memory. "And you disguised yourself with a straw hat, and a smock . . ." Darley could hardly contain himself. "And you drove that herd of pigs through Hyde Park at five o'clock."

Darley burst into laughter at the memory.

His companion made no comment, merely helping himself to another serving of the pie.

"And when you stopped Lord Petersham . . ." Darley was laughing so hard he could scarcely get the words out. "And asked if he could tell you the way to Smithfield Market . . ." Darley roared with laughter.

The viscount remained preoccupied with his pie.

Darley took out a handkerchief and wiped his brow. "Lord, but the Brown Dandy was near apoplexy," he gasped between chuckles. "I've never seen anyone so furious." Here Darley went off into gales of laughter again, though his cousin remained unresponsive.

Darley recovered himself at last. "It took them the better part of an hour to unsnarl all the carriages. I don't know how you escaped with your life, or how you kept anyone from finding out who you were." Darley had to chuckle again to himself. "Petersham still thinks it was a farmer."

The viscount gave the merest shadow of a smile. "And I delivered the pigs to market on time, just as I told the farmer I would."

"I remember!" Darley broke into laughter again at the thought. He looked up at his companion. "Fitzwilliam said he wished to see you. He said it's been too long since you've set London by the ears with one of your larks."

The viscount's expression hardened suddenly. "Larks are for schoolboys."

"You didn't seem to think so when you came back from Belgium," pointed out Darley, unruffled.

Aubrey raised his eyebrows and heaved a little sigh. "That was . . . different." He glanced up to see a look of cool inquiry upon his cousin's face, and he flushed. "I can't explain it. One was just so glad to be alive and to know that all that terrible agony was over."

William shook his head in disagreement. "I think it was Miss Fothergill who has made this difference." He held up a hand to stay the viscount's angry protest. "Even though you don't care to admit it."

Aubrey half-rose from his chair. His face was red with anger. "Cressida means nothing to me now, not that she ever did."

"Surely you can't deny—" began Darley mildly.

"I can't deny that I deceived myself, if that is what you mean," Aubrey interrupted hotly. "I can't deny that I was tired of suffering and death and ready to believe the first pretty girl who swore that she'd conceived an undying affection for me." He laughed with uncharacteristic bitterness. "In fact, you might say that I'm grateful to her; I certainly learned an invaluable lesson from her."

His cousin looked at him dispassionately. "If she affected you so little, why is it that you fly into a rage when I simply mention her name?"

The viscount laughed again, without amusement. "My so-called rage is directed at myself, for being such a naïve fool." He took a step toward the window, his eyes assuming a far-away expression. "I forgot the stakes a female plays for in marriage. The object of the game is simply to snare the biggest prize that comes along. A viscount is rather a tawdry trophy compared to a duke. I was unable to see that at the time."

Darley raised his eyebrows skeptically and the viscount turned and intercepted his gaze.

"She has her duke, and she's welcome to him." He sneered slightly. "She's paying the price for him now." He gave his cousin an ironic smile. "After all, wouldn't you say that she's done me a tremendous favor?"

"Yes, I would," Darley said meaningfully. "But, Aubrey, surely you can't believe that all—"

The viscount heaved a weary sigh. "You choose the wrong time to press your case, coz. You forget that I recently spent three dreary weeks in Dorset, interviewing my mother's latest candidate for the position of viscountess."

"Aubrey . . ." began Darley reproachfully.

A faint gleam of humor shone in his cousin's eye. "It's all very well for you to look like that. You haven't had to spend days upon days of boredom with some stammering miss. Let's see—this latest one spent the entire time discussing her lap dog. What was its name? Something entirely revolting."

"She sounds shy and charming to me," William said defensively.

The viscount shook his head. "Ah, but then you were not there to see the ambitious gleam in her eyes."

"Your mother has your best interests at heart," William protested.

"My mother, as always, has her own convenience at heart. She would love to see me safely settled, the responsible landowner." Aubrey looked at William with a trace of regret. "It's the sort of role you would fill to perfection. What a pity it is that I was born the viscount and not you."

"Aubrey," exclaimed Darley, deeply shocked. "I wish you would not say such things."

A smile curled his cousin's lips. "Even if they happen to be true?" He shook his head and put up a hand. "Never mind. I will not argue with you about something neither of us can change." He uttered a short bark of laughter as he observed the lingering dismay on his cousin's face. "Come, come, I acquit you of having any ambitions in that direction."

Darley's face relaxed while the viscount observed him with satisfaction. William's ability to be utterly content with his situation in life was one of the traits his cousin had always envied.

"Now the one before that," the viscount said, beginning on a diversionary track. "Let me recall . . . Oh yes, she was a trifle—how should I put it?—a trifle embonpoint, and she had a nervous giggle that still rings painfully in my—"

He was interrupted by the arrival of a footman bearing a silver salver.

"A letter for you, my lord."

Aubrey took the letter from the footman, then sent him on his way with a wave of his hand.

William seized this opportunity to reintroduce the topic he wished to discuss. "It's all very well to try to distract me, Aubrey, but I came here with the express purpose of seeing that you dine with me at the club tonight and I do not intend—"

"Blast!" Aubrey had opened the letter, and as he perused the contents, his face drew into a ferocious scowl.

"My dear fellow, whatever is the matter?"

Aubrey held the letter open so that William was able to recognize the distinctive handwriting.

"Your mother?" he queried.

"Yes, another urgent summons. Blast it!" Aubrey was unable to give full expression to his pent-up anger, so he relieved his feelings somewhat by crumpling the letter into a ball and hurling it forcefully across the room.

"Another young lady?"

"Undoubtedly." Aubrey began to pace back and forth. "Well, if she thinks I'm going to leap to obey her commands like some sort of trained animal, she is entirely wrong."

His cousin looked at him with sympathy, but ventured no comment.

"No. I refuse to play the dutiful heir again. Surely I deserve some peace in my life. Oh, she'll never be content until she's married me off." Aubrey spoke with a wholehearted bitterness.

Darley shook his head, although a slight glimmer of amusement shone in his eyes. "I feel for you, coz, but knowing Lady Herne, I should imagine there's little you can do."

Aubrey continued pacing. "You're right, of course. If I won't come to Dorset, she'd just bring the chit to London. I can see myself now, taking her for a drive in the park—at the fashionable hour, of course—escorting her to Almack's, to Drury Lane, to all the assemblies.''

Darley had to chuckle at the sarcasm in the viscount's voice. ''Surely there are worst fates, coz. Besides, what else can you do? Your only other choice is to vanish from the face of the earth.''

Aubrey halted in his pacing suddenly, a thoughtful expression upon his face. ''To vanish,'' he murmured. He turned and embraced a startled Darley abruptly. ''William, you're a positive genius!''

His cousin looked at him warily. ''Just what sort of trouble are you cooking up now?''

The viscount's eyes were dancing with their familiar mischief. ''It's just as you said. I intend to vanish from the face of the earth!''

''Now, Aubrey,'' Darley began warningly.

''No, it's the simplest solution. I can't imagine why it didn't occur to me before.'' He gestured toward his cousin. ''You yourself observed that my painting seemed rather dull. That's it. I have left London in order to search for fresh inspiration in bucolic settings.''

''You know what your mother thinks about your painting,'' William said disparagingly. ''She'll be furious to find that you ignored her request in order to roam about the countryside.''

The viscount clapped him on the back. ''That's the beauty of it, coz. I never received her request.''

Darley stared at him blankly.

The viscount raised his expressive brows. ''Don't you see? I was gone by the time her letter arrived.'' He rubbed his hands together. ''Perhaps I'll look up some of the other fellows in the regiment while I'm at it. It would be good to see St. Erth or Foxbridge.''

Darley shook his head. ''You'll never get away with it. She's too determined. She'll simply ask your servants where you've gone, then send a messenger after you.''

''My servants shan't know where I've gone,'' replied the viscount with a complacent smile.

Darley was skeptical. ''Even so, it would not be difficult for her messenger to trace your traveling carriage.''

The viscount's smile broadened. "I shan't have my carriage."

Darley frowned. "Just how do you propose to go, then? Wouldn't it seem just a bit premeditated to hire a post chaise and travel incognito?"

"Yes, that's why I shouldn't do it." The viscount paused, then had to laugh at the expression of perplexity on his cousin's face. "Come, you forget what hardships a soldier is used to. I intend to travel on horseback—a pack will hold all I need. That way, I may pause to sketch whatever strikes my fancy and abandon the road if I wish."

"You're mad," William said flatly.

The viscount laughed again, with more ease than William had seen him display in months. "I cannot please you. When you came in, you seemed to think I had become too dull. What was the word you used? Ah, yes, 'hermitlike,' that was it."

William shook his head again. "Laugh if you wish. I can foresee what the end of this will be. The viscountess undoubtedly will make my life miserable until she has sent me haring off into the wilds in search of you."

Some four days later, the viscount still was pleased by his little victory. He had packed and left that same evening, leaving even William in ignorance of his proposed destinations, though as he said, it was for William's "own protection." In these few days he had journeyed leisurely into northwestern Oxfordshire. Today had been spent blissfully sketching the scenic delights near Wychwood, the royal hunting forest beloved of the Tudor monarchs.

The day had been sunny and mild, perfect for pursuing his favorite pastime, but now the shadows were starting to lengthen, warning that evening soon would follow.

Aubrey finished the drawing on which he was working, heaved a little sigh, and closed his sketchbook. He walked over to his mount, a big rawboned black, and stuffed the sketchbook in his pack. The horse, who had been contentedly cropping grass, looked up at him in surprise.

"Time to go, Sligo," the viscount addressed him. "We must push on if we're to reach Burford tonight."

The horse made no protest as the viscount swung onto its back, and soon they were on their way.

As he left the confines of the forest, the viscount saw that the sun was dropping rapidly. Realizing that he still had several miles to go before reaching the main coaching road, he opted to ride across country and save a bit of time. The going proved rather rough, and it was with a sense of relief that he finally found a well-used track that seemed to head in the right direction.

By now the sun had abandoned them, but the viscount felt no sense of foreboding about traveling a strange road in the dark. He found the cool evening refreshing, and the leafy branches overhead seemed companionable to him as they murmured in the breeze. He felt a great sense of content at being in such a peaceful place all alone, with no responsibilities or obligations to worry about.

The horse also seemed relaxed, as if it appreciated having an easy road to cover. The minutes passed in perfect tranquility until suddenly Sligo startled the viscount by snorting.

"What is it, fellow?" The viscount patted the horse's neck reassuringly, but it shied and continued to dance a bit. Preoccupied as he was with his horse, the viscount did not hear the crack behind him, though he was abruptly conscious of a hot, searing pain in his right shoulder. Instinctively, the viscount clapped his hand over the spot and felt the warm trickle of blood between his fingers. The horse, frightened by the shot, began to rear as a second ball whistled just over its neck. Sligo reared backward as the viscount desperately attempted to transfer the reins to his left hand. For a brief second, Aubrey was aware that he would be unsuccessful in bringing the animal under control. Then, suddenly, all was black.

There were several moments of silence. The still-trembling horse returned from the short distance it had fled and nosed the motionless form on the ground. Another minute passed. There was a crackle in the bushes across the road, causing Sligo to snort with alarm once more. A short figure emerged from the bush and, avoiding the nervous horse, stepped over to look at the fallen viscount. A quick examination resulted in an exclamation of dismay and alarm, and after a few seconds' consideration, the figure rapidly took to its heels.

* * *

The viscount had no idea how much time had passed when he slowly became conscious of hushed voices. The pain in his shoulder was intense and his head throbbed. He was aware that he was lying in a featherbed and that he was the topic under discussion. With difficulty, he managed to open his eyes.

He received a quick impression of a portly middle-aged man and a statuesque, beautiful girl. The effort was too much and he closed his eyes again.

"Will he be all right, do you think, Doctor?" the girl was saying. Her voice, though worried, was melodic and cultured, soothing to the viscount's ear.

"I've seen worse," returned the doctor gruffly as he began to busy himself with Aubrey's shoulder.

Aubrey's eyes flew open at this agonizing intrusion. He saw that the girl was holding a lamp aloft, and he received an impression of a commodious, wainscoted room.

"Look, he's awakened," she exclaimed.

Aubrey tried to speak, but his mouth was dry and felt as if it had been stuffed with wool. He only managed to move his lips before his eyelids fell shut of their own accord.

"Is he conscious?" she asked.

The doctor's fingers had ceased their probing. "Not likely," was the curt reply. The chair creaked as the doctor rose.

"Lucky he didn't dash his brains out on that stone when he fell. Still, it will have knocked him silly for a few days, I imagine—if not longer."

"Longer?" There was concern in the girl's voice.

"Yes, you never can tell with a blow to the skull. And the gunshot wound is enough to give him a fever and make him delirious for a day or two all on its own."

Aubrey could hear a metallic clinking, as if the doctor were digging around in his bag.

"You'd best call a servant," said the doctor.

"No. They're all abed."

"You'll need someone to nurse him."

"I'll do it myself."

The doctor grunted noncommittally. Aubrey felt he must do something, must discover what was going on and why he was there and wounded. He made a supreme effort to raise himself, but the pain was excruciating and he fell back with a moan.

"I think he is conscious," he heard the girl say.

"Beginning to be feverish, more likely," returned the doctor.

Aubrey was abruptly aware of a damp sponge bathing his forehead. It felt delightfully cool. He tried to speak again without success. A gentle hand was laid on his forehead.

"Don't try to say anything. The doctor and I will take care of you. You're in good hands, and you're safe now."

He gave a little sigh as the doctor seated himself noisily next to the bed. The probing fingers began once again, then there was a sharp agonizing pain and mercifully the world returned to blackness.

Georgiana Chalford studied the inert form that lay on the bed before her. He certainly posed a mystery, whoever he was. A stranger who had been shot and abandoned on the road . . . There were no footpads or highwaymen to threaten the peaceful country lane. She could not quite accept the doctor's theory that it had been a poacher, though of course a stray shot was always possible. She shook her head to clear it. She was becoming as fanciful as Charlotte. The mystery likely would be resolved when the young man regained consciousness.

She bent over to examine her patient. Yes, he was still breathing, though he lay so motionless. He was dreadfully pale, but that was only to be expected, under the circumstances. He was a fine, healthy specimen in all other respects, according to the doctor's report.

She studied the face. Even in repose there was a sensitivity in it, a sensitivity that seemed to extend through him down to his hands, with their long, slender fingers. They were singularly beautiful hands for a man, she decided, and confirmed her impression that here was an artistic soul. He was doubtless one of those ethereal beings who didn't quite belong on this plane of existence and he probably would have a great deal in common with Charlotte. *I might have guessed that he was a drawing master even if we hadn't found the sketchbook,* she thought.

Of course, she had to admit, she had been a little puzzled until they had searched the pack for clues to his identity. His clothing was obviously expensively made, but it showed a certain amount of wear. Neither did it seem, in her limited experience, fashionable enough to proclaim its wearer as a true gentleman. No, the clothing undoubtedly consisted of castoffs from a wealthy employer.

The curious circumstance, of course, was why he would have been traveling on horseback. If he were on his way to a new position, his employer surely would have financed a journey by coach. The horse might make sense if he were headed somewhere far from a coaching stop, but she knew very well that no one in this neighborhood would have hired him. If only we might, she thought to herself hopefully, then dismissed the idea for the moment. He must be brought through this crisis first, and then, in the morning, she would have to face the formidable obstacle of her stepmother.

2

For Aubrey, the night passed in an agony of continuous nightmares. One moment he was waltzing with a laughing Cressida in a crowded London ballroom; in the next instant the ballroom had changed into a battlefield and he no longer held Cressida in his arms but a grinning skeleton clad in a silk dress. He dropped his arms in horror, but it continued to stand there, leering at him accusingly as the shells exploded around him. He suddenly was aware that someone was calling his name, and turned to see Jack, blood staining his chest and a red froth upon his lips. Aubrey was possessed by one idea; to get to Jack and help him. He began running toward him, dodging the shells as he called his friend's name. It seemed the harder he ran, however, the farther away Jack was. There was a look of reproach upon Jack's face, as if he were wondering why his friend wasn't coming. Exhausted, Aubrey fell upon the ground and tried to yell Jack's name again, to tell him that he was on his way, but all he could manage to produce was a harsh croak. Tears of desperation, encouraged by the smoke swirling about him, trickled out of the corners of his eyes.

Her patient gave a moan and Georgiana reached down to sponge his forehead once more. True to the doctor's prediction, the fever had come upon him in the middle of the night. He had begun tossing restlessly and murmuring in his delirium. She had been able to make out only a few words, though two names kept recurring. His eyes were open, but he stared at his surroundings without seeing them. Every now and then, he issued a sharp command, indicating that he thought himself on the field of battle.

It was sad to think that a former officer would be reduced to seeking employment as a drawing master, but she supposed he was more fortunate than many of the Waterloo veterans who had encountered raging unemployment upon their return to England. Those who had been disabled usually were reduced to begging in the streets.

"Jack," Aubrey exclaimed again, and she bent over to sponge his brow and whisper soothing words to him. It seemed to quiet him for a short space, at least, though she feared she finally might have to result to the laudanum in order to ensure that he rested. The doctor had warned her to employ it only sparingly, so she was reluctant to use it until absolutely necessary.

As the night wore on and her patient showed little sign of change, Georgiana began to be conscious of her own weariness. She wished there had been someone else she might call upon for assistance, but the servants were too elderly to help and Charlotte was of no use whatsoever in a sickroom. She laid a hand on the young man's forehead. Was it her imagination or did it seem a fraction cooler? She settled back into her chair with a yawn. Well, she would continue to keep an eye on him. Her eyelids were feeling very heavy. She fought them upward. She must contrive to stay awake somehow. That was her last thought as her head nodded forward and she fell asleep.

"Georgiana!"

She started and, opening her eyes, saw the sunlight streaming through the cracks in the shutters. She glanced down at her motionless patient and ascertained that he was breathing evenly. Stretching out a hand, she discovered that his forehead was cool.

"The fever must have broken during the night," she whispered to herself.

"Georgiana!" The voice outside the door would not be deterred.

Georgiana rose quickly, opened it, and with a finger on her lips to indicate the need for quiet, went into the hallway.

Her stepmother awaited her impatiently.

There have been women whose beauty has increased as they matured, the added depth of character compensating for the loss of some of their physical charms. Letitia Chalford, unfortunately, was not one of them.

Though no one could fault the regularity of her features, hers was a pallid, uninteresting countenance. The pale-blue eyes, without the sparkle of youth to recommend them, now clearly revealed her as a creature of limited understanding. Although not yet thirty, she appeared some twenty years older, which made her youthful, frivolous style of dress and coiffure seem all the more incongruous.

She fixed Georgiana with a cold look. "Wilkins told me about this strange young man that you took in last night. It seems to me that you might have asked my permission first." Her voice was high-pitched and affected, adding nothing to her charms.

"You were asleep and I didn't wish to disturb you, Mother," Georgiana said evenly.

"That is all well and good, but I do not think it appropriate that you should nurse him yourself. You could have called Betsey."

Georgiana fought back a sigh. "Betsey is no longer strong enough to take care of someone all night," she said gently. "The young man's illness is quite serious."

"It is, is it? Well, I suppose you have not even considered the consequences of what might happen if he dies."

"He is much better this morning," Georgiana said, hoping that her patient was still unconscious and so unable to hear this interchange.

"Hhmph. And had you considered that our neighbors might not feel that it was quite genteel for a young, unmarried lady of the house to be closeted alone for such a period of time with a strange young man?"

"I would think that our neighbors would view it as an act of Christian charity."

"It's not as if this young man were anyone important. Why, Wilkins told me he was riding alone, without even a servant."

Georgiana decided the time was right to play her trump card. "Well, of course I should like to do what you think right, Mother, but I did not wish to offend Lord Marwood."

"Lord Marwood?" As always, the name acted like a talisman.

"Why, yes," said Georgiana innocently. "Since it was his tenant who came to me about the young man, and since Lord Marwood was not at home . . ."

"But he was to have returned yesterday."

"Yes, so Jem thought, too."

"You mean . . . Do you mean that this young gentleman might be a friend of Lord Marwood's?"

Georgiana managed an effectively indifferent shrug. "Well, of course I do not know, since he has not regained consciousness, but I thought that since he was found in such proximity to Marwood House . . ."

Her stepmother had taken her hand and was patting it. "You did very rightly, my dear. If the poor young gentleman needs anything at all, you just let the servants know. And come to fetch me the instant he wakes. I would not like Lord Marwood to think that we have been remiss in any little attention to his friend." She smiled kindly at Georgiana. "You must be hungry. I will have Betsey bring up some breakfast for you."

Georgiana choked back a smile. "Thank you, Mother." She reentered the sickroom and stifled a giggle. How enraged her stepmother would be when she found out that the young man was merely an upper form of servant, a drawing master. Her eyes widened as she espied his pack. She hurried over and thrust it and its contents, including the telltale sketchbook, into the wardrobe. She resumed her place by her inert patient.

"We're safe for now," she whispered to him, "at least we're safe until you regain consciousness."

After a substantial breakfast, Georgiana felt greatly refreshed. It was clear that her duties as a sickroom attendant would be much less arduous today than they had been last night. Her patient seem to be resting comfortably, though he showed no sign of awakening.

Dr. Hodges came to examine him and pronounced himself well-pleased with his progress. He even had a quick word of praise for Georgiana, which she prized all the more for knowing how infrequent his compliments were.

After his visit, she decided that the time might be opportune for a nap, and so she settled herself comfortably in a chair. A quiet, hesitant knock sounded upon the door. Resignedly, she rose and went to open it. Her sister, Charlotte, stood there, an expression of mingled curiosity and horror on her face.

"I . . . I came to see if there were anything you might need," she said.

Georgiana smiled at her. "You can come in. He's still asleep," she said. Charlotte took a hesitating step forward. Georgiana repressed a smile. "You needn't be afraid—we've already washed all the blood off," she added.

The two girls provided a striking contrast to each other. Georgiana stood over a head taller than her sister. Her hair was a golden brown, while Charlotte's curls were of the palest blond. Charlotte was also more fair, Georgiana's skin being browned somewhat by exposure to the sun. Georgiana's eyes were an unusual greenish-gray, while her sister's were a more predictable blue.

Their features bore a marked similarity; it was easy to divine their relationship. Although they were both handsome girls, the likelihood was that most people would consider Charlotte the diamond. She had an ethereal sort of prettiness. Her expression also had a childlike quality that her older sister's lacked. They were both approaching twenty, but looking at them, it was hard to imagine that Georgiana was the elder by only a little more than a year.

Charlotte was busy studying the stranger. As Georgiana had foreseen, his appearance predisposed her in his favor, though she might have wished that he were a "bit more handsome."

Georgiana sat back down in her chair with an amused smile. "Really, my dear, no one is going to look his best when he's just had a shot dug out of him."

Charlotte repressed a delicate shudder at this overly frank method of speaking. "You don't know who he is?" she asked eagerly.

Georgiana shook her head.

Encouraged, Charlotte continued in a hushed voice. "I wonder if he's an earl, or maybe even a duke!"

"Really, Charlotte—"

"No, I mean it, Georgy."

Georgiana cocked an eyebrow at her. "And just why would a duke be riding a horse across country? Without even a servant to attend him?"

"He's traveling incognito, of course," Charlotte's face was beginning to shine with pleasure as she enlarged upon her theory.

"Why?" asked Georgiana flatly.

"Oh, there might be a thousand reasons for it," said Charlotte a trifle crossly. She paused for a moment, then her face lit up again. "I have it! Perhaps he has an estate agent whom he suspects of dishonesty and so he means to use this method to discover whether—"

"Charlotte!" Georgiana could not keep from laughing.

"Well, it happened just so in *The Absentee*. Don't you remember when—"

Georgiana could not control herself. "And why not make him an Italian prince instead, then? You read too many romances, Charlotte."

"Don't be silly," Charlotte said reprovingly. "Why, anyone can see that he's not foreign."

Georgiana shook her head hopelessly. "I hate to disappoint you, my dear, but the truth of the matter is that he's only a drawing master, doubtless on his way to a new position." She held up a finger. "Not a word of that to Mother, mind."

"I don't believe it," Charlotte said. "If he's only a drawing master, why would someone try to assassinate him?"

"He was unfortunate enough to be hit by a stray shot from a poacher's gun," Georgiana said patiently.

"A poacher would not have been shooting so near the road," Charlotte disagreed.

This was a point that had been worrying Georgiana secretly. "Well, perhaps the poacher was careless with Lord Marwood gone."

"Yes, but he was supposed to have returned last night," Charlotte reminded her.

Georgiana could think of no reply to that. "Well, we can't know the answer," she said. "We shall simply have to wait until he awakes and tells us what he knows." She gazed down at the pale, motionless form. "Which doesn't appear as if it will happen anytime soon."

Charlotte soon proved that she had an ulterior motive in visiting the sickroom. Georgiana easily yielded to her gentle persuasions and left the patient in her charge in order to snatch a few hours of needed sleep. Charlotte promised to fetch her if there were any sort of alteration in his condition, but when Georgiana returned to the sickroom some hours later, she saw that he was the same.

Charlotte gladly left her to her charge and Georgiana settled down for an uneventful evening. She had one unexpected visitor

in the person of the young boy, Jem, who had discovered the
stranger lying in the road the night before. He seemed frightened to see the patient lying so lifeless, though Georgiana
assured him that the young gentleman was much improved. He
also brought with him the news, unwelcome to Georgiana, that
Lord Marwood had finally returned.

I hope I can prevent Mother from writing to him in the
morning, she thought.

When Jem finally left, Georgiana was free to observe her
patient once again. It seemed to her that there was more color
in his face than before. She felt his forehead, but it remained
cool. There was little else that she could do, so she curled up
in her chair and was soon fast asleep. Her nap that afternoon
had not compensated for all the sleep she had lost the previous
night. Again she was oblivious to everything until she heard
her name being called the next morning.

"Georgiana! Georgiana! I have good news—Lord Marwood
has returned!"

"Oh, blast," she said as she sat up in her chair, rubbing her
face.

Automatically, she glanced over to look at her patient and
saw a pair of intelligent brown eyes regarding her with interest
and amusement.

"I see that you're awake," he said.

"I might say the same to you," she replied, a little irritably.

"Georgiana. Do I hear voices? Is the young gentleman
awake?"

Her eyes widened in dismay. "We're in for it now," she
whispered.

An eyebrow arched at her. "What's the matter?" he asked
in a conspiratorial whisper.

"It's my stepmother. She's sometimes a little difficult to
manage," Georgiana said as she desperately searched her brain
for an idea that would prevent the invalid from being thrown
out-of-doors.

"If he is awake, then the two of you shouldn't be in there
by yourselves."

Georgiana spun to face him. "I have it," she announced. She
looked at him with an expression of the utmost seriousness.
"Whatever you do, do not contradict what I say."

He had no time to reply before she swept to the door and opened it, revealing a somewhat ludicrous matronly figure in a youthful, beribboned gown of white muslin with an elaborately frizzed coiffure. Aubrey found it hard to maintain a grave expression as the caricature minced lightly over to him and simpered unbecomingly.

"My dear sir, we are so honored to have you as our guest, despite the unfortunate circumstances, of course. Lord Marwood is one of our dearest friends and—"

"Mother—"

"Georgiana, please do not interrupt me while I am speaking. As I was saying, I know that Lord Marwood will be greatly—"

"Mother, he wasn't on his way to visit Lord Marwood."

Letitia spun around in shock. "He's not a friend of Lord Marwood's?"

"No."

"Then what is he doing here and why are you alone with him?" Letitia said as she turned to glare icily at Aubrey.

Georgiana managed a tremulous little laugh. "Why, he was coming to visit us, instead."

Letitia's gaze became even more glacial. "I suppose I would remember if I had invited someone whom I do not even know."

Aubrey's eyes were beginning to sparkle with fun, but he maintained his silence.

"That's because he intended to surprise us," Georgiana said, a trifle weakly. "He only meant to stop in and pay his respects, as he is on his way to search for a new post."

"A new post!" Letitia's eyes almost popped from her head in outrage. "Do you mean that . . . that . . . this person is a servant!"

"He's a drawing master, Mother."

"You have been waiting hand and foot on a servant—"

"He's more than that, Mother," Georgiana announced boldly. "You see, he's our cousin."

Aubrey could have laughed aloud. Letitia was slowly turning a brilliant shade of crimson, and though her lips were moving, no words were coming forth.

Georgiana took advantage of the little lull to glance at Aubrey by way of warning. To her surprise, the brown eyes were dancing with delighted mischief and he slipped her a subtle wink of appreciation.

For no obvious reason, her heart suddenly gave a leap and she felt a little weak in the knees. She shook her head to clear her thoughts as her stepmother slowly regained the power of speech.

"Who . . . wwwhhoo . . ." Letitia said, pointing at Aubrey.

Georgiana smiled at her innocently. "Why, he's Uncle Thomas' son."

"Aaaaaaayyyyyhhhhh!" All the air she had been holding in abruptly escaped Letitia and she deflated like a balloon.

"You see, since we're cousins, you needn't have worried about our being alone all this time."

Letitia emitted something like a sob, and she turned toward the door, the spirit of battle within her utterly quelled.

Georgiana rushed forward to take her arm and help her out the door. Fortunately, Betsey, who had been attracted by the commotion, was standing by to help her along. Georgiana closed the door triumphantly and turned back to Aubrey. The look in his eyes brought a blush to her cheeks.

"And just who is my dear papa Thomas?" he asked her, his face alight with enjoyment of all this deviltry.

"He's the black sheep of the family, my father's younger brother."

Aubrey could not prevent an admiring chuckle. "No wonder that silenced her so effectively. But while I am here, what is it that I'm expected to know about him?"

Georgiana shrugged as she seated herself. "That's what's so perfect. No one knows anything about him. He was shipped out to India twenty years ago."

Aubrey directed a mocking gaze at her. "If I'm not presuming too much, then, what exactly is my surname?"

Georgiana's eyes widened. "Oh, that's right, I forgot to tell you." She smiled at him. "I'm Georgiana Chalford, though you may as well call me Georgy, since everyone else does."

"And since we're cousins, after all," Aubrey replied smoothly. "And I am Aubrey Tarrant, or rather Aubrey Chalford now, I suppose." His eyes twinkled at her. An imp of mischief had persuaded him to play out this masquerade a little farther to see where it might lead, and so he neglected to mention his title to her.

His mouth quirked up at one corner. "And if I may be so bold as to ask, how exactly did you discover my, er, my profession?"

Those brown eyes fascinated Georgiana. She had never seen any before that were quite so full of life. They seemed to invite you to share a secret joke, and they quite transformed that angular face. She felt magnetically attracted to him. With a start, she realized that she might seem to be lacking in decorum, so she reluctantly tore her eyes away from him and lowered them modestly instead.

"I'm afraid that in an attempt to discover your identity so that we might notify your relatives, I was obliged to go through your pack. Once I discovered your sketchbook, your profession was obvious."

She forgot herself and looked up at him again, sincerity shining out of the green-gray eyes. "You are quite good, do you know that? It's really like the answer to a prayer to have you here."

His eyebrows shot up in disbelief. "I can't imagine my being the answer to anyone's prayer."

"No, I mean your being a drawing master. You see, I have—"

A gentle knock interrupted her. "Who is it?" she called.

"It's Charlotte."

"Come in."

Charlotte entered, an anxious expression on her face. "Mother's in a terrible state," she said, closing the door behind her. "She says that he . . ." She blushed becomingly and corrected herself. "I beg your pardon, that you are a drawing master—"

"Charlotte had cast you as a duke," Georgiana confided.

"And that you're Uncle Thomas' son," continued Charlotte, ignoring the interruption. She looked accusingly at Georgiana. "Is that true, Georgy?"

Georgiana's brow wrinkled. "What would you say if it weren't?"

"Georgy," Charlotte said, scandalized.

Aubrey had been studying the two girls' interactions with some enjoyment. Admittedly, both were beautiful. Personally, he preferred Georgiana, with the air of innocence she used to mask the outrageous things she said. Charlotte was obviously a more transparent character.

All preferences aside, he turned his most charming smile upon her as introductions were made, and he remarked how fortunate he was to have been stranded where he would be surrounded by such remarkable beauty.

Charlotte, at least, proved herself impervious to his charm by coming straight to the heart of the matter. "Who was it that shot you?" she asked.

"Charlotte," reprimanded Georgiana, but Aubrey was more amused than offended. He confessed his ignorance, which caused Charlotte'e face to fall in disappointment, necessitating Georgiana's explanation of the assassin theory. He then listened with equanimity to the poacher postulate and agreed that it was the most likely solution.

The matter seemed settled and it was abandoned, though anyone who knew Aubrey well might have guessed that he was not entirely satisfied with the explanation. Georgiana was given a clue of this when, after Charlotte's departure, he asked quietly if Jem might be persuaded to pay him a visit.

"Why, certainly," Georgiana said, frowning slightly in surprise. She was not allowed to wonder long about his suspicions, however, for now there was a scratch at the door. She had no time to reply before the door burst open and a gigantic dog entered, pulling along with it a rather grubby little girl of about four, who was attempting to restrain it by the collar.

"Emmy," said Georgiana reprovingly.

The little girl abandoned her hold on the collar, whereupon the beast sprang forward to nose Aubrey eagerly.

"Down, sir," Aubrey said, vainly trying to ward off the kisses of the affectionate and ill-trained animal.

"Lion likes him," announced Emmy triumphantly as Georgiana grasped the animal by the collar and through a combination of force and threats managed to persuade him into a corner of the room.

Another little girl had appeared in the doorway, this one some two years older, her gown spotless and her expression angelic.

"I told Emmy not to bring him in here," Sophia announced.

The younger one's lower lip jutted out defiantly. "I just brought Lion in here so he could lick him and make him all better."

Georgiana sighed and put a hand on the girl's shoulder. "Well, that was very sweet, my love, but don't you think you should have asked me first?" She turned around to see a gloating expression on Sophia's face. "And you, miss, are old enough to know better. Why didn't you stop your sister?"

Sophia's face crumpled. "I tried."

"Did not."

"Did so."

"Did—"

"That's enough," Georgiana said with some severity. She looked at Aubrey. "There's no harm done, anyway?"

He shook his head with a little smile.

"Where is Augusta?"

"Here I am."

A third girl had appeared in the doorway; this one Aubrey judged to be about twelve. She had a rather grave, mature expression that her younger siblings lacked.

"I am sorry, Georgiana. I was preoccupied with that new volume of Horace that the vicar sent me; otherwise, I would have noticed where they'd gone."

Georgiana put an affectionate arm around her shoulders. "Never mind, my dear. As long as you are all here, may I present you to Aubrey Chalford. Aubrey, these are my sisters, Augusta, Sophia, and Amelia."

He acknowledged the introduction solemnly, though little Amelia burst out, "Are you our relation?"

"He's our cousin, dear," said Georgiana, causing Augusta to give her a suspicious look. "And he's a drawing master. I hope to persuade Mama to let him give us all lessons."

The younger girls greeted this pronouncement with delight. Aubrey's brows shot ceilingward at this depiction of his future. What in heaven's name had he gotten himself into now?

He was beginning to be thoroughly wearied by all these visitors, but this newest set showed a marked disinclination toward departure. Georgiana was having a great deal of difficulty in persuading them to leave this interesting arrival.

Just as she was becoming exasperated, Augusta put in a quiet word.

"I'll sit with Mr. Chalford while you take them upstairs, Georgiana."

This solution proved acceptable to all parties, and Georgiana soon had whisked the two youngest girls out of the room, though to Aubrey's regret, the dog was left behind.

Augusta seated herself sedately beside Aubrey.

"There's no need to be so formal," he told her. "You may call me Aubrey, if you wish."

She gave him a shrewd look. "Does it make you uncomfortable to be called by a false name?"

Aubrey might properly have been dismayed by her discovery. Instead, he let out a low chuckle, thereby unwittingly earning her approval. "How the deuce did you guess, you minx?"

She looked rather pleased than otherwise to be referred to by such an appellation.

"Well, you don't resemble any of us, do you? And I never heard of Uncle Thomas having a son. Besides, I can always tell when Georgiana is telling a bouncer." She leaned toward him with a confidential expression. "She disliked having to lie to us, but I understand that she could say nothing in front of the younger children. They cannot be trusted with a secret."

In an instant Aubrey had assumed a serious face. "I take it, then, that you would not think of betraying our confidence."

Augusta looked shocked. "Why should I? Besides, Georgy always has very good reasons for what she does—or almost always." She glanced at him archly. "I know all about it, anyway. Georgy had fooled Mother into thinking that you were a friend of Lord Marwood's in order to allow you to stay, and when Lord Marwood returned, she had to think of something else."

"Ah, yes, Lord Marwood. Tell me, just who is this mysterious person who ranks so high with your mother?"

"Lord Marwood?" Augusta shrugged. "He is a baron, one of our neighbors. Mother plans to marry Georgy off to him."

Aubrey's brows drew together darkly. "They have . . . an understanding?"

Augusta shook her curls. "No, it's just that he's available. He's of an age to need a wife, I guess, and Mother would like to save the expense of a Season. She says that since she married well without one, she doesn't see why the rest of us should need one.''

Aubrey's face relaxed slightly. ''And how does Georgiana feel about all this?''

Augusta looked sharply at him, as if she suspected he were mentally lacking. ''Well, females never have anything to say about these matters, do they? I expect she'll marry whomever they tell her to.''

A light sigh escaped the viscount. ''She has no sort of attachment to Lord Marwood, then?''

Augusta made a face of disgust. ''No, I can't imagine who would, though I daresay there are some,'' she added fairly. ''He reeks of scent,'' she offered. ''It's not as if Mother were so attached to him either. I daresay if anyone with a grander title or a greater fortune came along, Mother would marry Georgy off to him even more quickly.''

The viscount was frowning with a new thought. ''You mean that Georgy really has no choice in the matter? How does your father feel about all this?''

It was Augusta's turn to be amused. ''You don't know our mother.''

The viscount managed a little smile. ''This prospect does not seem to daunt you.''

Augusta drew herself up proudly. ''Oh, I don't have to worry about that. You see, no one will want to marry me. I am a bluestocking.''

Augusta's words were to ring in his ears long after she had left. Enough assurances had been given about his progress that Georgiana had deemed it safe to leave him alone for the night. Thus he had a great deal of time to think over his present situation.

Augusta was such a funny child, such a mixture of maturity and ingenuousness. She was both intelligent and perceptive, though, and he could not doubt that her assessment of Georgiana's situation was accurate. It placed him in a dilemma.

He was determined to remain until he had solved the mystery of his shooting, but he had to admit that the other reason behind his staying was Georgiana Chalford. She was definitely a woman he would like to know better. His experience with Cressida had made him cautious, though, and he had no intention of being thrust as a matrimonial prospect upon a girl he scarcely knew. It was clear from what Augusta said that Georgiana would have no voice in the matter. That revelation caused him to wonder fleetingly about Cressida and what part of her decision had been her own.

No. He knew only too well that if he were settled upon as a husband in advance, he and Georgiana would have little opportunity for getting to know each other or for changing their minds if the prospect displeased them. Augusta had given him a clear idea of what Mrs. Chalford was capable of doing. If I revealed my rank, since it is superior to Marwood's, she doubtless would say that I had compromised Georgiana by letting her nurse me all alone, he thought ironically.

What was the solution then? It came to him in a flash. Georgiana herself had provided it. He had no pressing obligations. His mother would be unable to trace him here. He was unlikely to encounter any acquaintances in this quiet rural neighborhood. All he had to do was to remain with the Chalfords for a while as their drawing master, a post for which, after all, he was qualified. In his spare time, he could poke about and see if he could find out who had shot him and why. Then, if he discovered that he and Georgiana would not suit, he could merely announce his resignation with no harm done. William would have been both gladdened and apprehensive at the wicked sparkle in his cousin's eye.

"A drawing master," he said softly to himself, then he threw his head back and gave a roar of laughter. "Lord, how Fitzwilliam would love it!"

3

By the time Georgiana went to Aubrey's room the next morning, she was surprised to find that he had already breakfasted, shaved, and received a visit from the doctor. He was sitting up and she noted with satisfaction that his color was much improved.

"Well, I won't ask you if you slept well," she remarked jestingly, "for it's evident that you did."

He smiled at her, and the warmth sent by those brown eyes set her heart to racing.

"Then, I am afraid, you would be wrong." He gestured to a mound of golden fur in the corner. "My, er, companion over there snores rather loudly."

Georgiana looked at the dog in dismay. "Lion! You mean he was left in here last night?"

"Yes. Your butler—Wilkins, is it?—made an admirable attempt to evict him, but without success." Aubrey cast a sardonic eye upon the dog. "It seems that the misbegotten cur has developed a fondness for me."

As if aware that he was being spoken of, the dog looked up and thumped his tail on the floor.

Georgiana turned a disapproving eye on the dog and was about to scold him when she remembered the errand that had brought her here. "Oh, I almost forgot. Jem Thornby is here to see you, as you requested yesterday."

"By all means, send him in."

In a few moments an urchin appeared. He was smaller than Aubrey had expected. He appeared to be only about eight, but upon questioning, he revealed his age as twelve. His clothes were well-patched, but quite clean. He managed a creditable bow upon his introduction, and the viscount was surprised by his well-bred manner of speaking.

The boy could shed little light on the mystery. He had found Aubrey lying in the road, his horse beside him. He hadn't heard any shots, nor could he guess how long Aubrey had been there. He hadn't seen any suspicious-looking persons about that night. Knowing that Lord Marwood was not at home, he had simply come to Chalton Hall looking for help.

"Well, I suppose we know it wasn't a footpad, anyway, since no one took my purse," Aubrey commented. He extracted the aforementioned item and tossed a guinea to Jem.

The boy blushed bright red and handed it back to him.

"Small thanks for saving my life," Aubrey said gently.

"No, sir. I cannot take it," Jem said determinedly.

"Can you not? Then I will give you another chance to earn it," Aubrey said with a smile. He rose from his chair somewhat painfully.

"If you will wait for a moment while I attire myself properly, then lead me to the spot where you found me, the guinea is yours and there'll be another to match it."

The boy had been eyeing the coin hungrily as Aubrey spoke, but now he turned a fearful gaze upon him. "Surely, you're not well enough to do that, sir. It's near a mile from here."

Aubrey smiled as he took off his slippers and began to put on his boots. "The doctor was here this morning and he seemed to think that moderate exercise might be of benefit to me."

Although Jem showed a more-than-ordinary reluctance, Aubrey knew how to be persuasive and soon he and the boy were making their way along a wooded drive, the faithful Lion trotting at their heels. Jem's disinclination to make this journey became more and more apparent as they traveled along. By the time they reached the spot of the mishap, Jem actually was hopping from one foot to the other in his impatience to be gone. His discomfort did not escape Aubrey's notice. He pressed the guineas into Jem's hand, over his objections, and told him that he could easily find his own way back. After a few more protests, the little figure sped away in some relief.

Aubrey watched the retreating back with some interest. His first impression of the boy wouldn't have led him to suspect Jem of cowardice, but what other explanation could there be? Surely it was peculiar, too, that the boy had avoided meeting his eyes when he gave him the money. He sighed. Perhaps the lad was just proud. Judging from his manner of speaking, he might well be from a family that had fallen into difficulties.

Aubrey gave a shrug and dismissed these questions. He had more important matters to resolve. He leaned over to study the road. It was lucky the ground had been soft, for the road still retained the hoofprints where Sligo had reared in terror. The sight of a small boulder beside the site caused him to rub his head ruefully and reflect that the doctor had been right: he had been lucky not to have dashed his brains out.

He turned his back to the road. He had been facing in this direction when he was shot, therefore . . . He spun on his heel to determine where the shots had come from. He walked across the road, retracing the shot's trajectory as best he could. He took a step into the knee-high brush and frowned. His assailant certainly need not have ventured far from the road to conceal himself.

He looked about him rather hopelessly. He did not know exactly what it was that he was attempting to discover. Lion came up and nosed him helpfully.

"Begone, you beast," he said, nudging him away with one boot.

Stare as hard as he might, there was nothing to distinguish this area from any other. He could not even be positive that this was the spot where his attacker had hidden. He took a few aimless steps, then sighed. He had not learned a great deal from this expedition, except to confirm his idea that there was plenty of cover where an assassin might conceal himself.

His shoulder was beginning to throb uncomfortably, so he decided to return to Chalton. He looked about for Lion and saw that he was nosing interestedly in a bush beside an oak tree.

"Come, Lion," he called as he stepped back to the road, still pondering the mystery. His instincts told him that the shots were not the accidental discharges of a poacher. They had been aimed deliberately at him. But why? No one could have known his destination, for he did not know it himself. The footpad theory also might be discarded, for his purse had not been touched. He thought it unlikely that Jem would have been enough to frighten a desperate criminal away.

He looked up and saw that Lion was now scrabbling at the bush with his enormous paws. "Come, Lion," he called in some irritation, without making any impression on the animal.

The dog was whining in his eagerness to get at whatever was beneath the bush, and it was clear that force would be necessary to drag him away. Aubrey temporarily considered the idea of abandoning him, then discarded it as he pictured little Emmy with an accusing expression in her eyes.

"Come, Lion," he said again, halfheartedly, then he sighed and turned back into the brush to retrieve the dog.

He reached Lion and began to tug on his collar, but the dog only strained harder to dig away at the desired object. Aubrey gave a heave with his good arm and managed to pry the dog back a few inches, but Lion only began barking excitedly and dragged him back to his original position.

"What am I to do with you?" Aubrey asked him.

Lion replied with a series of preoccupied growls and snuffs. Aubrey bent down to see the cause of all this activity. Lion's efforts had managed to knock away the few branches that had been thrown down quickly in order to disguise this little cache. Unfortunately the natural depression in the ground in which his prizes lay had been enlarged by his digging, causing them to settle ever deeper into the earth.

With some difficulty, Aubrey thrust Lion aside and reached down to grasp them. He rose, brushing the dirt from a huge, ancient, but nonetheless menacing-looking pair of horse pistols. He frowned to himself as he studied them. They effectively eliminated the poacher theory, in any case.

Feeling a nose on his leg, he looked down to see Lion panting up happily at him, his tail wagging with pleasure.

"Well, done, lad," he said appreciatively. "And here I was, doubting your intelligence."

He took a quick look about, but could see nothing more of interest. A sharp twinge in his shoulder reminded him that he had better be on his way.

Pistols in hand, he fought through the underbrush to the road and began the journey back. Lion now trotted along happily at his heels once more.

He frowned to himself as he walked. This discovery had raised more questions than it had answered. It confirmed his feelings that the attack had been deliberate, but he still had no clue as to the reason for it. Furthermore, why should his assailant flee the scene, leaving his weapons behind? Jem had said he had seen no one else on the road that night. It was deuced odd.

By the time he reached Chalton, the problem no longer seemed as pressing as his need to lie down. The walk had wearied him far more than he had expected. Fortunately, there was no one about to question him regarding his little expedition. He quickly sought the sanctuary of his room. He tucked the pistols in his pack, which he had discovered in the wardrobe. Then, pulling off his boots, he lay down upon the bed and sank into oblivion for the better part of the afternoon.

It wasn't until several hours later that he was awakened by a gentle tapping at the door. "Come in," he called, sitting up and rubbing the sleep from his eyes.

Georgiana entered, a little shyly, a leather pouch in her hands. "Did I disturb you?"

He shook his head and swung his legs down onto the floor.

"We eat dinner in an hour, and I wondered if you felt well enough to join us."

"Certainly," he replied, though he could not quite suppress a yawn. "What time is it, anyway?"

"Four o'clock," she said apologetically. "I'm afraid that we dine early here in the country, you know." She hesitated for a moment. "How did your—"

"Georgiana!" There was no mistaking that voice.

Aubrey noted curiously that Georgiana thrust her hands defensively behind her back as Letitia entered.

"Where have you been? I have been searching for you all morning."

"I was working in the garden, Mother."

Letitia eyed her suspiciously. "You're certain that it was the garden?"

Georgy looked at her innocently. "Why, I thought you might like me to arrange some fresh flowers for the dinner table."

"Hmph," replied Letitia, but clearly she could think of no objections to raise. She turned a cold eye upon Aubrey. "Will he be joining us for dinner?"

"Yes, Mother."

"He'll need time to dress, then," she pronounced, correcting the error that had yet to be committed.

"Yes, Mother."

As Letitia turned on her heel and left, Georgiana leaned down and hissed desperately at Aubrey. "We can talk later. I must go fetch those flowers now."

As she left the room, Aubrey could have laughed aloud. What mischief was the girl up to now? Whatever it was, she had gotten her hands and skirts filthy, and it certainly hadn't been in the garden. Just what was she concealing in that pouch, too? He chuckled to himself, the pain in his shoulder temporarily forgotten. I couldn't have landed in an odder household, he thought, if what I have seen so far is any example.

Aubrey's opinion was not to be altered by his experiences during dinner. It was true that the only family member he had not met before was Georgiana's father. This gentleman at first glance did not seem at all out of the ordinary. He was tall, with a rotund figure and a florid countenance that bespoke a more-than-average fondness for the bottle. He appeared the epitome of the simple, hard-drinking country squire.

Upon his introduction, he responded with a frankness that did not surprise Aubrey. "So you're Thomas' boy. I suppose you know our relations haven't been exactly cordial all these years. My father disapproved of him, y'know. Always a bit of a rapscallion, was Thomas." Feeling his wife's frosty gaze upon him, he concluded quickly, "But you're very welcome, for all that."

"Thank you, sir." Aubrey bowed and took his seat, inwardly entertained by the critical look his hostess was giving him. Even she could find nothing to object to in his correct attire of pantaloons and dark-blue tailcoat, with a white satin vest underneath. Even his neckcloth, though very simply tied, was spotless and boasted an adequate amount of starch. She gave a little sniff of disappointment and turned her attention to her daughters.

"You should have allowed me to arrange the flowers, Georgiana," she said disapprovingly as an elderly manservant began carrying in the first course. She honored Aubrey with a condescending smile. "I'm afraid that none of the girls has my talents in that direction."

He managed to arrange his features into a politely interested expression. As she prepared to elaborate, though, she was cut off by her husband, who was busily applying himself to the soup.

"So how is old Thomas, anyway? I haven't heard any news of him in years."

Aubrey was at a stand as to how he should reply. He drew in a deep breath. "Well, actually—" he began to improvise.

Georgy cut him off. "I thought you knew, Papa. Cousin Aubrey told us that his father is dead."

Aubrey couldn't help but admire the way in which she carelessly slew her kinsman with such a blandly innocent expression on her face.

"Dead?" Harry Chalford's beetling brows ascended ceilingward. "How?"

She continued easily. "He was carried off by a fever. You know what a dreadful climate India has." She looked at Aubrey wide-eyed for confirmation. "You said it was some five years ago, didn't you?"

"Four," Aubrey amended, managing to hide his amusement with the strategic use of his napkin.

"Four years ago?" Harry looked either stunned or disbelieving. He glanced at Aubrey, and the latter had the sudden, uncomfortable feeling that he had misjudged this country squire. The bloodshot blue eyes beneath that iron-gray hair were surprisingly shrewd, and Aubrey fancied that they held a look of suspicion. Once again, Georgiana rescued him.

"Well, yes, Papa—and rather naturally, it is painful for Aubrey to talk about him. He hadn't seen him since he was a little child."

"He thought it was healthier for me to remain in England," interjected Aubrey in mournful tones.

"So, you see, that's why he was forced to take up a position as a drawing master," Georgiana added helpfully.

Harry turned his gaze to her, and for a moment Aubrey could have sworn that an unspoken form of communication passed between the two.

Her attention attracted by this sudden lull, Letitia seized the opportunity to thrust herself into the conversation once again.

She directed a patronising look at Aubrey. "So, tell us, then, how is it that you decided to visit us just at this moment?" She managed to sound both civil and resentful at the same time.

Aubrey put down his wine glass. "I just left my old position and thought to take advantage of this little respite to call upon my relations."

"You were dismissed?" she accused him rudely.

He gave her a half-smile. "Actually, I'm afraid that with this type of post, one's students are eventually bound to outgrow one's talents for instructing them."

"It is a pity that you could not have written to advise us of your coming," she said in a sweetly icy voice.

Remembering his scheme of being hired as a drawing master, he assumed an expression of abject humility. "Actually, I must apologize to you, Mrs. Chalford. I was on my way elsewhere and I merely intended to stop in and pay a brief call one afternoon. Unfortunately, my mishap has caused me to intrude upon your kind hospitality."

She was not to be so easily mollified. "Won't your friends he concerned about you?"

He paused for a moment's thought while pretending to busy himself with his napkin. "Oh, they never stand on formality," he replied at length. "Actually, it is rather a joke with them that they never know when to expect me. You see, I was on my way to see my mother's family," he added confidingly.

"Your mother's . . ." Letitia looked as if he had slapped her across the face with the slice of mutton he had on his plate. Charlotte, silent throughout the meal, was not able to prevent a little gasp. Georgiana maintained an admirably noncommittal look on her face, but her father was unable to keep his eyebrows from ascending.

The next few minutes of the meal passed in a stony silence while Aubrey wondered just exactly what it was that he had said. Whatever it was, he could not help but be grateful that, for the moment at least, Letitia was utterly quelled. At last, Harry manfully stepped in and broke the spell.

"I've seen your horse in the stables. Quite an animal. You didn't earn that in your position as a drawing master, I'll wager." The shrewd eyes rested on him once again, and Aubrey had the uneasy feeling that Harry knew more than he was saying. Fortunately, during the few minutes of silence, he'd had time to perfect his story.

"In a roundabout way, I did," Aubrey replied smoothly.

"You see, my last employer was the Viscount Herne. He gave me the horse as a farewell present."

The title had attracted Letitia's attention. "What a generous gift," she breathed.

Harry's gaze remained fixed on Aubrey, but he merely said casually, "It's a valuable gift, for certain. Thoroughbred, isn't it?" At Aubrey's nod, he continued on with his new topic. "They're fine for flat courses, but for hunting, I myself say that they can't touch a cocktail horse. These Thoroughbreds lose their speed in deep ground, and their thin skins make them fear a blackthorn fence. No, I'd take one of my half-bred brutes over a Thoroughbred any day."

Aubrey, rather than being offended, was instead diverted by this plain speaking. "I collect, then, sir, that you are a Melton man."

He regretted his words instantly, for a look of gloom descended upon Harry's face.

Letitia jumped in immediately. "I can't imagine why someone would feel the need to travel away from home merely to hunt," she tittered angrily. "Why, Mr. Chalford has his own pack of hounds—and nasty, dirty animals they are—while the rest of us must make do with outmoded dresses so that his precious hunters may be kept in hay."

Since she was the only one at the table in obviously new raiment, Aubrey was not able to feel a great deal of pity for her plight.

"Mother, you know—" began Georgiana gently.

"No. I won't hear a word of it," stormed Letitia, red-faced. "A gentleman must have his pursuits. Well, what about a wife, then? Do you know just how long it's been since I have gone to London? I didn't know when I married that I would have to spend the rest of my days locked away in the country raising children, with no amusements at all, and forced to associate with a very inferior class of people."

Her family sat silently, not daring to raise their voices.

Letitia turned to Aubrey for sympathy. "Well, it's been three years since I've been to London—three years! And since then, I've had to rely on outmoded fashion plates for my gowns."

His cousin would have been made nervous by the sparkle of mischief in Aubrey's eyes. "No one would ever know that to look at you, ma'am," said the viscount sweetly, dampening the fires of her explosion.

A muffled noise came from the other end of the table. Aubrey glanced down to see that Georgiana was turning purple as she apparently choked on her dinner.

Seemingly unaware of Georgiana, Letitia gave Aubrey a gratified look. "Well, I thank you for saying so. Goodness knows that I have done my best, though it is not easy."

"I can imagine," Aubrey commiserated.

Her eyes lit up. "Of course, since you have been used to move in the first circles—among them, I mean—you doubtless are an expert on all the latest modes."

Aubrey thought of how his cousin would laugh at his being described as an expert on fashion. He assumed a humble expression and replied, "Yes, I have been accustomed to observe my betters, if that's what you intended to—"

"Precisely!" The faded blue eyes showed more animation than Aubrey could have believed possible. "And doubtless you have spent a great deal of time in London."

"I have just come from London," replied Aubrey as if awed by her perceptive powers.

"That settles it, then." Letitia turned to the rest of her family proudly. "Mr. Chalford, I think it is our duty—since our young cousin finds himself without a position—to offer him at least a temporary one with us." She inclined her head to Aubrey graciously. "You may instruct the girls in drawing. As Georgiana says, there are many people—though I do not feel this way myself—that think that a lady cannot be truly genteel without such an accomplishment."

She turned back to her family as if to see whether they had any objections before she continued. "And in his spare moments, perhaps our cousin would be so kind as to advise me concerning the latest modes."

"I shall be at your disposal," Aubrey promised.

It was difficult for him to keep a straight face throughout what remained of dinner, particularly as Georgiana herself was having trouble concealing her amusement, but fortunately he managed somehow. After dinner, he excused himself on the grounds that he needed some fresh air, and fled into the garden.

Georgiana found him there a few minutes later. With one look at her face, he was ready to dissolve into laughter. She shook her head and put a finger to her lips, then took his arm and pulled him through the formal rose garden into a holly maze, where they both dropped down on a bench. She immediately burst into shrieks of laughter, although she made a vain attempt to muffle herself with her hands. Aubrey could not help but join her. They laughed until the tears came streaming down their faces. Every time they attempted to speak, they would go off into fresh gales of merriment. By the time the fit had passed, it took them several minutes more to recover their breaths.

"You were wonderful," gasped Georgiana at length. "Tell me, is it true about the viscount or did you make that up, too?"

He assumed an injured expression. "My dear girl, it is perfectly true that I have given the viscount a great deal of instruction."

"And did he give you the horse, then?"

He gave an other shout of laughter. "So, you decided that I was a horse thief?"

Georgiana could only shake her head helplessly as she giggled.

He smiled at her. "I assure you, the viscount and I are closer than brothers. He would vouch for every word I said if he were here." He grinned at his own secret jest.

Her shoulders shook helplessly. "If only I'd known," she whispered hoarsely, "I needn't have made up any of the rest about Uncle Thomas. The viscount was enough to impress her."

He began to chuckle slowly. "As long as we are speaking of my late parent, what exactly is it about my mother's family that inspires such silence?"

Georgiana's eyes widened in surprise, then her mirth began to overtake her again. "You mean I didn't tell you?"

He shook his head.

"Oh, I thought you did that deliberately," she moaned, laughing. Aubrey waited patiently for her to recover, a process that took about five more minutes. At length, she wiped the tears from her eyes and began.

"Well, as I told you, we don't know a great deal about Uncle Thomas." She had to pause again for breath. "We don't even know that there was a child." An irrepressible giggle escaped her. "All we know is that after Grandfather cast him off, he supposedly took up with an opera dancer—"

"What?"

"—and married her."

"You . . . you minx!" Aubrey could not help but be entertained by her outrageousness. Her merriment had brought a sparkle to her eyes and a flush to her cheeks. Her curls shook about her face as she giggled. Aubrey felt an abrupt, fierce urge to take her in his arms and smother her with kisses. "Oh, Georgy," he said, unexpected tenderness in his voice.

She abruptly stopped laughing. A little breeze had sprung up, carrying the scent of roses to them. She looked at him for a second or two without speaking, then she drew herself up rather rigidly.

Aubrey was sophisticated enough to recognize a cue when he saw one. He rose to his feet and offered her a hand.

She took it and rose, looking at him wonderingly. "Do you always have this effect on people?"

He lifted an inquiring eyebrow.

She dropped her eyes, almost blushing. Hesitantly, she raised them again. "It's just that, well, our lives seem to have been turned topsy-turvy—and you've just been here three days."

He gave a low laugh. "My dear girl, you can't imagine the effect you've had on mine."

They walked back to the house without speaking, each lost in his or her own thoughts. Aubrey was beginning to realize that this adventure might not be entirely the lark he had imagined. Georgiana was musing upon problems of her own.

It wasn't until they reached the house that Aubrey recollected the other mystery that had been puzzling him. He halted in his tracks.

"You must satisfy my curiosity on one other point," he told her gently. "What precisely did you have in that pouch earlier?"

Georgiana opened her mouth to respond, but just then a voice floated over to them. "Georgiana!"

She put a hand on his sleeve. "I'll show you in the morning," she whispered.

He watched as she slipped into the house and her stepmother greeted her with the news that the younger children must be put to bed. Georgiana disappeared meekly up the stairs.

As he watched her go, Aubrey thought to himself that she shouldn't have to be here. A beautiful nineteen-year-old girl should be out dancing at assemblies instead of playing nursemaid to her younger sisters and dancing attendance upon a vain and selfish woman. The idea that they would marry her off without consulting her enraged him.

The ridiculousness of his situation hit him with a jolt. He gave a low, bitter laugh. Wasn't he an unlikely candidate to play Sir Galahad? He could just imagine what Fitzwilliam would say to see him in such a role. He gave a shrug of his shoulders. Perhaps this Lord Marwood was an amiable fellow. Perhaps what Georgiana needed was a safe and secure marriage to such a man. After all, she'd never know what she had missed.

His thoughts were becoming too serious. In spite of his attraction to her, he knew it was ludicrous to be so concerned over a girl he'd only just met. He gave his head a little shake to clear it, and became aware that his shoulder was once again throbbing dully. It reminded him that he had a mystery yet to solve.

"Blast," he said succinctly, then he made his way into the house.

For Aubrey, the toll he had taken on his body proved a blessing in at least one respect: as soon as he went to bed, he fell immediately into a deep and dreamless sleep.

Georgiana was not so fortunate. After reading the children a bedtime story and tucking them in, she made her way to her own room. She felt fortunate that Charlotte had her own bedroom, for she did not feel that she could face all Charlotte's questions just now. She made all her preparations and lay down in bed, but sleep eluded her. She stared at the ceiling with eyes that refused to shut. It had all seemed such a frolic when it all started. Now she had to face the fact that she felt a dangerous attraction to a charming and entirely ineligible young man, a man she scarcely knew. It undoubtedly would have been for the best had he gone away, but she herself had paved the way for him to stay.

She frowned. She must be practical. Her stepmother had delineated her future clearly to her and Georgiana knew that this time there would be no getting around her. Her one attempt at approaching her father had been useless.

Georgiana never had been one for dwelling on matters that could not be changed. This was, after all, one of the first young men with whom she'd had more than a nodding acquaintance. It was conceivable that she would feel the same way toward Lord Marwood. Her memories of him were rather indistinct. She comforted herself with the thought that at last she had found a drawing master—and a good one. Now she might begin to make some actual progress on her project.

Even with such sensible thoughts, the memory of a pair of laughing brown eyes was to deprive her of sleep for much of the rest of the night.

4

Aubrey had scarcely finished his breakfast the next morning when an anxious Georgiana appeared at the table.

"Thank goodness, you're here," she said.

He raised his eyebrows inquiringly at her, but she crossed quickly to his side and took him by the sleeve.

"I thought you'd never awaken. Come, we must go. Mother sleeps late in the morning, so it's the only time we have."

He put his napkin on the table as he rose. "Where are we going?"

"You'll see. Now, come," she demanded, tugging at his sleeve.

He followed her obediently as she made her way hurriedly through the house. She paused only to snatch a tired straw bonnet from a peg and jam it on her head. As she tied the ribbons carefully under her chin, she looked over her shoulder at him impatiently. "Come—we haven't much time."

He had no idea what could be causing this urgency, but he raced after her as she went through the doorway and down the steps into the back. She led him at a brisk march up a broad avenue, past the kitchen gardens beside the house, into a picturesquely shaded area, where he saw a small structure of some sort.

He had lagged a few steps behind, thinking wryly to himself that it was fortunate that he hadn't been shot in the leg.

Georgiana, having reached the neglected-looking building, glanced at him with some irritation. "Hurry," she hissed, the gray eyes scanning the grounds worriedly as she spoke.

He did his best to comply and in a few moments they had slipped into the cool dimness of the little house. A pleasing and familiar odor assailed his nostrils as Georgiana shut the door hastily behind them. She gave him an apologetic look.

"It's just that Mother mustn't know." She crossed over to the far side of the cottage and opened a set of curtains, permitting the sun to come filtering inside.

"What is that scent?" he asked, half to himself.

"This used to be a lavender house," she said, "though no one's used it for years."

His eyes now adjusted to the light, he began to take note of the surroundings. In contrast to the rundown appearance of the outside of the building, the inside was clean and neat, free from cobwebs and dust, and the wooden floors well-swept. The walls were lined with shelves on which rested an assortment of boxes, all carefully labeled. Mystified, Aubrey turned to Georgiana. "What is all this?"

She had an unexpectedly shy look on her face. "I told you that I had been praying for a drawing master," she said. She walked over to a shelf and selected a box. She lifted it down onto a table and opened it. He drew close to her, peeping over her shoulder.

At first glance, the box appeared to be filled with an assortment of irregular stones. As he took another step forward, though, he could see that they were actually shaped like shells.

"Fossils?" he asked.

"Mother doesn't approve," she explained. "She thinks it an unladylike pastime."

He looked around him admiringly. "But this is quite a collection. Surely you didn't find all this on your own."

She blushed slightly. "The former rector here was the one who awakened my interest in them several years ago. He showed me where to find them—and occasionally I have hired help." She smiled. "But, then, you've met Jem."

Aubrey walked over and picked up a box labeled only with a question mark. He opened it to discover an odd-looking bone.

Georgiana opened her hands expressively. "You see why I need you? The rector moved away two years ago and now I have no one to help me identify them."

He looked at her quizzically. "My dear girl, if you're imagining that I'm an expert on fossils . . ."

She laughed and, taking the box from him, replaced it. "No, I just need someone to draw the fossils so that I might send the rector a representation of them."

"This rector must be a very learned fellow," Aubrey said, beginning to feel the slightest twinge of jealousy.

"Oh, well, he is, of course. He's the one who took it upon himself to tutor Augusta. He found her trying to read one of Father's Latin texts one day when she was just a little girl, and he said that he could not bear to see such an inquiring mind go to waste."

"A young man, then, is he?"

Georgiana shook her curls, a little frown of puzzlement on her face. "No, I would say that he's about sixty years of age." She didn't notice Aubrey's shoulders relaxing slightly. "But, you see, he has several connections at university, so he is able to get other opinions about his findings."

Aubrey extracted another box and discovered some peculiarly shaped teeth.

Georgiana saw his questioning look and took the box from him. "These belonged to marine animals of some sort—giant fish, if you like."

He gave her a shrewd look. "And just what does the rector plan to do with all this information?"

"He would like to publish a treatise on it, comparing his findings in different parts of the country. That is why it is important that I send him information of my latest discoveries." She looked at him with some anxiety. "Would you mind helping me?"

He shrugged as he replaced the box. "I have no objection, though it may be difficult to conceal what we are doing from Mrs. Chalford."

She shook her head optimistically. "We shall contrive somehow."

Aubrey returned to study the shells on the table. "Just where is this clergyman living now?"

"Dorset. He lives quite close to Lyme Regis." She let out a little sigh. "Oh, how I should like to visit there. He says that there is an abundance of fossils."

Aubrey had picked up a snaillike object and was turning it in his hand. "Yes, I myself saw the giant sea creature—"

"The one that was discovered five years ago?" she interposed hastily. At his nod, she continued, eyes sparkling, "Oh, how I should like to see it. It is immense, is it not?"

"Some twenty feet long, I should guess."

"And imagine! A complete skeleton, and it was a girl of about my own age who discovered it. What good fortune!" She remembered herself and gave a little sigh. "But here we find only bits and pieces of creatures. Dr. Browne says it is because of the different nature of the rock."

"Differing conditions when the bones were deposited, you mean."

"Precisely."

He could see by the gleam in her eyes that she was about to engage him in a discussion of this favorite topic, so he held up a hand to stop her. "I've already warned you that I was not an expert on fossils. Neither do I know much about stratification of stone, so it is useless to discuss your theories with me."

She gave a merry laugh. "Do I seem such a bluestocking? I assure you, I leave all such matters to the rector. I'm concerned only with the animals themselves."

He replaced the shell in the box and gave her an ironic look. "You have relieved my mind. I had suspected that I was about to hear a lecture on the formation of the planet."

She startled him by giving a sudden gasp. "I had not meant to stand here talking so long. We must return to the house or Mother will be wondering where we are."

She closed the box upon the table and tied it with a bit of string. "I thought I might give you these to sketch in your spare moments," she said, handing it to him. She paused for just a moment. "Of course, I am willing to pay for whatever supplies you need . . ." She hesitated. "And for your effort."

Repressing a smile, he took the box from her gravely. "I think I should have enough supplies to begin with," he said. "Perhaps you can obtain more for me when I start the drawing lessons."

Her eyes brightened. "That's a good scheme."

They were interrupted by a scratching upon the door. Aubrey opened it to see Lion regarding them eagerly. Augusta was just a few steps behind.

"You'd best come back to the house right away," she addressed them. "Mama has her fashion plates spread out all over the parlor and is calling for Cousin Aubrey."

Georgiana could not be sure exactly what had transpired

during their discussions, but when she encountered her mother in the parlor some hours later, it was evident that Aubrey had not lost his talent for conciliating her. Georgiana inquired politely whether their cousin had been of any service to her. Letitia gave her a smug look.

"Well, of course you girls, having spent all your lives in the country, have never developed the discerning eye that someone with a great deal more experience—such as I—have. I could tell immediately that he was a perceptive young man, and he shows the most remarkable taste. Why, would you believe that he agreed with all my selections, protesting only against those designs that he thought would be too ordinary for me."

She looked at Georgiana complacently from the fauteuil in which she was reclining. "He said that he could tell immediately that I was a lady out of the common way, and he said that my clothing must reflect that." Here she paused and her eyes became dreamy. "He said that I must never make the mistake of giving in to popular taste, that I should never allow myself to feel obligated to wear the humdrum sorts of dresses favored by all the other ladies."

Georgiana had some terrible suspicions, but she merely asked politely, "So you have selected a design for the Evershams' ball next month?"

"Yes, and some others besides. Oh, I shall be the—what did he call it?—the *dernier cri*," she said exultantly. Her forehead puckered with a sudden thought. "It's a pity that our cousin isn't female. I should have liked him to accompany me to the dressmaker's tomorrow morning."

Georgiana drew a little breath of relief. "If you will be gone, then I may call upon my godmother tomorrow . . . with your permission, of course," she added quickly.

The mention of Georgiana's godmother did nothing to lessen Letitia's frown. "I suppose if you feel you must," she said reluctantly.

"I haven't seen her since our cousin's arrival," Georgiana reminded her gently.

"Very well, then," Letitia agreed petulantly. Georgiana turned to go, but her stepmother stopped her with a question. "By the way, have you seen your father this morning? Do you know where he might be?"

Georgiana had to repress a smile at her mother's questioning such an obvious certainty. "I would imagine that he went out hunting this morning."

Letitia scowled in earnest. "He is so very disobliging. I meant to invite Lord Marwood to dinner Saturday, and I wished your father to deliver the invitation himself." Georgiana was about to speak, but Letitia forestalled her. "Well, I suppose it's of no consequence. I shall simply send him a note myself." She looked up at Georgiana as if to see whether the girl would make any objections. "I should not like Lord Marwood to feel that we have been remiss in any little attention."

Georgiana schooled her face to remain carefully expressionless. "No, Mother." She was about to depart, but she hesitated for a moment. A little too brightly, she inquired, "Will we be expecting many on Saturday? I will need to make plans with Mrs. Turner."

Letitia studied her for several seconds before replying slowly, "No . . . I think it will just be a family party. I would not wish to overwhelm Lord Marwood, since he doubtless is weary of London crowds."

Georgiana heard her with a sinking heart. Letitia obviously did not intend to allow anyone or anything to interfere with her plans for a match. The circumstances were hardly unusual, in any case. The Chalfords' invitations, though infrequently issued, were frequently declined.

Determining that her presence was no longer required, Georgiana left the room. Low in spirits, she retreated to the sanctuary of her own bedroom. She had foreseen this eventuality, but not that it would come upon her so quickly. She supposed she should have been warned when she first heard the news of Lord Marwood's expected return.

It was frustrating. She was certain that if she had only a few more months, she might be able to make some significant discovery, some sort of lasting contribution, and then she could leave her fossil-collecting happily and settle down as a wife. Letitia had warned her repeatedly that it was not the sort of avocation a man tolerated in a wife. Though Georgiana often doubted her stepmother's opinions, she felt a sad certainty that, in this case, Letitia was right. It was an unladylike pursuit, and she knew it.

She heaved a sigh and sat for a moment in depressed silence. There was a quiet knock on the door.

"Come in," she called.

Charlotte's eyes were sparkling with excitement and she wore an air of mystery that Georgiana particularly distrusted. She looked about the room as if searching for hidden spies before she softly closed the door behind her.

Georgiana waited tolerantly as Charlotte tiptoed dramatically toward her. "What is it, Charlotte?" she asked.

"I have solved the mystery," Charlotte hissed. At Georgiana's blank look, she continued, in a whisper, "I know who our 'cousin' is."

Georgiana regarded her skeptically. Undaunted, Charlotte seated herself beside her sister.

"I don't think you need to whisper, Charlotte. We're the only ones here."

Charlotte gave her a look that neared reproach. "We would not wish for a casual listener to learn of his true identity from us," she said, still in a lowered voice.

Georgiana heaved a little sigh. "Very well," she said. "Who is he?"

Charlotte's eyes sparkled. "Do you recall last night at dinner when he mentioned the Viscount Herne, his supposed patron?"

Georgiana nodded, a trifle wearily.

"Well, I thought to myself that the story of the horse was unlikely, and I began thinking about who he could actually be." Charlotte paused to look directly at her sister. "You realize, of course, that we know absolutely nothing about him."

Georgiana had sunk her chin onto a hand.

"Anyway, I was thinking to myself, Why should he mention a name at all in fabricating such a story? He might have made up a hundred more likely tales otherwise."

Georgiana offered no encouragement.

"And that's when it came to me," Charlotte said, excitedly. She paused for a moment before making her big pronouncement. "That's when I realized that *he* is the Viscount Herne!"

In spite of herself, Georgiana gave a startled chuckle.

"Don't you see? It makes perfect sense," Charlotte told her seriously.

Georgiana shook her head, much amused. "Don't tell me that

you're back to the theory that he's traveling incognito to investigate a scurrilous agent.''

Charlotte was offended. "And why not?"

Georgiana shook her head. "Has it ever occurred to you, you goose, that the Viscount Herne does not have an estate in this vicinity—nor does any other viscount, earl, or duke, for that matter.''

Charlotte stubbornly refused to give up her postulate. "I think you're being unfair. You don't know any more than I. Why, there might be some other reason for his traveling incognito.''

"There is." The words took Charlotte by surprise. Georgiana's eyes were dancing with their familiar mischief, but Charlotte did not heed their warning. "What do you mean?" she breathed.

Georgiana motioned for her to draw nearer. "He confessed his true background to me last night," she said in a low voice.

Charlotte leaned forward, wide-eyed.

"He must conceal his identity," said Georgiana mysteriously.

Charlotte took the bait without hesitation. "Why?"

"The horse isn't his at all," Georgiana whispered gravely. "It was stolen."

Charlotte was rapt upon her words.

"You see, the truth is that he is the illegitimate son of an earl. Since he had no resources of his own, he took to highway robbery."

Charlotte gave a little gasp.

"He became the leader of a band of ruffians, and when they had a falling-out over dividing their latest booty, they shot him and left him for dead." Georgiana could maintain her composure no longer. She burst out laughing. "Charlotte, your face!"

Charlotte drew herself up haughtily. "Did you really expect me to believe such a ridiculous story?"

Georgiana could not reply for laughing.

"Why, any child would know that if he really were involved with a band of ruffians they would have taken his horse when they shot him."

Georgiana was still busy giggling.

"Really, Georgy. I don't see what is so funny about it," Charlotte said crossly.

Georgiana shook her head and fought to regain her self-control. "I'm sorry," she gasped at length, "but, honestly Charlotte, it's no more ridiculous than his being a viscount."

Charlotte frowned and was about to retort, but Georgiana forestalled her. "Would a viscount take a position as a drawing master?"

Charlotte had to agree that this seemed an unlikely possibility. "But, Georgy, he does not seem like a drawing master to me," she said, unwilling to relinquish her argument entirely.

"I know," Georgiana hesitated for a moment. "Perhaps I should not tell you this—he has not told me himself—but when he was feverish, he said things that made me realize that he had been an officer in the war." Georgiana looked at her sister seriously. "Doubtless, like so many others, he has fallen into difficulties and was forced to take a position as a drawing master."

Charlotte's face was alight with sympathy. "Poor young man."

"It may be that it embarrasses him and he does not wish it to be generally known."

"You need not worry. No one shall hear of it from me," Charlotte said sincerely.

Georgiana studied her face. She might have erred in betraying his secret to Charlotte, who was not known for her discretion, but it had been necessary to put her sister's foolish surmises to rest. She took her hand and patted it. "I'm afraid that viscounts don't fall upon one's doorstep, my dear." A sad thought came back to her. "Mother is inviting Lord Marwood to dinner Saturday."

"Oh, Georgy!" Her sister needed to say no more to her. Charlotte knew as well as anyone what Lord Marwood's presence meant to Georgiana's future.

Georgiana saw the bleak look upon her sister's face and adjusted her own expression to a more cheerful one. She patted Charlotte's hand again and released it. "There's no need to wear such a Friday face. Perhaps he'll take a violent dislike to me, or perhaps we shall both fall madly in love—that would please you."

Charlotte bit her underlip. She was determined not to

remonstrate with her sister, having learned that it only caused her more pain and did not alter her circumstances. She rose silently to go.

Georgiana could not bear to see her sister's gloomy expression. She made one more attempt at lightness. "If he is a viscount, then I hope that his brother, or cousin, or best friend, may come along and fall madly in love with you."

Charlotte gave her a sad little smile and exited, closing the door after her.

Georgiana heaved a sigh. Poor romantic Charlotte, with her dreams of a handsome, wealthy young nobleman. Mother undoubtedly would marry her off to some fat, middle-aged country squire. Georgiana's thoughts had traveled this path before. If I do marry Lord Marwood, she thought, I may be in a position to help her, and all the other girls, too.

She shook her head. There was no sense in worrying about Lord Marwood until Saturday. She deliberately turned her thoughts in a more pleasant direction. There was the visit to her godmother tomorrow to look forward to, after all. Somehow she always felt reassured after meeting with a lady of such solid good sense.

The next morning she had her horse saddled and ready at an early hour. She had decided that if they were to maintain the pretense that Aubrey was a cousin, it would be best for him to accompany her.

"You see, she has known our family so intimately for such a long time," she explained to Aubrey as the groom helped her mount, then went to fetch Aubrey's horse. "And since she is a semi-invalid, she could not easily come here to call."

Aubrey was eyeing her horse critically. "Is that nag what you usually ride?"

She smiled and patted the neck of the sleepy old mare. "What, don't you admire Tinderbox?"

He gave a guffaw at the name. "I should think Somnambulist would be more appropriate."

She shook her head in mock reproof. "You shouldn't disparage her so. We are well-contented to have her. Mother favored the purchase of a donkey instead."

Aubrey grimaced at this disclosure as the elderly groom led

a restive Sligo out with difficulty. Aubrey mounted and brought the animal under control and they set out.

For the first several minutes there was no more conversation. Aubrey had to concentrate upon convincing Sligo that he would not be allowed to stretch his legs; Georgiana had to use relentless persuasion to convince her mare into a steady amble.

By the time that both these purposes had been accomplished to lasting effect, they were well out on the main road and passing through territory that was new to Aubrey. As they rode, he saw that they were approaching a large farmhouse that stood in need of some repair. There was a garden beside the house, and a familiar small figure was hoeing it in earnest.

"There's Jem," remarked Georgiana, whereupon she gave a shout of greeting.

The boy paused long enough to acknowledge them, but then returned to his work with a fury.

As they passed out of earshot, Aubrey commented upon the neglected state of the house.

Georgiana frowned. "It's a sad case. Ever since their father died two years ago, Jem and an older sister have been trying to make a go of the farm, but luck has been against them. The crops failed last year and I fear that they will not recover from the setback."

"How old is the sister?" Aubrey asked curiously.

"Only eighteen—and there are two younger children to care for also." Georgiana's scowl deepened. "When their parents were alive, they used to hire additional labor, but now I don't know if they are able to."

"Didn't you say that they are Lord Marwood's tenants?" Aubrey asked.

"Yes. Maybe he will be able to do something for them now that he has returned," she said, but her voice lacked conviction.

Aubrey's brows drew together. A decent agent would have kept Lord Marwood informed of the situation, even though he spent most of his time in London. Either his agent was dishonest or lazy, or Marwood was a careless landlord. Aubrey did not feel free to express his sentiments to Georgiana, so he diverted the conversation.

"My talk with Jem made me curious. He seems unusually cultured for a farmer's son."

"His background in unusual. His mother was an educated woman. I do not know her story, but I believe she was a curate's daughter who suffered some misfortune in her life. Her husband was quite a prosperous farmer when they married, so the match was not as unequal as it may seem. She insisted upon all of her children being tutored by the rector, and her husband continued sending them, even after her death. Jem, in particular, has a quick mind and had begun studies in Latin and Greek when his father died." She shook her head. "He also used to help me with my fossil collection, and he was invaluable. Of course, now he must spend every spare minute working on the farm."

"It seems a great pity. Such a boy could be useful elsewhere."

"That's what I think." She squared her shoulders. "I mean to speak to Lord Marwood about it when I have the opportunity."

Seeing that this conversation brought up painful associations, Aubrey again changed the subject and began asking her about her godmother, obviously a more pleasant topic.

Georgiana brightened immediately and responded to his questions eagerly.

"Well, of course I think that she is a remarkable woman. She was crippled by a fall from her horse when she was quite young, just after her marriage, I believe. She is in constant pain, and it is agony for her to walk even a few steps, but she keeps the estate in excellent order, riding over it herself, and did so even while her husband was alive. Sir Roger Dowles was a member of Parliament, and naturally his duties there took up a great deal of his time."

"They had no children, then?"

Georgiana shook her head, and with a flash of insight he saw that she probably had filled that role for Lady Dowles. As Georgiana chatted happily on, he began to develop a picture of her godmother as a shrewd, capable, and strong-willed person, and one who had served as a mentor to her goddaughter.

This impression was confirmed when they arrived at Lady Dowles' home and they were introduced. Lady Dowles remained in her chair as they entered, but she sat serenely erect. The only sign of her invalidism were the two canes tucked discreetly beside her chair.

She took Aubrey's hand in her own small firm one and looked

up at him with bright assessing eyes. She was somewhat younger than he had supposed, being just forty years of age. Her face had the lines pain causes, but her chestnut hair held not a trace of gray. Her features were good and her figure was still elegant, and she appeared a remarkably vital and attractive woman.

When Georgiana introduced him as Thomas' son, Aubrey was almost certain that he detected a look of surprise upon her face, but she hid it quickly and contented herself with making bland small talk. She quickly extracted the information that Aubrey now was employed as the Chalfords' drawing master; she learned of his accident and made polite protestations of shock and dismay. The conversation passed into more innocuous channels, though Aubrey was aware that he was being studied quietly.

At length, Lady Dowles smiled at Georgiana and said, "As the day is so fine, I think we might enjoy our tea al fresco. Would you be a dear and fetch my India shawl from the great chest and tell Molly that we wish for tea in the garden?"

As Georgiana rose, Lady Dowles turned to Aubrey apologetically. "You must forgive me," she said, "but I've grown so tired of depending on my servants that I am apt to abuse my friends."

"Oh, Godmama, you know I don't mind," Georgiana said as she slipped through the doorway.

"Such a sweet girl," Lady Dowles remarked before fixing Aubrey with a hard steely gaze. "Just who are you anyway?"

Aubrey was so taken aback, he could only blink in surprise.

"There's nothing of Thomas in you," Lady Dowles said, "so that tale won't wash and you're no drawing master either."

Aubrey began to stammer out an explanation, but she stopped him with a look. "I won't have my goddaughter trifled with," she said calmly, "so you might as well tell me who you are."

Aubrey could not help a reluctant smile. "You are very perceptive, Lady Dowles."

She waited quietly for him to continue.

"As a matter of fact, the notion of my masquerade as her cousin was her idea, not mine. It was done to conciliate her mother."

"To conciliate her?" Lady Dowles' face was expressive of her disbelief.

He had to smile again. "Well, at least to permit me to remain."

"Why should you wish to?"

He regarded her seriously. "I was determined to solve the mystery of my shooting, and Georgy required a drawing master for her fossil collection."

Lady Dowles pursed her lips. "Those rocks," she said disapprovingly. "But you still haven't answered my question. You're not a drawing master."

"No, I'm not." For the first time, Aubrey dropped his head. He studied the carpet for a moment, then gazed up at her again. "Lady Dowles, would it be satisfactory if I gave you my word as a gentleman that I am interested only in your goddaughter's happiness and wish to keep her from harm?"

"Georgy has a *tendre* for you," Lady Dowles said flatly. He could not prevent a slight flush from rising to his cheeks. She observed this shrewdly. "So that's the way it is, then."

"I give you my word of honor that Georgy has nothing to fear from her association with me. There is nothing in my background that—"

"There's something familiar about you," said his companion abruptly, scanning his face.

"Lady Dowles, it is most important—"

"I do not forget a face," she said, scrutinizing him carefully. "Your features . . . I have seen before—"

"Lady Dowles—"

"Parliament," she said suddenly. Her eyes widened. "Herne—" she breathed.

"I must beg you—"

"Sir Roger supported your father's antislavery stand in the House of Commons."

"Lady Dowles—"

"I knew I'd seen that nose before," she said in an unflattering way. She looked at him. "Well, you're not going to attempt to deny it, are you?"

He shook his head.

"Your father was a great man," she began earnestly.

"I know," he said, preventing her from continuing. "I must ask you to keep my identity a secret, however." She frowned as he went on. "I admit that I am attracted to your goddaughter. I wish to know her better. Having become acquainted with her stepmother, though, I think it would not be possible if my title were known."

Lady Dowles gave a sniff of disgust. "You're right there. Encroaching creature." She shook her head. "I knew from the first how it would be. A middle-aged widower who marries the first pretty piece of tinsel that comes along. She had money, yes, but he had plenty of his own. No breeding whatsoever, and yet she acts as if she's the one who married beneath herself." She sniffed again. "The most nip-farthing creature alive, too—where everyone else is concerned."

"You can see, then, that I would not wish Georgy forced into marriage with me—as she's being pushed upon Lord Marwood."

Lady Dowles' expression darkened. "That's what concerns me," she said softly. "The Marwoods always were a bad lot, and I have no reason to believe that this one is any different." Her brow creased with anxiety. "My acquaintances in town move in different circles than he, but if my suspicions about him are confirmed, then he is the last person I should wish my Georgy to marry."

She lifted her chin and looked at him warningly. "I would have you know that I am not one of those females who are filled with romantic nonsense—and neither is Georgiana. My own marriage was an arranged one, and I daresay that both Sir Roger and I were happy in it. However, I should not wish to see Georgy married to a man she cannot respect."

"I would say it is her sister who has the romantic notions," Aubrey said with a smile.

"Charlotte," Lady Dowles sniffed. "Why, she can't hold a candle to Georgy. Not that she isn't an amiable sort of girl," she added fairly. "But Georgy, Georgy has the potential to be more than just a pretty ornament on a man's arm."

"Lady Dowles," Aubrey said, "before Georgy returns, may I have your word that you will not reveal who I am?"

"Oh, she won't be back for a bit yet," said Lady Dowles unconcernedly. "I sent her on a wild-goose chase." She saw the earnestness in his eyes and her own face became serious.

"Georgy's mother was my dearest friend," she said. "And I have an obligation to her memory. First, I must ask you—is she in any danger through her association with you?"

Aubrey blinked in puzzlement.

She frowned impatiently at him. "Come, man, you were shot. Have you discovered who did it? Do you believe that another attempt will be made?"

He shook his head. "I still do not know who shot me or why, but I do not believe that the attack was made on me personally, as no one knows my whereabouts. My suspicions are that it was a case of mistaken identity."

"Very well." She gave him a hard look. "And do I have your word that you will not take unfair advantage of your situation?"

"Georgy considers me to be a drawing master, and so it will remain until when and if I decide that I wish to declare myself."

"I don't like it," she said flatly. She glanced at him and heaved a little sigh. "The worst of it is that since I am an invalid, there is nothing I can do about seeing that Georgy has a Season as she should."

"I am sorry, but I cannot promise to marry your god-daughter," said the viscount. "That is not my purpose in remaining here." He saw her inflexible expression and added, "I will promise you this: if Lord Marwood is what you believe him to be and I see that Georgy is being forced into marrying him, I shall use all my influence to prevent it, even if it means removing her to London and enlisting my mother's aid."

Lady Dowles still looked far from satisfied, but she gave a sigh and capitulated. "I dislike any kind of deceit," she said, "but I have little choice. I rely upon your word as a Herne."

He acquiesced, wondering silently what a coil he had gotten himself into now.

5

Although he could not have anticipated it, the visit to Lady Dowles was for several days Aubrey's last opportunity to see Georgiana alone. Letitia apparently had decided that she had exercised enough leniency, for when he arrived at breakfast the next morning, he was informed by the servants that the nursery party was awaiting their first drawing lesson. Accordingly, he dutifully armed himself with drawing paper and charcoals and made his way upstairs.

From the beginning, it was apparent that this task would be more difficult than he had first envisioned. Augusta, as might be expected, listened carefully and applied herself diligently in accordance with his instructions. Sophia made a rudimentary effort at sketching the flowers he had arranged on the table, but she quickly became bored and abandoned the attempt halfway through. Emmy's brief attention span did not enable her to make more than a few doodles on the paper before deciding that a great deal more enjoyment could be derived from tearing it into small bits. After an hour's effort even Augusta was beginning to be impatient, while the two younger children were openly mutinous.

He accepted defeat and dismissed them with a sigh. The most discouraging aspect of the whole business was that none of the girls—not even Augusta, with all her effort—showed the slightest aptitude for art. He began to feel a great deal of sympathy for the lot of drawing masters in general.

It had been decided that the two older girls should have lessons separate from the nursery crowd. When he came downstairs, he encountered Charlotte alone. She informed him that, Letitia having retired for a nap, Georgiana had taken the opportunity to slip away to her beloved fossils. He felt a pang of disappointment, but recovered quickly and suggested to her that they sketch outdoors, in order to help prevent detection of Georgiana's escape. Charlotte assented and soon returned sporting a fetching leghorn hat.

He led her from the front of the house into the park, where he found an imposing old oak tree for her first attempt. She seated herself carelessly on the lawn and began her sketch, though he suspected that she listened with only half an ear to his instructions. He was amused by the artless way in which she asked him the most probing questions. The deft way he side-stepped them did not seem to discourage her in the least. She really was an enchanting picture with her fair curls peeping from under her bonnet, and he thought that had he not already been captivated by the elder sister, his heart might have been in some danger. His surprise was profound when she handed him her sketches at the end of the session, and he realized that out of all the family, this was the one who possessed some artistic inclination. He complimented her and offered to continue the lessons, but she professed her weariness and skipped gaily off, leaving him to deal with the materials.

The next few days saw little alteration in Aubrey's schedule, though one day was brightened when Georgiana actually attended a drawing lesson. Somehow, it did not come as a shock that she exhibited no more talent for drawing than her youngest sisters. Teaching the little ones was rapidly becoming an onerous task, and the hardships were not lessened by the realization that his pupils suffered every bit as much as he himself did. His friendship with them was beginning to unravel from the continued strain. He racked his brain trying to think of a way to end the lessons, but had no success. Every night Letitia asked him how the instruction was proceeding, and every night he lied to her with a smiling face.

It was Friday night when inspiration struck him. Letitia had been rambling on about the portrait of Mr. Chalford's great-great-grandfather, which hung in the dining room, saying that it drove away her appetite.

"I do not say that we must rid ourselves of it," she was saying in her querulous voice, "but surely there is somewhere else where it might be hung." Searching about the table for an ally and finding none, she appealed to Aubrey. "You are a connoisseur of art. Don't you agree that it is a pitiable piece?"

Aubrey had no strong feelings about the portrait of the gentleman, whose Royalist sympathies were envinced by his long curling locks, rich lacework, and the ostrich plumes adorning his hat. Nor was Aubrey attending greatly to what Letitia had to say.

"Cousin Chalford," she repeated, "isn't that a dark and gloomy painting?"

"The age of it would be enough to darken it," he was replying absentmindedly when the idea seized him.

"It lends the room such a dreary, old-fashioned appearance," Letitia was saying when he startled her by leaping in eagerly to agree with her.

"I think that you have hit upon the precise problem, Mrs. Chalford," he said earnestly. "I was just studying your family, thinking what handsome subjects they'd be, and then it occurred to me: what could be more modish than a family portrait?"

"A family portrait?" asked Letitia, intrigued.

"Oh, yes. All the best families have them done. While I was in his employ, I did a portrait of the Viscount Herne and his family."

"But didn't it take a long period of time?"

"No, that's the beauty of it. I arrange individual sittings with each subject and then simply paint them together, so that there is as little inconvenience as possible."

With only a trifle more persuasion, he was able to convince Letitia of the worth of the idea. This was an acquisition that none of her neighbors would be able to match.

Georgiana was able to see through his scheme, and giggling, she cornered him in the hall after dinner. She led him hastily upstairs where, safely out of earshot, she gave vent to her amusement.

"What a bouncer," she chortled.

"I beg your pardon," Aubrey said innocently.

"You never painted a family portrait for the viscount."

He pretended shock. "You suspect me of an untruth?"

She laughed. "I saw the expression in your eyes when you told her that. You've merely decided that it would be easier to paint us than to teach us to paint, since we're all so miserable at it.''

''My dear girl, I can't imagine what would make you think such a thing.''

His expression changed suddenly. ''Besides, now I will be able to go on your expeditions with you and sketch the fossils. Had you thought of that?''

Her eyes widened. ''That's right. How clever you are.''

He walked to the wardrobe and extracted a folder. ''I have this for you also.''

She opened it up and saw beautifully detailed sketches of each of the fossils she had given him. She gave a little gasp of admiration.

Aubrey, unsure of her reaction, added, ''I did a front and a side view of each of them. If that is not sufficient—''

''Oh, they're lovely,'' said Georgiana. She noticed the name that had been penciled in the top corner. ''How did you know they were ammonites?''

He grinned. ''You're giving me too much credit. I read the label on the box.''

''Oh.'' She gave a little laugh at her own oversight. She looked up at him appreciatively, meaning to thank him, but she surprised an expression there that made her cheeks grow warm. Abruptly she was aware that she had imprudently closeted herself with a strange young man and, even worse, that her heart was racing dangerously fast. The first thought that came to her mind was escape.

''T-thank you,'' she stammered awkwardly, her cheeks bright red, then she turned and fled the bedroom hurriedly.

Aubrey stood looking at the door some time after she had gone, pondering his own secret thoughts.

From the moment Aubrey awakened Saturday, the air of tension in the household was apparent, and it only deepened as the day wore on. The demands of entertaining Lord Marwood were proving too much for Letitia's already fragile nerves, and she snapped irritably at her unhappy daughters and servants. She refused to accept Georgiana's assurances that everything had been taken care of, and she insisted of interfering with the arrangements that had been made, criticizing the choice of this sauce or that pastry until the cook threatened mutiny.

When Aubrey encountered Georgiana on the stairs, he expected to find her exasperated, but instead her eyes twinkled with humor. He was surprised and told her so frankly. Georgiana chuckled. "Well, it's all so ridiculous, you see. Mother considers that it would be extravagant to hire a French chef—as I do myself—but then she becomes so angry with poor Mrs. Turner because she made a simple pudding for dessert."

Aubrey had to chuckle himself. "She'd prefer Carême's set pieces—a ruined temple of marzipan, perhaps."

Georgiana had to laugh at the picture he presented. "Exactly." Her eyes sparkled mischievously. "But you needn't think that you are to be permitted simply to enjoy all our misfortunes. Mother asked me specifically to fetch you to consult with her about her dress for tonight."

Aubrey's face assumed an expression of dismay. He glanced about him. "Then I must make my escape," he whispered, and began sidling quietly down the stairs. A sharp-edged soprano voice stopped him in his tracks.

"Oh, Cousin Chalford, there you are," said Letitia. "I need your assistance. I would not wish Lord Marwood to think us dreadfully behind the mode."

Aubrey looked pleadingly up the stairs at Georgiana. She gave him a very bland look, the effect of which was marred somewhat by the wicked gleam in her eyes.

"Cousin Chalford . . ." began Letitia fretfully.

Resigned, he bowed to her. "I shall be happy to be of service to you, however I may."

It wasn't until she was up in her own room that Georgiana was struck by how odd Aubrey's remark about the cooking had been. She did not think that most gentlemen paid a great deal of attention to such matters. It seemed peculiar that he should be able to describe a set piece that she had only read about in a magazine. Of course, she was forgetting about Viscount Herne. If his story were true about his employment there, he might have observed such a culinary masterpiece as the chef was finishing it in the kitchen. She sincerely doubted that even a well-respected drawing master would be invited to sit at a viscount's table.

A similar sort of problem had been troubling Letitia's mind.

It seemed vastly improper to her to seat a drawing master at the same table with a baron. The thought had crossed her mind as her obliging nephew had approved her selection of a gown and made some startlingly original suggestions as to finishing touches. She had watched him leave her chamber with a vague sort of regret and immediately expressed her doubts to Charlotte, who also had been marshaled to participate in the fashion consultation. Charlotte had attempted to overcome her objections by pointing out that Cousin Chalford was a relative, after all.

"Yes, but since his father disgraced the family name, I am not sure that we should allow that to weigh with us," replied Letitia, unconvinced. "It might give Lord Marwood the wrong sort of idea as to the type of family we are."

"He will even out the numbers, and he is a very gentleman-like person," Charlotte reminded her.

"Yes, but one never can tell," said Letitia, frowning. "What if he should blurt out something inappropriate and embarrass us all?"

Charlotte thought the likelihood rather remote of Aubrey's being the one to embarrass the family, but she wisely held her peace.

"He is, after all, a common drawing-master."

"But we need not mention that."

"I think it might seem peculiar to Lord Marwood if we included him."

Charlotte privately felt that if Aubrey indeed had been a cousin, it would be more peculiar not to include him, but she tried a different tack, instead.

"Surely someone who is accustomed to living in a viscount's household knows how to conduct himself with propriety."

Letitia considered this point for a moment. As Charlotte had envisioned, the mention of the title had its usual impact upon her. At length, however, she shook her head.

"No. Being a servant, even in so great a household, does not mean that one has the ability to conduct oneself properly as a guest." Letitia looked at Charlotte sternly. "I believe that he behaves with a great deal too much freedom for a drawing master. Despite his amiable qualities, I have noticed an unfortunate inclination toward independence in his speech. No,

I do not think that we should take the risk. The occasion is a great deal too important.''

Her words reminded Charlotte of why she was making this effort to have Aubrey included. She doubted the honor of sitting at the same table with Lord Marwood would mean a great deal to him personally. But she wished to save Georgiana from a forced marriage, and though she knew little about Aubrey, she had an inkling that he might be her ally in that matter. It was a slender hope, particularly since she did not know that there was anything he might do about it either, but it was a hope! Aubrey must be at that dinner party. She drew in a breath and took her last gamble.

"There is a reason why he is so independent, Mother. Cousin Chalford was an officer in the war, although apparently he does not like to talk about it.''

"An officer?" The speech was making the desired impression.

"Yes, Georgy said that was clear from the things he said in his delirium.''

"I wonder what regiment he was with . . . Oh, we shall have to find out all about this.''

Charlotte suddenly was filled was misgivings. "Georgy says that he does not discuss it. She thinks that it probably embarrasses him, given his present position.''

"Of course it would.''

"So, naturally we should not mention it,'' Charlotte said. "Though you see, you need not fear that he cannot conduct himself with propriety.''

"Of course. Of course. We could not think of excluding him, one of our brave veterans.'' Letitia's eyes held a strange gleam that Charlotte could not like, but at least she had won his inclusion at dinner. She made a last feeble attempt to win Letitia's silence.

"You see why we cannot say anything about it to him.''

Letitia drew herself up, offended. "If you are implying that *I* should be the one who would embarrass the poor young man, I should think that you would know that *I* am the very soul of discretion.''

Charlotte had to content herself with that. She murmured apologetically and left the room.

* * *

By dinnertime that evening, the tension in the house had reached an almost-unbearable peak. Anxiety and curiosity, dread and impatience, all swirled about the parlor where the family, with the exception of the youngest members, had gathered to await Lord Marwood's arrival. Mr. Chalford had been persuaded into a pair of old-fashioned black knee breeches, accompanied by a long-tailed coat. He looked distinguished, if uncomfortable, and pretended to be oblivious to the dark looks cast at him by his wife. She contented herself by making remarks about gentlemen who refused to adopt modern manners of dress. Aubrey was glad to have escaped this reproach by wearing the form-fitting pantaloons that had come into fashion as evening wear after the war's end.

Letitia herself was resplendent in a highly beribboned and flounced satin gown, which seemed more suited to a ball than a simple dinner party. Acting upon Aubrey's advice, she had added knots of matching jonquil ribbons to her torturously frizzed coiffure, rendering her appearance even more ludicrous. Georgiana had to repress a gasp when she first saw her stepmother, but it was apparent that Letitia was smugly pleased with her ensemble.

To Aubrey's eye, Georgiana presented a charming picture in a simple and elegant gown of jaconet muslin trimmed with lace worn over a peach sarcenet slip. He gave her a warm, appreciative gaze as she entered the room. Georgiana could not help but color slightly, and she quickly took a seat at the opposite corner of the room. The little action reminded him of the purpose of the finery and he scowled.

Charlotte was not far behind her sister, and she also was attired most becomingly in a gown of pink, which accentuated her fair complexion. Aubrey, watching her, noted that the strain of the evening was much more apparent on her delicate features than on those of her sister, who entered into small talk with her stepmother as they waited. All conversation halted abruptly when Lord Marwood was announced.

Aubrey was admittedly curious to see Georgiana's prospective husband for himself. He studied the man carefully as he came into the room.

In one sense, what he saw might have disappointed him. Lord

Marwood was not an aging gentleman of sixty; Aubrey judged him instead to be in his mid-thirties. When Lord Marwood politely bowed upon being introduced, Aubrey was displeased to see that they were of much the same height, though Lord Marwood was some pounds heavier. One could not fault his figure either, though he lacked Aubrey's slimness. Aubrey had to content himself with imagining that Marwood likely would run to fat in his old age. The visitor bore Letitia's fawning with good grace, made polished compliments upon the beauty of the two girls, and treated Mr. Chalford with respectful deference. Nor could Aubrey carp at his clothing. It was well-cut, certainly, but not ostentatious, and his powerful figure enabled him to dispense with padding.

Worst of all, in Aubrey's eyes, was Lord Marwood's countenance. The features were strong, but blended harmoniously so as to create a pleasing aspect. The dark eyes seemed rather bold to Aubrey, and personally he found the black curls that cascaded carelessly over the brow, a bit too contrived. With his experience of woman, however, Aubrey had to admit that the faint lines of dissolution upon Marwood's countenance would probably only add to his appeal in the eyes of a young girl.

Since Georgiana was to have the place of honor next to Lord Marwood, it was she whom he escorted into dinner. Aubrey did not like the proprietary way in which he took her arm or the manner in which he leaned over to whisper some little remark in her ear. Aubrey observed them as well as he could as dinner began, but he was at somewhat of a disadvantage, for Letitia clearly considered that he should devote his attention entirely to her.

She managed to catch Aubrey's interest completely with one remark that seemed to spring out of the blue. "You know, Cousin Chalford, I hope that you may be able to advise me on continental fashion also. I should like to know what sorts of dresses the ladies were wearing during your time there."

Taken aback, he could only blink at her in surprise. As if the thought were just occurring to her, she called across the table to her husband.

"Mr. Chalford, I don't know if you realized our young cousin here—though he has been too shy to mention it—is a veteran of the late war."

Her voice successfully interrupted all the other conversations at the table.

Mr. Chalford turned interestedly to Aubrey. "Saw action in Belgium, did you?"

"Yes." Aubrey was still reeling under the shock of it. Who could have found out about that part of his background? He looked across the table at Georgiana. There were two bright spots of color on her cheeks and she was staring angrily at Charlotte. Her sister was doing her best to avoid meeting her gaze.

"He was one of our brave officers," Letitia informed Lord Marwood, emphasizing the last word.

"Ah, one of our celebrated Waterloo heroes." There was no mistaking the sneering tone in Marwood's voice.

Aubrey looked up in surprise to see that the expression of polite boredom had changed to one of positive antipathy. "I should not choose that term myself."

"What regiment did you happen to be in?" Marwood asked casually, perhaps with the hope of diminishing his status.

"The Life Guards," Aubrey said flatly, resenting this questioning, but powerless to do anything about it.

"Might have guessed that from your height," remarked Harry Chalford jovially. "What an action it must have been," he added with enthusiasm.

Marwood's eyes were now locked onto Aubrey's. "Yes, do tell us of your daring exploits," he said coldly. "I daresay the ladies would be enthralled."

Aubrey had forgotten about the rest of the company as he entered into the verbal duel with Marwood. "I do not find that battles make pleasant dinner conversation, my lord."

Marwood's eyes narrowed. "Oh, no? Then you must be an unusual young gentleman indeed. Most veterans I have met seem to think that they themselves defeated Bonaparte singlehandedly. I myself suspect that they have done more slaying of hearts than they ever did Frenchmen."

Aubrey's eyes darkened with anger. "Then I must regret that your lordship is only acquainted with such empty-headed fellows."

Marwood had abandoned all pretense at politeness. "You

yourself, then, might speak more knowledgeably on war's glories.''

Aubrey's first instinct was to jump to his feet and throw his glass of wine in the fellow's face. Fortunately, Letitia, who was oblivious to all this verbal sparring, leapt into the conversation.

"Oh, yes, indeed. How glorious it must all have been. I remember an article—I did not read it myself, but—''

Her interruption gave Aubrey the opportunity to regain his self-control. He cut her off before she could proceed farther. ''I am afraid, Mrs. Chalford, that I myself cannot tell you about war's glories.'' He paused and took a deep breath. ''I saw only its horrors.''

This statement had the desired effect of silencing his questioners, though Marwood's thwarted anger was clearly visible on his face.

Harry Chalford was the first to break the quiet. ''I daresay that's true.'' A wistful gleam came into his eyes. ''But blast it—if I'd been ten years younger myself, how I should have liked to have been there.'' He saw that Letitia was about to reprove him for his language, so he turned hastily to his guest. ''Tell me, Marwood, weren't you tempted to buy a pair of colors yourself?''

Marwood smiled in a condescending way. ''Actually, my dear sir, no. As a responsible landowner yourself, you can appreciate that one cannot go gallivanting off to parts unknown for long periods of time and expect to find things in order upon your return.'' He heaved a little sigh. ''No, unfortunately, I am one who has always taken my duty to my tenants far too seriously for that.''

Aubrey had to press his lips together to keep from making some response to that speech. He happened to glance at Georgiana and was happy to see that her face was pink and her eyes bright with anger, though she too forbore comment.

Harry, either from politeness or ignorance, appeared not to notice the irony in Marwood's words. ''That's true enough,'' he said. ''Not to mention the damage poachers do in your absence.'' He indicated Aubrey with a nod of the head. ''Why, our young cousin there was shot on the road recently by one in your woods.''

"Indeed?" Marwood's eyes rested on Aubrey for a moment, their expression enigmatic.

"Yes. Fortunate he wasn't killed."

"Fortunate indeed."

"I daresay that you'll find game sadly diminished, too, if you mean to try for some sport."

"I had meant to ask you about that very point, sir, knowing your reputation as a sportsman. Please tell me . . ." The two men were soon involved in a lively discussion of the different types of game to be found and likely locations for shooting, which soon turned into a comparison of the latest developments in firearms. Marwood pointedly excluded Aubrey from the conversation.

When the ladies retired, Aubrey therefore mumbled some apology and excused himself also. He was seething with an inward anger he found difficult to conceal. It added nothing to his equanimity to see the various significant glances that Letitia directed at her husband as she left the room. Fortunately, her husband seemed oblivious to these hints, apparently absorbed by the conversation instead.

Aubrey escaped to his room, glad to get away from the final scene of this little drama. He doubted whether his self-control would have proved adequate to the occasion. His blood boiled at the thought of the charm Marwood undoubtedly would lavish upon Georgiana as soon as they rejoined the ladies.

His original antipathy toward the man had deepened into decided enmity. He felt more certain than ever that Georgiana should not wed that man. It was clear, however, that Letitia had received no such unfavorable impression of her guest. Even if she had, he mused, it was unlikely to serve as a check to her ambition.

He had been tempted at least once during dinner to leap to his feet and announce his own name and rank, for he knew Letitia well enough to realize that by doing so he would scotch Marwood's chances with Georgiana. Such an action would only place him in a new sort of predicament, however. Attracted as he was to Georgiana, he still had no wish to be thrust into marriage with her. The alternative of flight would leave the mystery of his shooting unsolved, and some obstinate streak in his personality could not be content to leave it so. Besides, he thought, recalling Marwood's eyes upon him, I have the distinct impression that he knows something about this matter. Thinking back upon the conversation, surely it was odd that Marwood had expressed no surprise about the mishap.

Aubrey's eyes narrowed in speculation. It would appear that the key to solving both Georgiana's dilemma and the mystery lay in discovering more about Lord Marwood. Where should he start? An eyebrow flew up as the idea suddenly occurred to him. Why not begin with those pampered tenants of whom Marwood boasted? He already had an introduction to Jem.

Accordingly, as the next day was Sunday, Aubrey took himself off into the afternoon to visit Jem and his family. He had the good fortune to find the entire family at home, and he was welcomed in politely, if not cordially. Indeed, Aubrey's curiosity was aroused by the uneasy way in which Jem received him and by the quick glance he exchanged with his elder sister before the invitation was extended.

Crossing the threshold, Aubrey found that the inside of the cottage was consistent with what the exterior had promised. There was a pleasing cleanliness and order to it, which did not manage to disguise the fact that the inhabitants were in straitened circumstances. The children similarly were well-scrubbed and they exhibited a decorum in their behavior that at first took Aubrey by surprise. A few minutes' observation provided him with an explanation: every one of their young faces showed the stamp of care. Clearly they all felt the uncertainty of their situation, and this early responsibility had given them a maturity beyond their years. This was particularly evident in the eldest, Susan, who exhibited a great deal of self-possession for a maid of eighteen. After the brief interplay with Jem, she welcomed Aubrey in briskly and proceeded to pour him a glass of homemade perry.

She was more than ordinarily pretty, with blond hair and blue eyes. The quick intelligence that shone in her face gave her a beauty beyond that of the average country maid. She was tall for a woman, and her figure had a comely roundness.

She immediately took efficent charge of the conversation, directing commonplace sorts of questions to Aubrey, including a brother or sister when she could, and keeping a stern eye on the rest. In fact, the tension Aubrey had sensed upon his arrival seemed to dissipate with time, and he was beginning to feel quite comfortable with this unusual family.

The situation changed abruptly when he mentioned Marwood's name. An unexpected hush fell upon the room. As Aubrey glanced at Susan, he saw that she was gazing at Jem, a warning look on her face. He turned to observe Jem and saw that his face had flushed with some unspecified emotion and that he held his fists tightly clenched.

"James, you'd better go see to Mr. Chalford's horse. It's a warm day and it may want water."

Jem gave a quick nod of acquiescence and escaped the room. Aubrey looked at Susan again and saw that she had assumed an air of nonchalance, though her complexion was pinker than before. She made an attempt to turn the conversation, but Aubrey could not abandon his inquiries so soon.

"Judging by his remarks last night, Lord Marwood seems to feel that his duties to his tenants come before all else."

He directed a sharp glance at the girl. "I suppose you must consider yourself fortunate to have such a landlord?"

There was no mistaking the spark of anger that flew from her eyes, but she mastered herself quickly. "I suppose that since we have never had another, it is difficult for us to make comparisons," she said haltingly.

Hoping to learn something more, Aubrey shot an arrow at random. "He is quite well-respected in these parts, then?"

An exclamation burst from one of the younger children.

Susan turned and silenced them with a look, her mouth grimly set. She turned to Aubrey coolly. "Why, is there some reason he shouldn't be?"

Remembering Georgiana's godmother's agitation, Aubrey played a hunch. "I believe that his reputation in London is rather different."

He was disappointed to see that this statement produced no reaction. Susan merely shrugged as she took his empty glass from him and busied herself with refilling it.

Aubrey really could not blame them. Why should they confide in a stranger, particularly one so insignificant as a drawing master? He decided to lay his cards on the table.

"You must forgive me if my questions seem impertinent,"

he said, "but after making Lord Marwood's acquaintance yesterday, I feel strongly that he is not the man to wed my cousin Georgiana." He looked at Susan with all the appeal he could muster. "My problem is that I need to discover more information about him in order to have a hope of preventing their marriage."

"They're to be married?" Susan asked, turning around to glance at him sharply.

It was Aubrey's turn to shrug. "I understand that is the family's intention."

There were a few moments of silence. Aubrey waited eagerly for a confidence, but none was forthcoming. Susan handed him his glass in an abstracted manner. He was shocked by the bleak expression on her face. He thanked her, and the words seemed to recall her to her present surroundings.

"I am sorry that we cannot help you," she said indifferently. "He is gone from Marwood a great deal. Perhaps someone in London could tell you what you wish to know."

Try as he might, Aubrey could not make the slightest breach in this wall of reserve. Even the youngest children viewed him with a new wariness. He eventually abandoned his attempts at light conversation, gulped down his glass of perry hurriedly, and made his awkward farewells.

He found Jem outside, stroking Sligo's nose admiringly. As Aubrey approached, he was surprised to receive the first smile he had ever seen upon the boy's face.

"He's grand," Jem said.

One corner of Aubrey's mouth curled upward in a grin. "Sligo seems to have a high opinion of you also."

An eager inquisitiveness had seized Jem. "Sligo? He's Irish, then?"

Aubrey nodded as he untied the reins from the fence post. "You're a horse-fancier, I see."

Jem almost blushed. "Oh, no. But this one—he's finer even than Lord Marwood's black."

Aubrey could not help but be touched by the boy's enthusiasm. He held out the reins to him. "Do you care to try him? Just take him down the road a little way."

Jem obviously was overwhelmed by this offer. His eyes shone

with excitement and he could not manage to speak, but instead nodded slowly. His hand was stretched toward the reins when his sister's voice reached him. "Jem!"

He turned and saw her regarding him warningly from the doorway. His small shoulders slumped with disappointment, but he turned to Aubrey bravely.

"Thank you, sir, but I am afraid that I need to get back to my chores."

Aubrey gave him a sympathetic smile. "Well, another time, perhaps."

"Yes, sir." His forlorn expression belied the possibility.

"Well, good-bye, then. And thank you for your hospitality," called Aubrey as he swung aboard Sligo and started on his way. He glanced once behind him and saw Jem trudging slowly back to the cottage, his sister still watching him keenly.

Aubrey was both puzzled and irritated. He could understand why a family so dependent on Marwood's good graces might not wish to carry tales about him. On the other hand, why should that sister be so determined to prevent the least intimacy from forming between Jem and him? What secret could a twelve-year-old boy reveal that would place their family in jeopardy?

He shook his head. Despite what they said, or chose not to say, it was evident that Marwood was not the ideal landlord he claimed to be. When he had mentioned Marwood's name, the fear and loathing in that house had almost been tangible. Here was a fresh mystery to solve, although Aubrey had an inkling that it was not unrelated to the other.

"I mean to find out why they feel that way about you, my dear Lord Marwood," he whispered. "And then I mean to prevent your marrying Georgy."

6

Just having made his resolution, Aubrey was less than pleased to see the object of his thoughts riding toward him, Georgiana mounted on Tinderbox beside him. As Aubrey came within earshot of the couple, he could hear Marwood laughing appreciatively at some remark of Georgiana's. Marwood's whole attention was devoted to Georgiana, and as she kept her eyes modestly downcast, the couple was almost upon Aubrey before they noticed his presence.

Georgiana happened to glance up and regarded him with a startled expression. "Cousin Aubrey!"

Marwood was obliged to turn his eyes from his fair companion. He looked at Aubrey unpleasantly. "Ah, if it isn't the Waterloo veteran," he sneered.

Aubrey was determined to keep his temper in check. He nodded briefly at the two and would have continued on his way if Georgiana hadn't stopped him.

"Wait, cousin. I've been searching for you."

Taking a deep breath, he reined in Sligo and turned to her, his face expressionless. "I should hate to interrupt your tête-à-tête."

Georgy flushed with embarrassment. "Oh, but we weren't . . . That is, Lord Marwood was just . . ."

Aubrey made no attempt to extricate her from her difficulties.

"Lord Marwood just happened to be riding in the same direction that I was so—"

Marwood gave her a dazzling smile. "So I took advantage of such a splendid opportunity, naturally."

Georgiana turned to him, a little stiffly. "My lord, since I have found my cousin, I shall be returning home now."

"Ah, must you?" He took her gloved hand and kissed it. "I

should be desolate, except for the knowledge that your beauty will brighten my eyes again on the morrow.''

The dazzling smile was cut off abruptly when he turned to Aubrey and gave him a curt nod. He wheeled his big black around and cantered off in the direction of Marwood House. At the back of his mind, something about that black horse bothered Aubrey, but the thought eluded him. If he had been in a fair-minded mood, he would have had to admit that Marwood cut rather a dashing figure. He was in no such mood, however.

Georgiana attempted a slight, conciliatory smile. Aubrey's face remained expressionless. Sligo pawed at the ground in boredom.

At length, Aubrey spoke. ''Well, why did you wish to see me?''

Georgiana heaved a little sigh. She had expected him to be upset, but obviously he was angrier than she had anticipated. ''We might as well ride,'' she said softly.

Accordingly, they urged their horses forward into a walk, though Tinderbox, as usual, was disinclined to move from the comfortable stance she had assumed. With persistence on Georgiana's part, however, she finally joined Sligo in an ambling walk.

Georgiana sneaked a glance at Aubrey's face, which still retained its forbidding expression. Well, there was no point in delaying any longer. ''I wanted to find you to apologize—'' His face did not relax one whit, so she added hurriedly, ''For last night, I mean. I know you were placed in an awkward position.''

Aubrey still did not take his eyes from the road, but he responded coolly, ''My dear girl, you are much mistaken if you believe that I hold you responsible for Lord Marwood's manners, or want of them.''

A tinge of color rose to her cheeks. ''That's not what I was speaking of.''

He lifted his eyebrows in a manner Georgiana found offensively supercilious. ''Indeed! Well, surely you don't imagine that I would attempt to censor your choice of companions.''

Georgiana was flabbergasted. ''My choice of . . . What in heaven's name are you saying?''

He shrugged slightly. ''I should have thought it obvious. I

myself am not used to country manners; however, I would imagine it is not quite the thing for a young lady to ride unescorted with an unmarried gentleman.''

Georgiana's temper was beginning to rise. "Oh, then perhaps I shouldn't be here with you."

He shook his head. "You are forgetting that I am a relation, at least in the eyes of the world."

If they had not been on horseback, she would have been tempted to give him a good shaking. As it was, she was forced to take a deep breath to regain her self-control. She reminded herself grimly that he was the injured party and that he was owed an apology. She spoke in the most reasonable tone that she could muster.

"This discussion has distracted me from my original purpose. I did not search for you in order to talk about Lord Marwood. Rather, I came to apologize to you for discussing your military background with my family."

Aubrey was boiling with rage. First of all, it was apparent that Georgiana had been enjoying herself with Marwood. Else why would she defend him so vigorously? He had also heard Marwood mention an assignation for the morrow. She undoubtedly had her mother's full blessing for these clandestine meetings, too. It was as he had foreseen. Just like any other silly, opportunistic schoolgirl, Georgiana couldn't resist a title, and Marwood's dubious reputation only rendered him more attractive. Aubrey ground his teeth. Why had he bothered to imagine that she was any different? He could barely hear what she said, he was so angry.

"Although I didn't know if you wished it to be a secret, since you had not mentioned it to any of us, I should not have taken the liberty of—''

He finally managed to take in what she was saying. On top of everything else, it seemed unforgivable. He yanked a startled Sligo to a dead stop and turned to glare angrily at her. "You are saying that you felt free to reveal to your family everything I said in my delirium?"

Georgiana was taken aback by this fresh blaze of rage. "Yes . . . That is, no . . . That is, I only told Charlotte and she promised she wouldn't tell anyone else," she began to stammer.

"Oh, so you only told Charlotte," he sneered. "You might

as well have told the *Morning Chronicle*, or didn't you realize that?''

Georgiana made another attempt to defend herself. ''Well, she was convinced that you were some sort of earl or an Italian prince in disguise, and I couldn't let her go on dreaming that—'' She abruptly choked off what she was about to say and instead looked at him contritely. ''You do act in a commanding way for a drawing master, you know.''

By now Aubrey's fury would not let him admit the justice of this observation. ''And would it have done such great harm for her to have imagined that?''

''I thought—'' Georgiana began weakly.

''Surely you didn't imagine it in the least likely that anyone else would give the slightest credence to any of Charlotte's romantic theories?''

Georgiana could only shake her head dumbly.

''So, tell me,'' he continued bitterly, ''what other fascinating bits of information did I reveal while I was out of my senses? Doubtless there were other tidbits too delectable not to be shared with Charlotte.''

Georgiana colored hotly. ''No! That is, I did not tell Charlotte anything else.''

He had leaned over from his horse to take her wrist in an iron grip. ''But there was more to tell.''

She was caught between anger and embarrassment. She hadn't realized before the enormity of what she had done. The words came reluctantly from her lips. ''Not much.'' She hesitated. ''There were just two names that you kept calling.''

His grip tightened. ''And they were?''

She could not meet his eye. ''Jack . . . and . . . Cressida.''

He dropped her wrist abruptly.

She looked up, startled. His face was white. ''Aubrey.''

He was not looking at her. ''I suppose a mere drawing master should not expect to be entitled to privacy,'' he said, as if to himself.

Tears started to her eyes. ''Aubrey,'' she said again, but he did not appear to hear. Instead, he touched his heels briefly to Sligo's flanks and the two were off in a cloud of dust.

''Aubrey . . .'' Georgiana began, but it was too late. He was gone. There was no help for it. She could never hope to overtake him on her sleepy old mare. She heaved a sigh and managed to convince Tinderbox into a walk. She rode toward home, feeling more guilty and miserable than she had ever felt in her life.

Georgiana did her best to avoid the rest of the family when she arrived home, and she took to her bed early, pleading a headache. Bed could not provide the respite she sought, however. She lay tossing uncomfortably all night, tormented by the stricken look she had seen upon Aubrey's face. It was in vain that she reminded herself that he was only a drawing master, and a mere acquaintance at that. She thought of how uncomplainingly he had followed her outrageous lead, of the jests they had shared, of the beautiful and detailed drawings of fossils that he had been presenting to her regularly without compensation. How willingly he had halted his life for her convenience! And she had repaid him with betrayal. She had taken him for the merry, heedless being he appeared on the surface, ignoring the possibility that he might have feelings he chose to keep hidden.

She remembered the anguish with which he had called the names in his delirium, and winced to herself. How could she have imagined that revelations about his past would make no difference to him? An officer reduced to earning his living as a drawing master! How it must have wounded him. She recalled his last words, that he supposed "a mere drawing master should not expect to be entitled to privacy." How could she have treated him so? She would only receive her just deserts if he left in the morning.

She turned her face into her pillow and wept. She never paused to wonder why the prospective departure of a mere acquaintance, even one undoubtedly useful to her, should render her so entirely wretched.

Once his anger had cooled, Aubrey too began to feel remorseful about the incident. It was not fair to blame Georgiana for her sister's featherheadedness or her mother's insensitivity. She undoubtedly had thought it for the best when she told Charlotte, however mistaken she might have been. After all, she had no way of knowing what an unpleasant topic it was for him or what

awful memories it dredged up in his mind. He closed his eyes
for a minute, trying to erase the picture of Jack as he had seen
him last. Of course it was no use. It never was.

He opened his eyes again. He was a fine one to take offense.
After all, he was masquerading in her home under a false
identity. What would she have to say if she knew he wasn't
a drawing master, since he'd never indicated otherwise during
these several days? He shook his head. Well, it was too late
to give up his role now, with the mystery yet to solve and
Marwood clearly intent upon marrying Georgiana.

Marwood . . . Aubrey had to admit that it was Marwood who
had driven him into such a rage. The notion that Georgiana
might enjoy, or even prefer, his company was too painful even
to contemplate. Of course, she did not know that Aubrey suspected Marwood was a blackguard. Aubrey unconsciously
clenched his hand into a fist. It was up to him to prove his
suspicions; he would need evidence. He thought of the
unexpected way in which Jem had opened up to him, even
though it was just for a moment. I must get that boy to trust
me, Aubrey resolved, and somehow that will be Lord
Marwood's undoing. With sweet thoughts of vengeance, he took
to his bed and fell asleep instantly, unmindful even of Lion's
snores.

Georgiana took advantage of the first faint rays of sunlight
to rise and dress. Though she knew it would likely earn a scold
from her stepmother, she took her digging materials and fled
to the quarry. She had left a promising specimen half-embedded
in the stone. Its extraction might help to take her mind off her
difficulties for a while.

When Aubrey awakened later the same morning, the thought
uppermost in his mind was that he must find Georgiana and
apologize to her. The task was not as easy as it seemed. She
was not to be found in the breakfast parlor or in the morning
room. He went outside to investigate the lavender house but
found it deserted. Could she have slipped out to meet Marwood
early? He realized with a sinking heart that his angry words
of the previous day might well have driven her into Marwood's
arms.

He was making his way back through one of the kitchen

gardens when he encountered Augusta. He greeted her in an absentminded way.

She, shrewdly noting the direction whence he had come, asked him bluntly, "Are you looking for Georgy?"

When he assured her that he was, she gave a satisfied little smile. "I thought so. Well, you'll probably find her at the quarry." Her face assumed a look of anxiety. "But please don't mention it to Mother."

He gave her his promise that he wouldn't, and after extracting directions from her, he headed for the stables. A few minutes later, he was galloping down the same dusty road that he had taken the day before, passing Jem's family farm.

Augusta's directions proved more than adequate and he was able to find the quarry road without any difficulty. Half-choked with weeds, it exuded a desolate loneliness that made Aubrey wonder that Georgiana should not be frightened to be here by herself.

As he approached, he saw that she was not quite alone, for Lion had evidently deserted his chamber in the early morning to provide his mistress with companionship. The big dog looked up alertly at him as he drew near and then the great tail began to wag back and forth in happy recognition.

Georgiana evidently was preoccupied with her task, for she did not even seem to hear as he rode into the quarry. Her bonnet had fallen off in her struggle to wrest the fossil from the surrounding rock, and her gloves had been discarded as impediments to her work. Her curls clung damply to her face, which was flushed from the heat of her exertions. Aubrey watched in fascination for a moment as she took up her chisel with exquisite care and tapped her hammer firmly against it. This blow produced the desired effect of dislodging the fossil and it sank into her waiting hand.

"I say," Aubrey said admiringly, without thinking, "it's almost like sculpture, isn't it?"

Georgiana started in fright, nearly dropping the fossil. She turned to see Aubrey and let out a gasp of relief. "Oh, it's you."

"I'm sorry. I didn't mean to startle you." He swung down from Sligo and knotted the reins about a nearby tree branch. He looked up with a smile, but saw that she was watching him warily. He noticed the dark smudges underneath her eyes and the tension in her attitude, and his conscience smote him.

"I came to apologize to you."

She looked at him uncomprehendingly.

"I shouldn't have lost my temper so yesterday. It was just that—"

She shook her head, interrupting him. "You had . . . you had every right to be angry with me. What I did was inexcusable."

"You thought it was for the best," he said, defending her.

She refused to be pardoned. "Still, I never should have mentioned it without your permission."

"You couldn't have known that it would bother me so."

Her face paled and he saw that he had said the wrong thing. "It was bound to come out sooner or later," he added hastily. "In any case, I hope you will forgive me for acting in such a childish manner."

"No, it's you who must forgive me, though I don't know how you can. I behaved reprehensibly."

He took a step toward her. "No, my reaction was entirely out of proportion to what you did." He took in a deep breath. "Perhaps you might understand it better if I explain it to you."

He took her by the arm and led her to a nearby block of stone upon which they sat. She turned her eyes upon his face and the pain in them served as a reproach to him. Unthinkingly, he took her hand and patted it.

"I was a great beast yesterday. I only hope that I can make you understand why I acted as I did." He pursed his lips. "I guess I will begin by telling you that I was fresh out of university when Napolean made his escape. I suppose I was no different than any other eager young fellow. We all bought our commissions thinking it would be a great lark to take care of the French." A shadow passed over his face. "We had no more idea what we were about than a pack of blind, newborn puppies."

Georgiana was beginning to forget her guilt in her fascination with his story.

"Nothing I had ever read, or heard, or seen, prepared me for the realities of war." He closed his eyes for a moment. "Nothing could prepare you for it, to see, not three feet away from you, a man's head carried off by a ball." He grimaced.

"When we charged, our horses trod upon the bodies of the dead and dying. The screams, the smoke, the stench, the mangled pieces of bodies that once were your childhood friends . . .'' He shook his head as if to dispel the picture and gave a heavy sigh.

Georgiana scarcely dared breathe. He looked up painfully.

"I am wandering from what I meant to tell you.'' He took his free hand and rubbed his forehead with it, unconsciously retaining her hand in the other. "I don't suppose that there are many people we know in our lifetimes whom we can admire wholeheartedly.'' He tightened his lips again, revealing the difficulty with which the words came. "My friend Jack was one of those.''

He took another deep breath and launched into his tale resolutely. "We were boys together at school and all the way through university. I never had a brother of my own, but Jack filled that role for me.'' He shook his head wistfully, his thoughts far away. "He was the brightest student, the champion cricketer, and the best of good fellows. There aren't many men whom you could say this of, but he was respected and liked by everyone who was fortunate enough to know him . . .'' Aubrey's voice trailed off.

Georgiana waited silently for him to begin again.

"He was the first to go, naturally. His fearlessness and the devotion he inspired made him a far better soldier than I ever could have hoped to have been. He seemed almost unaware of the danger, as if no ball, or shot, or sword could touch him.''

Aubrey was clenching Georgiana's hand rather tightly now, but she made no protest. His face was pale as he continued.

"I suppose his own attitude made us all believe it. It seemed unthinkable that anything could touch him. But then, the day was almost over and it was clear that the victory was ours.'' His voice took on a bewildered tone. "Jack hadn't even received a scratch. The rest of us each had a half-dozen minor wounds. And then the shot came, a stray. He had just made some joke and I was smiling when I saw him fall.'' There was a look of incredulity on his face. "It happened so suddenly. There was absolutely no warning.''

"He was killed,'' murmured Georgiana.

"No. Not instantly.'' Aubrey took another deep breath before continuing. "I took him to the surgeon myself." He put his free hand up to his forehead again. "I don't remember exactly how I got him there, but when I did, they said I had wasted my time. His condition was hopeless. The shot had penetrated his lung and lodged in his spine. Jack himself seemed to know it was useless. When he had been hit, he had looked up at me and said, 'I'm done for, old man.' I simply refused to believe it."

There was a pause before Aubrey continued. "I stayed with him all night. It was against regulations, but I couldn't bear to leave him to die alone there. I sat beside him and held his hand while he lay there, in great pain, gasping for breath while his lungs slowly filled with blood. All around us we could hear the sounds of other wounded men screaming in anguish. And I didn't even have a canteen to dampen a handkerchief with which I could sponge his lips. It took him all night to die."

Aubrey fell silent. The horrified Georgiana clasped his hand in sympathy. There was a long silence before Aubrey seemed to rouse himself. He looked at Georgiana in surprise, as if he had forgotten that she was there.

"I don't know why I told you all that," he said. "I didn't intend to. I never have told anyone the entire story before."

Her eyes were full, but she gave him a tremulous little smile.

How beautiful those eyes were. He realized that he was still holding her hand and dropped it abruptly.

Aubrey was at a loss. He was embarrassed by the depth of his disclosures and couldn't quite think of what to say. Fortunately, rescue was at hand. Both he and Georgiana heard the voice at the same time.

"Mr. Aubrey!"

He looked up to see Jem scrambling down into the quarry.

"Mr. Aubrey, I need to talk to you." The boy ran up to them, his chest heaving as he recovered his breath. He looked appealingly at Aubrey, who gave him a sympathetic smile.

"How may I help you?"

Jem cast a glance at Georgiana. "How do you do, Miss Georgiana?" he said, dipping his head and shoulders in a hasty bow. He turned again to Aubrey. "Please, sir, I need to talk to you in private."

Aubrey's eyebows rose slightly, but he gave no other sign

of surprise. "Very well. I suppose we may leave Miss Georgiana to her work." He gave her a quick smile, then went to untie Sligo.

She watched them walk off, the tall young man and undersized boy. She noted the deferential way in which Aubrey bowed his head to listen to Jem. She wondered when they had become confidants. It was only natural, she realized. Jem's father had been dead for two years. Jem undoubtedly missed an older man's companionship.

She sat upon the rock and watched them as they walked out of view. A beam of sunlight caught Aubrey's rough shock of hair and turned it to a bright gold before he passed around the bend and disappeared from view. What a different picture she had of him now. She considered the case dispassionately for a moment.

"I'm in love with a drawing master," she whispered softly.

It could not be, and yet it was. She had longed to fold him in her arms and comfort him after hearing his story. She did not try to deceive herself into believing that it was merely pity she felt. She longed to run her fingers through his hair, to press him to her, to kiss that mouth.

She stopped her daydream abruptly, shocked at herself. How could she have fallen in love with someone so ineligible so quickly? She was not Charlotte. She knew better than to imagine that her parents would have no objections or that he would suddenly escape his poverty by inheriting a fortune or other nonsense. There was only one person in whom she could confide. She rose hurriedly and ran to snatch up her bonnet and gloves.

"I must go see Godmama," she said to herself.

It wasn't until they were well out of Georgiana's earshot that Jem abandoned the seemingly random topics of conversation he had introduced and gave Aubrey a hard look.

"Mr. Aubrey, I have a question to ask you," he said seriously.

Aubrey gave him an inquiring look.

Jem's face flushed slightly. "Is it true . . . That is, my sister said that Lord Marwood intends to marry Miss Georgiana."

Aubrey shrugged. "He certainly seems serious in his

attentions to her.'' He was unprepared for the sudden, urgent grip on his sleeve. Startled, he looked over to see that Jem's face wore a look of desperation.

"But you can't let him. You mustn't let him. Miss Georgiana has always been so good to my family and me. She can't marry him!''

Aubrey was taken aback by this fierce appeal. "I'm sorry, Jem, but I don't know that there is a great deal that I can do about it at this point.''

Jem held on to his sleeve even tighter. "But you're her cousin. Maybe you could talk to her, or her father, or someone.''

Aubrey detached the boy's hand gently. "I assure you, I like Lord Marwood no better than you, but I don't think that my opinion has much weight with Miss Georgy or her family.''

Jem's eyes were beginning to fill with emotion. "But you've got to do something,'' he said, gulping back a sob. "He's an evil man, a horrible man. Miss Georgiana shouldn't marry him.''

Aubrey laid a sympathetic hand on the boy's shoulder. "But I have no way to prove that to anyone else. All I know is how I feel about him.'' He patted the boy's shoulder. "After all, Lord Marwood hasn't actually proposed yet. You may be worrying yourself unnecessarily.''

It was the best Aubrey could do, but the boy looked at him disbelievingly. "I have to return to my chores now,'' he said, curtly, and then took off as fast as his heels could carry him. Aubrey shook his head as he watched him go. What an odd, contradictory boy Jem was. Aubrey had a definite feeling that the boy knew more than he was telling. Well, trust might come with time. I only hope it's in time to do me some good, he thought.

When Aubrey arrived back at Chalton, he found the entire household in an uproar. Upon espying him, Wilkins gave an audible sigh of relief.

"Ah, there you are, sir. Mrs. Chalford has been seeking you this past hour or more.''

Aubrey was not allowed time for questions as the butler rushed him hurriedly in the direction of Letitia's chambers. The familiar petulant voice could be heard within, ascending in volume with some complaint. It ceased abruptly when Wilkins knocked and announced Aubrey, nearly thrusting him through the door. Inside, Aubrey found a peevish Letitia and a harried Charlotte, while Betsey was close to tears.

Letitia's face brightened instantly at the sight of Aubrey. "You may go, Betsey," she said sharply to the maid, then tossed her youthful curls. "Useless wench," she commented.

Aubrey saw it was time to be at his most ingratiating. "My dear lady," he said with simulated concern, "whatever is the matter?"

Letitia sniffed with displeasure. "We are to dine with Lord Marwood tonight, and since my new gowns are not yet ready, I have little that is suitable to wear." She glanced at the unfortunate Charlotte. "And naturally, I can expect nothing but the most countrified notions from my family."

Aubrey's eyes lit up with an expression Georgiana would have recognized instantly as wicked delight. "I should be happy to offer you my own humble ideas, madam."

Aubrey parted from her an hour later, well-satisfied with himself. After all, since he had not been included in the invitation, he should not have to spend his dinner hour looking at her. It might have been hard to keep a straight face otherwise. Charlotte might have been scandalized by the notion of a rather dated aigrette with towering ostrich plumes as suitable headgear for a quiet country dinner party. She also might have found Aubrey's combination of yellow and purple for Letitia's ensemble rather too original. She knew better than to remonstrate with her delighted parent, however, and so managed to keep her mouth firmly shut during the entire interval. Letitia was so pleased by Aubrey's choices that she did not even notice Charlotte's lack of enthusiasm when called upon to second them.

Letitia could not know it, of course, but she had done a great deal to lift Aubrey's spirits. On the one hand, she had gratified his sense of the ludicrous. More importantly, however, she had let him know that Georgiana's meeting with Marwood was to be in the nature of a family outing, rather than the clandestine assignation Aubrey had imagined. Therefore, it was likely that she had no more fondness for Marwood than he himself had. He felt a great sense of relief. It should make his task a great deal easier. He broke into a whistle as he made his way to his own chamber.

He would have been a great deal less complacent had he been able to foresee the events that would take place that evening. As it was, he went to bed with a light heart.

When he awoke the next morning, he recalled that he had been remiss about his assumed occupation and determined to set to work accordingly.

The three youngest girls had been attired in white muslin dresses with blue sashes for their portrait; so, finding a well-lighted area, he began to work on their likenesses jointly. He had arranged them to his satisfaction, Sophia and Amelia sitting on a richly brocaded sofa while Augusta leaned on its arm. He picked up his charcoal and had made a few preliminary strokes when Charlotte burst in upon them. He looked at her inquiringly.

"I thought we might have your sitting this afternoon."

"I must speak to you." Her voice and expression were unusually serious.

He made a few more strokes, sighed, and put down his charcoal. "You may take a rest now."

Emmy whooped with joy as she bolted from the sofa. Sophia followed her more sedately from the room. Augusta cast a curious look at her sister, but she also departed.

Aubrey picked up a cloth and wiped his fingers delicately. "What did you wish to discuss?"

"You must stop him."

"Stop whom?" he asked calmly.

She nearly stamped with impatience. "Lord Marwood. Last night he asked Papa for permission to pay his addresses to Georgy."

Aubrey's face assumed a grim expression. "And your father consented?"

Charlotte flung herself onto the sofa in despair. "You know our mother. What else could he do?"

"And Georgy, has she also consented?"

Charlotte's forehead puckered in a frown. "No, or at least I don't think so. She won't discuss it with me." She looked at him with something approaching panic in her eyes. "It's only a question of time, don't you see?"

Aubrey shook his head. "I don't know what you expect me to do."

She leaned toward him, a pleading look upon her beautiful

countenance. "I don't know either, but you're our only hope."

Aubrey had not expected a complication so early. What a pickle he was in. He was certainly fond of Georgiana, but he was not ready to make her an offer yet himself. Possibly he was a fool, but he had learned his bitter lesson well at Cressida's hands. He didn't even know how Georgiana herself felt about this match. Charlotte's eyes had not wavered from his face and the trust in them bothered him.

He heaved an unconscious sigh. "Well, I'll see what I can contrive."

She leapt up and, to his annoyance, proceeded to embrace him. He was busy attempting to extricate himself from her grateful clasp and so hardly noticed that a visitor had entered and was being announced. He was trying to peel her arms from about his neck when the name caught his attention.

"Mr. William Darley," announced Wilkins ponderously.

Aubrey swung to face the doorway and beheld his cousin standing there openmouthed.

"Aubrey," exclaimed William in shocked disapproval.

7

The exclamation caused Charlotte to turn her attention to the door. Her shock was extreme when she realized she was being surveyed with a look of disapprobation by the handsomest man she had ever seen, clearly a pink of the *ton.*

"Oh," she gasped, and quickly relinquishing her hold upon Aubrey, she fled from the room.

"Really, Aubrey—" William was beginning when Aubrey frowned and put a finger to his lips.

"Be silent and let me do the talking. Above all, do not mention my title or surname."

"Come now—" William was protesting when an extraordinary creature issued into the room. She turned an ingratiating smile upon him, clearly impressed by the air of fashion he exuded. Indeed, William was looking very dapper for a man who had spent the last week in very inadequate country inns. Thanks to the loving attentions of his valet, Smith, William's pantaloons were immaculate, his topboots shone like mirrors, and his linen was as crisp as if he'd just stepped out onto Bond Street for a morning stroll. The many-caped driving coat he wore seemed a little unseasonable to Aubrey, but Letitia certainly found no fault with it.

It was perhaps unfortunate that, given her obvious amiability, she made no such positive impression on him. She was wearing a pink muslin, which only served to exaggerate the color brought on by too-tight lacing. It was richly trimmed with French work, which in addition to the triple flounce about the hem and the wreath of artificial roses in her hair combined to make the sartorially sensitive William feel rather ill. He glanced at Aubrey involuntarily and saw that worthy observing his reaction with a gleam of mischievous appreciation.

The creature extended her hand to William while giving

Aubrey an arch glance. "Pray, cousin, don't you mean to introduce me to your handsome young friend?"

William's brows drew together in puzzlement at the mention of the word "cousin," but he obediently took her hand and kissed it as Aubrey smoothly leapt in and prevented his speaking.

"Pray forgive me, I was startled by my *friend's* unexpected visit. Mrs. Chalford, allow me to present Mr. William Darley of London. William, my *cousin* Mrs. Chalford."

William did not miss the slight emphasis Aubrey placed on the two words. He wondered what kind of havey-cavey business Aubrey was engaged in now.

"Please," Letitia was simpering, "there is no need to stand on such formality, since you are, after all, our cousin's good friend. I wish you would call me Letitia." She gave him a confiding glance. "It makes me feel such a fossil to be called Mrs. Chalford. I married quite young, you see."

William was taken aback somewhat by this sudden intimacy. He looked at Aubrey to see his eyes brimming with amusement, and determined to pull him aside and demand the truth at the first opportunity.

"But what a poor hostess I am," Letitia continued. "You must be in need of refreshment after your travels. Let me ring for some sherry."

After giving instructions to Wilkins, who had removed the driving coat, Letitia offered her arm to William in a manner that did not allow for refusal.

He did his best to mask his reluctance as he took it. She leaned upon him heavily, assuring him that he must catch her up on the latest *on-dits* of London. "For," she said, looking at Aubrey kindly, "Cousin Aubrey of course was not in a position to know all the latest gossip."

This was true enough, though William wondered how she would know it.

As they seated themselves on the sofa, she inclined herself toward William in an intimate way. "So tell me," she said, "how is my dear Mr. Brummell?"

Aubrey was forced to look away in order to control his laughter as William gravely informed her that Mr. Brummell had fled to Calais that spring in order to avoid being thrown in debtor's prison. Another person might have been deterred by this, but Letitia, never bothered by sensitivity, merely remarked, "That is the misfortune of being able to go to town so little. I am so dreadfully behindhand with all the news." She turned to give Aubrey, who had recovered, an engaging look. "Had it not been for our young cousin there, I'm sure I might despair of appearing in the least modish."

William, who was at the moment accepting a glass of sherry from Wilkins, nearly dropped it at these words. He threw Aubrey an accusing glance, but the latter once again jumped into the breach.

"My dear lady, with your sense of style, I am certain no one could ever stigmatize you as a dowd."

William, who was taking a sip of sherry, nearly choked on it, whereupon Aubrey leapt up to pat him on the back helpfully.

"My friend should not attempt to partake of spiritous liquors," he informed Letitia. "They often induce these little fits."

Letitia looked at William anxiously. "Oh, dear, I shouldn't have offered it had I . . . Tell me, do they last long?"

A warning pinch kept William from speaking. "Usually not above half an hour or so."

"Half an hour, good gracious," she said anxiously as William continued to cough dutifully. "Perhaps he should lie down somewhere," she suggested.

"An excellent idea. I'll just help him to my chamber."

"There's no need for that. He may have the gold bedchamber. I think the poor young man may be more comfortable there," she said, eyeing William curiously.

"That is very kind of you," said Aubrey, hauling William to his feet, while the latter managed a nod of appreciation between coughs. Aubrey threw his arm about William and, following Wilkins, assisted him to the designated chamber.

"My friend's man might be of aid to him at the moment," Aubrey advised Wilkins, who thereupon went to fetch the valet.

As soon as they were alone, William ceased his coughing and gave Aubrey an irate look. "Very well, Aubrey. What's all this nonsense?"

The viscount had some difficulty in replying, for he was convulsed by gales of laughter.

This merriment did not improve William's temper in the least. "Out with it," he demanded.

His eyes brimming over with mirth, Aubrey looked up at William and gasped, "If you could have seen your face, especially when she told you that *I'd* been assisting her in matters of dress."

The humor of that situation had not escaped William. His face relaxed slightly and his mouth curled up in a reluctant grin. "Well, it was too clear that you had. After all, you are the last fellow on earth that I should wish to advise anyone on . . ." He frowned suddenly. "But you haven't explained anything. Why does that female mushroom call you her cousin? And why did you tell her that I was merely a friend?"

Aubrey's eyes sparkled. "Come now, old man. I couldn't very well be cousin to both of you, could I?" He could not resist the impulse to tease William a little further. "I'm afraid that's not the only shock I have in store for you. You see, I've obtained a position. I'm not only a cousin, I'm also their drawing master."

"The devil you are!"

William was not allowed further comment, for a discreet knock sounded at the door. Aubrey gave him a warning look and turned his back to the entryway, while William coughed feebly, "Come in."

Smith entered the room, concern upon his face. "I understand you are indisposed, sir, though I was given the most nonsensical explanation for—" His words broke off as Aubrey slowly revolved toward him. "My lord," he exclaimed joyfully, "we have been combing the countryside for you."

He halted suddenly as Aubrey motioned to him for silence. William shook his head at the valet. "He doesn't want anyone here to know he's a viscount, Smith. Somehow he's managed to pass himself off as a drawing master, though God knows the reason for it."

Aubrey smiled sympathetically at his cousin, although his eyes still twinkled with amusement. "I intend to put you in full possession of the fact, coz. And Smith will need to be in on the secret also, if you intend to remain here for any amount of time." He looked about him and selected a comfortable chair. "Now it all began the evening I was *shot* . . ."

He held his audience spellbound for the next twenty minutes or so as he recounted his story. When he had concluded, Smith started abruptly and exclaimed, "Pray excuse me, sir, but I think I should go warn the groom, Hodges, in case he might accidentally let some information slip." He exited the room while Aubrey shook his head in disgust.

"I might have expected you to travel with a full retinue of servants. Tell me, did you take the traveling chariot with the family arms emblazoned on the side? I expect that Mama will be joining us at any moment."

William colored hotly. "You know very well that I didn't," he said indignantly. "I came in my curricle and you know that I could not travel without Hodges or Smith. Besides, Lady Herne is waiting for word from me."

He glared suddenly at his cousin. "And that was an unpleasant scene, I can tell you. You needn't look so amused. Not to say what I've endured this past week, staying in obscure, flea-ridden inns, eating tough mutton and drinking watered wine. And the trouble I had in finding you—why, if I hadn't happened to stop and ask for directions I might still be wandering blindly through Oxfordshire now." His voice became peevish. "Honestly, you seem to think that you're the only one who can keep a secret."

"My apologies, coz," Aubrey said gravely, although a suspicious sparkle remained in his eyes. "I was unaware of the extent of your sufferings." He frowned slightly. "But do you think you can keep Mama from coming to pursue me for a few more weeks? I am determined to solve this mystery."

William looked profoundly shocked. "Why, you don't imagine that I intend to abandon you here when you are living every moment in danger for your life?"

"Rubbish."

"I do not care what you say. I intend to remain in this vicinity as long as you are here."

Aubrey looked thoughtful. William tried to reassure him. "See here, I am certain that your mother could not trace me unless she were willing to send out a Bow Street Runner, and I think that she would wish to avoid that possibility for scandal for some time at least."

William brightened with a fresh idea. "And I can continue to post her letters explaining that I have not located you."

Aubrey sniffed, but William forestalled his objections by adding, "And I can send Hodges in the curricle to post them from different villages if need be."

Aubrey was still far from satisfied. He looked at his cousin with real seriousness this time. "You are determined to stay?"

William set his chin stubbornly. "Yes."

"Very well, then." He rose, took his cousin's hand, shook it, and grinned. "I am glad to have you. This performance was badly in need of an audience."

The two cousins put their heads together and formulated a plan of action. It was agreed between them that William should pose as a friend of Viscount Herne, in case his inquiries in that direction should accidentally surface. He would have known Aubrey from that context and also since they had been at school together.

"After all," said Aubrey with a twinkle, "I am presumed to be from a family that has fallen upon hard times."

The connection with the viscount was to prove enough to produce an invitation from Letitia immediately. She insisted that she could not be so inhospitable as to let a dear friend of her "cousin's" stay in the tiny and uncomfortable inn that the village offered. William was properly grateful for her kindness, though Aubrey warned him in an aside, "She means to have you for one of her daughters, old boy."

Georgiana meanwhile was unaware of the happenings that had been taking place at the hall. The peace of mind she had sought at her godmother's yesterday had not been forthcoming. That shrewd, usually forthright woman had been extremely reticent when Georgiana delicately began to broach her dilemma. Georgiana had expected Lady Dowles to condemn outright an attraction to one's drawing master, but that lady had seemed indecisive and uncomfortable and finally Georgiana had been forced to let the matter drop. Possibly she had shocked her godmother with such a discussion.

The evening's events had done nothing to improve her peace of mind either. Though Lord Marwood had not talked to her himself, Letitia could not resist the urge to tell her daughter about his conversation with her father, and Georgiana was dismayed to discover that her father had given his consent already. In light of his circumstances, she could not blame him, but she had expected at least a token show of resistance. To find herself so totally without an ally in this matter was dispiriting in the extreme. She could hope she wouldn't have time alone with Marwood, but with a sinking heart she realized that Letitia somehow would contrive to thrust them together.

The worst part of it was that she herself felt so indecisive. It might be that marriage with Marwood would be a good thing for her. It would free her from her stepmother's tyranny and she might be able to assist her sisters in her new position. After all, she did not know him that well. It was possible that the slightly repulsive feeling that came over her whenever he was near would disappear when she became better acquainted with him. Unbidden, Aubrey's face rose before her eyes. She had certainly felt an attraction to him from the first.

"You must stop this," she told herself sternly. "He is entirely ineligible."

Attracted by her voice, Lion rose and, tail wagging, trod over to her. She gave a sigh and began to gather her things. She had hoped that by fleeing to the quarry she might be able to sort matters out, but instead, she was more confused than ever.

She picked up her hammer and chisel from where she had left them and absentmindedly brushed the dust from them with a glove. She dropped them into her bag and began to trudge wearily back along the stone's face toward the end of the pit. A commotion attracted her attention.

A squirrel, hunting for food among the vegetation that had sprung up, was discovered by Lion, who felt that an immediate execution was in order. Accordingly, the squirrel fled, with Lion in hot pursuit. The little animal went scrabbling straight up the stone face of the quarry, leaving Lion to bark and fling himself uselessly against it.

"Lion," she called, but she made no impression. She sighed again and marched resignedly over to where the dog stood rearing and yelping. "Come on, fellow."

He still ignored her, so she caught his collar and tried to tug him away. Intent on his intended victim, he refused to budge.

"Come on," said Georgiana emphatically, but he merely whined and wagged his tail while continuing to stare longingly at the top of the rock.

"Idiot dog," she said, beginning to flush from her exertions. He whined once more and she glanced up the stone herself to see if the squirrel was still in sight.

Evidently a cautious animal, it had long since departed. She tugged again at Lion, and this time felt the resistance weakening. She was about to exhort him again when the ghost of an idea flashed across her brain. Puzzled, she looked up at the rock face again. Was there something unusual about it? She peered up at it intently. Lion, by now resigned to the loss of the squirrel, abandoned all resistance and looked at her, tail wagging.

It was no trick of the light. There was something up there. She would need a ladder to examine it properly, though. Lion recalled her to the present with a penitent lick on her hand. She realized that she was still holding his collar and released it. There was no help for it. She certainly would be missed at home by now and doubtless would receive a good scolding. This problem would have to wait for another day.

She needed to mark this spot, though. She emptied her bag and found a rag that she used for cleaning specimens. She tore a strip from it and tied it to a nearby bush. That should suffice. She turned and began on her way.

With some hours remaining yet until dinner, William insisted that he immediately be made acquainted with all the particulars of Aubrey's shooting. Leaving the efficient Smith to unpack William's traveling cases, Aubrey conducted his cousin to his room and showed him the antiquated horse pistols. Even the phlegmatic William could not hide his surprise at this choice of a murder weapon, and he turned them over and over in his hands curiously. He gave a slow whistle and then looked up at his cousin.

"You're lucky this is all your attacker had. With a modern weapon, he might have killed you."

Aubrey's lips twisted into a wry smile as he reclaimed the pistols and proceeded to hide them again. "That aspect of the matter had occurred to me also. But come, coz, what do these suggest to you, if anything?"

"Well, I'd say that your attacker was not a person of means"—he could not resist a slight attempt at humor—"unless it's someone's grandmother, of course."

Aubrey's eyes twinkled appreciatively. "I think we can assume that it was a little late for Granny to be out with her rheumatism." His expression became serious again. "But if it is a poor laborer of some sort, why would he have abandoned what were obviously his only weapons?"

William was nonplussed. Aubrey shrugged. "Do you feel up to a walk?"

"Yes. Why?"

"I'll show you the site of the shooting and then you'll know as much as I do."

William listened with only half an ear as Aubrey described the events of the night of the incident. Though he asked a few relevant questions, his brain was preoccupied with the problem Aubrey had raised. At last they reached the site and Aubrey pointed out where the various bits of action had occurred, concluding with the area where the pistols had been found. William studied the ground gravely.

"You say they were hidden in haste?" he asked Aubrey abruptly.

"Yes."

A vague theory was forming in his mind. He attempted to put it into words. "Perhaps they examined you and found you were not dead," he began slowly, "and thought they'd leave the pistols here for another attempt."

"And why not just finish me off then?"

"No more shot?" William shook his head with dissatisfaction at his own theory.

A little frown settled between Aubrey's eyebrows. "Actually, coz, I've been over and over it in my mind. I can't see what anyone had to gain by shooting me. They didn't rob me, and no one knew I would be traveling this road."

William looked about him, studying the locale with new eyes. "I see what you mean. This spot was chosen very carefully, wasn't it? That bend in the road, the cover—it was some kind of a planned ambuscade."

"My thinking exactly." Aubrey gave William an appreciative smile.

"Then you think it was simply a case of mistaken identity?"

"That's my best surmise. But it still doesn't explain why the pistols were abandoned."

"The assailant panicked when he found he'd shot the wrong man?"

Aubrey shook his head. "No. If those pistols are his only weapons, then they mean a great deal to him."

"Hmmm. Well, if he were a small man, perhaps they would be too heavy to carry a great distance. No, he carried them here, didn't he?"

Aubrey sighed and prepared to turn back toward the house. "I've thought about it a great deal and I can't explain it. The pistols are large, and they are heavy and obtrusive, but I can't understand why . . ." His words hung in the air for a moment.

William was nodding in agreement when Aubrey suddenly took him by the sleeve. "That's it!"

"What?"

"That's the problem. They're obtrusive. You could not conceal them easily."

William was beginning to follow him. "You mean that your attacker was afraid that someone might see him carrying them."

Aubrey waved an impatient hand. "If he were simply returning home, he might have managed it well enough. But he was going somewhere where he would be seen and he could not afford to have the pistols on his person."

"But surely that wouldn't have been the original plan."

"No. I disrupted it somehow." There was silence for a few moments as Aubrey considered this new information. "Blast," he said. "I'm no better off than before."

William shook his head sympathetically. "Maybe given more time—"

"And time's just what we're lacking." Aubrey sighed again. "Well, there's no use moaning about it. We might as well return to the hall."

They were nearing the long drive that led to Chalton Hall when they espied a figure approaching from the other direction. William saw that it was a tall young lady in a tired and rather dirty walking dress of white muslin. A straw bonnet with no pretension to fashion was jammed carelessly on her head, and her gloves were gray with dust. She apparently was preoccupied, for she stared at the ground as she walked along, absentmindedly swinging the leather pouch she carried. William was about to call his cousin's attention to this unusual phenomenon, but he was forestalled.

"I say, it's Georgy!" William was shrewd enough to notice the sudden sparkle in Aubrey's eyes when he identified this person. He tugged at William's sleeve. "Come along, you must meet her."

William found himself being dragged rapidly toward the young woman as his cousin hailed her in carrying tones. She looked up, startled, as she heard him. There was no mistaking the soft-pink color that flooded her cheeks as she recognized Aubrey. William drew his own conclusions from that also.

As they neared her, William could see that he had under-estimated the young woman rather badly. It was true that her dress revealed an inattention to current modes and that she looked remarkably as if she had been grubbing in the dirt. Her features were good, however, and the large, grayish-green eyes beneath the disheveled brown curls were quite beautiful. The animation of her countenance added to her charms. In all, she was an exceptionally lovely young woman, if not quite the nonpareil he had glimpsed in Aubrey's arms earlier.

She smiled shyly at him as Aubrey introduced him as an old friend and seemed not in the least surprised to hear that he was to be a houseguest. She murmured politely how pleased they would be to have him, before falling awkwardly silent. William wondered how this bashful young woman would have managed to capture Aubrey's interest.

Herne managed to solve the mystery of her besmirched appearance by explaining to William that she was a fossil-hunter. He then proceeded to quiz her in what seemed to William quite a knowledgeable manner about her day's work. Feeling decidedly *de trop*, William, feigning an interest in the local flora and fauna, fell back a few paces as they conversed.

"So," Georgiana was telling Aubrey, "I think it could be something interesting, but I shall need a ladder in order to examine it better. It's hard to tell much from below."

"I didn't have the opportunity to ask you yesterday about what you discovered. Was it anything significant?"

"Oh." She shook her curls. "It was a particular type of bivalve mollusk which is quite common in this type of stone— much more common than an ammonite, for example. It was a particularly well-preserved specimen, however. I'll show it to you later, if you like.'' She looked at him a trifle curiously. ''I suppose Jem had an urgent matter to discuss with you?''

Aubrey shrugged. ''I think he thought so at the time.''

This enigmatic answer left her little to pursue. A silence fell between them. Aubrey knew that now was his opportunity to ask her about Marwood and his proposal, but somehow he hadn't the nerve to do it. Surely it was up to her to confide in him if she wished.

Apparently, she had no desire to, for this constraint continued between them until they reached the house.

A piercing voice reached their ears. ''Georgiana!''

Her face assumed a look of comic dismay. ''I must go,'' she said, and fled into the house.

William sneaked a glance at his cousin's face and was surprised to see the troubled expression upon it. The signs of a romance had been plain as day. It was patent that his affection was returned. What was bothering him, then? It was clear that Aubrey had neglected to tell him everything that had occurred since his arrival here.

By dinnertime, William had other thoughts with which to occupy his mind. In the first place, he could not help but be sensible of the admiration he inspired when he appeared downstairs in suitable evening attire. The elaborate arrangement of his snowy stock, the height of his shirt-collar points, and the wasp-waisted coat could not fail but to impress the female members of the family, who had never seen a Bond Street beau in full regalia before.

In the second place, his presence obviously had inspired Letitia to see that the family was arrayed in its finest attire also. Letitia herself wore a dress in a violent shade of scarlet that flattered neither her complexion nor her figure. Georgiana was dressed more subtly but more pleasingly in a quiet dress of green, which, though it showed no pretension to fashion, was certainly a vast improvement over what she had been wearing before. William also for the first time made the acquaintance of Mr. Chalford, who clearly would have preferred not to be wearing his black satin knee-smalls. The one person at the table who held William's gaze, though, was Charlotte.

She had not required Letty's strictures in order to choose the

most becoming gown in her wardrobe. The round dress of a
fine jaconet muslin boasted a triple fall of lace at the throat and
was complimented by a flounce of the same work at the bottom.
It was a credit to Charlotte's skill with the needle that she
managed to appear both modish and *jeune fille* at the same time.
She kept her eyes modestly lowered as introductions were made,
though a pinkness tinged her cheeks as she recalled the situation
William had surprised her in earlier. She tried to keep from
imagining what he must think of her.

As for William, any harsh thoughts he had harbored
evaporated at the sight of this angelic picture. It was evident
that this was not the brazen hussy he had pictured to himself.
This innocent beauty could not be capable of throwing herself
at a gentleman. He frowned as he thought of the warmth with
which Aubrey had greeted Georgiana earlier. It was true that
Herne was careless to a fault in many ways. But surely even
he would not trifle with the hearts of two gently bred young
ladies at once, particularly sisters. He shot Aubrey a dagger
glance, but the latter was busy finishing the introductions.

Preoccupied as William was, he missed the rather skeptical
look he was given by Harry Chalford upon his introduction,
but fortunately so did everyone else in the room, with the one
exception of Aubrey. The viscount could tell that Harry was
not entirely pleased to have yet another stranger dropped into
their midst. It was certain that Harry's feelings had little to do
with the matter, however, as Letitia officiously thrust William
at the embarrassed Charlotte, announcing that they were to be
dinner partners. Charlotte's mortification might have kept her
silent throughout the meal, but William's well-bred conversation
enabled her to relax sufficiently to reply to his courteous
inquiries. Not surprisingly, the two discovered that they had
a great deal in common and were soon engrossed in each other.

Aubrey watched these proceedings with a slight frown of
concern. He knew his cousin well enough to be sure that William
was exhibiting more than his customary good manners. It was
most unlike him to take such a fancy to a girl immediately. Not
that Charlotte wasn't beautiful, but he had never known mere
beauty to make that deep an impression upon William.

There was no harm in it, of course. That is, there was no

harm in it unless Letitia decided to set a trap for the unsuspecting William. Surely any trap she set would be clumsy enough to be spotted. However, he might warn William to avoid spending time alone with Charlotte.

His train of thought was broken when Letitia, observing his gaze, remarked with satisfaction what a handsome couple his friend and her daughter made. Aubrey had no choice but to agree, though it required an effort to mask his dislike of her obviousness.

Having made this preliminary remark, Letitia found the time opportune to introduce several less-than-discreet questions about William, his social position, and his fortune. Not for the first time, Aubrey regretted the humble nature of his role. He dearly would have loved to give her a set-down and put an end to her impertinent questions. As a humble drawing master, however, all he could do was to sidestep them as adroitly as possible. He toyed momentarily with the idea of painting a black portrait for Letitia, then discarded it. William was all too clearly a man of means, and Aubrey was quite certain that a dubious reputation would prove no hindrance to Letitia's plans. His lips curled for a moment at the picture of honest, stolid William as a scheming blackguard. His attention suddenly was recalled by something Letty was saying.

"And such a smart curricle, too. I am sure that it must have cost a fortune, but then, young men must be dashing, I suppose, in order to make an impression on the young ladies. Why, Lord Marwood himself never uses the family coach with his coat of arms. He always sends it along with the servants and baggage and insists upon riding that black horse of his, even to London. I am sure I would be dreadfully fatigued after so long a ride."

Aubrey clearly was not expected to participate in the conversation, so he managed a noncommittal murmur, freeing Letty to continue her soliloquy.

"Mind you, I don't know why he doesn't buy a modern conveyance like your friend. But then I have always observed that titled gentlemen are often the most cautious when it comes to spending. Doubtless your friend the viscount is the same." She gave a philosophical little sigh. "Well, perhaps Georgiana can persuade Lord Marwood to spend the money on a new carriage. How I should like to see her in a really smart equipage." Visions of glory began to fill Letty's head. "Oh, I can just imagine driving in the park at five o'clock with her in a new landau with postilions and outriders in . . ."

A thought had been tugging at the back of Aubrey's mind. Instantly, Letitia had his full attention.

"What was that you were saying?" he asked.

Gratified by his interest, Letty continued her remarks. "Do you mean about driving in the park at five? Well, doubtless Lord Marwood has a large acquaintance in town and—"

"No, no," said Aubrey, a little impatiently. "What you were saying earlier, about Lord Marwood never riding in his coach."

She shook her head. "Well, I certainly do not blame him. It is very old-fashioned and must be uncomfortable to ride in—"

"But do you mean that he always rides?" Aubrey asked. "He has never been known to hire a post chaise, for example?"

Letty looked a little surprised. "Why, no, not since I have been acquainted with him, at any rate. In fact, I always have thought it would be extremely inconvenient to arrive a day ahead of one's luggage, not to mention the danger of being set upon by highwaymen, since he often travels at night." Here she gave a delicate shudder. "But then I suppose a titled gentleman must have his little eccentricities."

"He does not take a manservant with him?"

"No, and that is what seems so very peculiar to me, riding alone about the countryside in that fashion."

Struck by the thoughtful frown upon Aubrey's face, Letitia endeavored to clarify what she had been saying. She patted his arm gently to recall his attention.

"Of course, I do not mean this as a criticism of him. Such a delightful person and such charming manners, don't you agree? We all have our own little foibles, after all."

Herne nodded absentmindedly at her, reassuring her that he hadn't misinterpreted her remarks as criticism of Georgiana's prospective fiancé. She felt free to resume the delightful topic of her plans to travel to London after Georgiana's marriage.

The subject of her conversation, like Aubrey, had been disgruntled by Letitia's machinations, though for different reasons. How could Mother be so lacking in sense, she thought angrily to herself. Poor romantic Charlotte has rarely been given the opportunity of conversing with a young gentleman in her life, and what does Letitia do but thrust her together with a veritable Adonis? It is too much to expect her not to fall in love with a gentleman who looks as if he stepped out of the pages of one of her favorite romances.

Georgiana saw her sister's dreamy expression and shook her head. She'd hardly met him and she was lost already. The poor young man was undoubtedly only being civil to her. Georgiana flashed an angry glance at Letitia and was even more irritated by her stepmother's smug expression. Just then Letitia's voice peaked, as it did so often when she mentioned titles, and the words "Lord Marwood" floated clearly over to Georgiana's ears. She felt suddenly sick to her stomach and laid down her fork. She had managed to put that problem out of her mind for an hour or so. Now she could not avoid it. Involuntarily, she glanced at Aubrey, but he was lost in a brown study. A feeling of despair washed over her.

As soon as dinner was concluded, she pleaded a sick headache, which was hardly a fiction by then, and excused herself. She went to her room, threw herself down upon her bed, and even her pillow could not quite muffle her sobs.

8

Charlotte and William passed the meal in blissful ignorance of the undercurrents of tension that swirled around them. After dinner, it seemed only natural that they should find themselves alone together in the gardens; neither would have thought for a moment to question how they had arrived there.

To Charlotte, it was almost as if a fairy-tale prince had dropped into their midst. William's handsome, regular features, his superb dress, and his exquisite manners were the epitome of everything she had ever dreamed of in a gentleman. He was more than just a romantic picture, though. Whenever she dared to meet those clear blue eyes, she encountered a gaze of such sincerity and warmth that she could feel her face grow hot beneath it. She knew instinctively that this was no trifler merely amusing himself. At the same time, she was almost overawed by the notion that this paragon truly could be interested in her.

As for William, he was swept away every bit as much as Charlotte. Never had he encountered such unspoiled beauty. It seemed incredible that such an exquisite creature could retain such modesty. With Charlotte, there was none of the flirtatiousness that he had come to expect of even a passably handsome girl in London. She seemed almost unaware of her own loveliness, meeting the compliments he ventured with blushes of embarrassment. Surely even though she lived in the country she should have had an opportunity to break some hearts. But whenever she dared to peep at him with those glowing blue eyes, he felt certain that her guilelessness was not merely an act.

Time stood still for the two as they strolled and talked, and the minutes turned into hours. Only belatedly did William realize that night had fallen and reluctantly suggest to Charlotte that they should return to the house. She was grateful for the darkness, which covered her flush. What must he think of her? Surely only a wanton would go strolling alone with a strange young gentleman after dark. When they said their good evenings upon reaching the house, she could not quite meet his eyes and fled rapidly upstairs to her room. William gazed after her dreamily. What an enchanting creature, he thought.

It was with an air of happy unconcern that he made his way to his own chamber. When he opened the door and encountered his cousin there, he evinced no surprise, but merely gave him a bemused smile as he entered.

Aubrey leapt up from his chair and exclaimed testily, "Lord, William, where have you been this age?"

His expression unaltered, William replied, "Just out. Walking in the garden. Such a delightful evening."

Aubrey observed him with narrowed eyes, but decided to let the topic drop for the moment. "See here, I've been waiting all this time for you because I've finally discovered the answer."

William yawned slightly as he removed his cravat. "The answer?" he asked incuriously.

Aubrey could have shaken him. "The answer to why I was shot."

At last he had his cousin's attention. William settled into an ancient damask-covered chair in a listening attitude.

Aubrey paced nervously as he spoke. "Mrs. Chalford gave me the key tonight." He glanced at his cousin. "You remember that I had decided that *I* could not have been the intended victim." At William's nod he continued. "Well, now I know who the assassin's target was—it was Marwood."

"Marwood?"

"Lord Marwood, a baron who owns a nearby estate. I have reason to believe that he is not well-loved by all his tenants."

"But how do you know?"

"It's all too clear. I can't believe that it took me so long to see it. He rides a big black, similar in appearance to Sligo. He's of much the same height as me. He prefers to ride alone instead of traveling in his coach. He was known to be returning from London about that time, and it was dark, so that his assailant could not see clearly. They shot me thinking I was Marwood, and when they saw I wasn't, they panicked and fled."

William frowned. "That seems likely enough. But it still does not explain why the attacker left his guns, even if he did depart in haste.''

Aubrey's brows drew together. ''I have a theory regarding that, too, but it's only half-formed as of yet.''

''Do you have any idea who the assailant might be?''

''No . . . no certain idea, at any rate.'' Aubrey's face assumed a look of determination. ''But I think I have a way to find out.''

Georgiana intended to rise early the next morning, obtain a ladder somehow, and examine her interesting new find at the quarry. Unfortunately, her own misery had prevented sleep for most of the night with the result that when she awakened, the sun already was shining brightly. She grimaced as she dressed hastily. She felt more in need of an escape today than ever. She hoped she was not too late.

As she began to tread cautiously downstairs, she was halted by a voice that confirmed her fears.

''Georgiana!''

She steeled herself to turn and address her stepmother politely. ''Good morning, Mother.''

''Where are you going?'' Letitia asked suspiciously.

''Why, nowhere in particular,'' she lied.

''Hmph.''Letty eyed with disfavor the ancient mull gown Georgiana was wearing. ''Well, you'd better go and change your dress. Lord Marwood has sent word that he will be calling upon you this morning.''

Georgiana's heart sank within her at these words. ''This morning, Mother?''

''Yes,'' replied Letty irritably. ''Well, don't stand there gaping at me. You would not wish Lord Marwood to see you in that frock, would you?''

Georgiana murmured an inaudible reply as she began to make her way back up the stairs. This was all too soon, much too soon. She tried to comfort herself with the thought that Lord Marwood could not be intending to make her an offer yet. He has already spoken to Father, though, an unkind little voice reminded her. She did her best to shrug away the idea. Whatever Marwood's intentions, there was no way to avoid seeing him.

She permitted herself one small act of defiance by choosing to wear a gown in a most unbecoming shade of pink. Since it had scarcely been worn, she knew it would meet with Letty's approval, anyway. She considered arranging her hair into an unflattering style, then decided there hardly could be anything less attractive than drawing it up simply, the way she already had. She looked in the mirror and was satisfied with her reflection. She was disagreeably pale from lack of sleep and in addition boasted dark smudges under her eyes. Those eyes gazed back at her with considerable anxiety. She attempted a brave smile, but managed only a weak, trembling one.

"Courage, girl," she whispered to herself. "Lord Marwood cannot help but be frightened off by such a hag-ridden appearance." She rose and with head erect made her way downstairs.

Had Aubrey been present, he might have disabused her of the notion that she looked positively hideous, but fortunately for her sense of confidence, he was otherwise occupied at the moment. He had determined to ride over to Jem's farm this morning and, if necessary, shake the boy's secret from him. Like Georgiana, he was forestalled by Letty.

The first portion of her new gowns had arrived this morning and she was faced with the momentous task of deciding which to wear to the Eversham's ball. She had discovered the unsuspecting William at breakfast and tried to show him the gowns for his opinion. That honest soul could not quite mask his horror at the monstrosities she exhibited. She was forced to conclude reluctantly that although he was certainly *au courant* with male fashions, he lacked the spark of originality that made her young cousin's opinions so much in agreement with her own tastes. Accordingly, she was forced to abandon William as a possible fashion consultant and so sought out Aubrey instead.

She was well-rewarded for her decision, for he managed to conceal his irritation at being distracted from his purpose. And once she actually showed him the gowns, the sparkle of enthusiasm in his eyes was obvious. He declared himself to be in raptures over them, and Letty herself could not but admit that the seamstress had done a more-than-adequate job of executing the gowns they had envisioned. With Aubrey's help, she soon had selected not only the gown to wear to the Eversham ball, but also an appropriate choice for the family portrait. The mention of the portrait served to jog her memory, and she inquired meaningfully what progress he was making.

"Why, I meant to have Georgiana sit for me today," Aubrey replied smoothly, hoping to ensure his own escape.

Letitia frowned. "No, I am afraid Georgiana will be busy today."

"Perhaps Charlotte, then," he suggested.

Letty might have agreed, but she suddenly recalled how well Charlotte and William had been getting along the previous night. Perhaps a tête-á-téte today might serve to further cement that relationship.

"I think she might be occupied. I would sit for you myself, but I shall be quite busy, as we are entertaining Lord Marwood today."

"Oh?" asked Aubrey politely. He hoped that his face was expressionless. This explained why Georgiana would be busy. A worrisome thought assailed him, but he dismissed it instantly. Surely the fellow would not be boorish enough to press his suit so soon.

Letty's brow was wrinkled in thought. "I suppose Mr. Chalford is out hunting somewhere," she decided. "That leaves the younger girls, then. I will send word for them to make ready."

Aubrey had little choice but to assent. He was truly beginning to tire of this masquerade. Being even a superior sort of servant definitely became less amusing the longer one kept at it. Having to follow orders was fine as long as one had nothing better to do. Well, he could not expose himself now, with the mystery so tantalizingly close to being solved. He had a fair idea that while Jem might be tempted to confess his secrets to Aubrey Chalford, he would have nothing whatsoever to say to Viscount Herne.

Lord Marwood arrived while Aubrey was busy with his young subjects. Letty observed with some smugness that Marwood was dressed with particular care. She lost no time in suggesting that since it was such a fine day, perhaps he might care to have Georgiana show him through the rose garden.

Georgiana was embarrassed by her mother's lack of subtlety, but Marwood appeared oblivious to it as he thanked her and agreed gladly. Georgiana's nervousness, encouraged by her stepmother's arch glances, increased as they stepped outside and she found herself alone with him. She could not keep from babbling madly at him. The fact that he kept the conversation firmly upon topics of horticulture did nothing to ease her tension. There was something in his gaze that she could not like.

After a certain amount of time spent admiring the roses, he indicated an interest in the holly maze. Nothing would serve but that they should explore it. Her reluctance to enter it alone with Marwood was heightened by her memory of the last time she had entered it, on the occasion of Aubrey's first family dinner. She thought of that laugh, those sparkling brown eyes, then compressed her lips tightly together. She must put him out of her mind.

Marwood noticed her troubled expression. "Is there anything the matter, my dear?"

"No, my lord."

"Ah, I wish you would not be quite so formal with me. My given name is Bevis. Would you do me the favor of calling me by it?"

There was no graceful way to refuse. He was looking at her in an expectant way.

"Very well . . . Bevis." She nearly choked on it.

"And in return, may I have the privilege of calling you Georgiana?"

She would have liked to shout "No!" But since she had begun this whole fiasco, she might as well see it through. She nodded reluctantly, which apparently satisfied Marwood.

"Ah, Georgiana, such a lovely name, and such a lovely young lady."

Since she was not feeling very lovely today, his words struck her as especially insincere. They had reached the center of the maze now, which Marwood plainly had intended for their destination.

"Here we are." He took her hand in his and seated her on the bench, selecting a place close beside her. She wished desperately that he would relinquish her hand, but instead, he closed his other one over it also.

"Georgiana . . ."

The butterflies in her stomach increased. She lowered her eyes to gaze at the ground, hoping he might take it for modesty rather than revulsion.

"You are clearly a most intelligent young lady. Therefore, I will speak frankly to you." Here he paused for a moment. "I have come to the age where a person in my position must consider taking a wife."

In spite of herself, a tiny sound of surprise escaped her.

"No, please hear me out, my dear."

She disliked the oily way his voice lingered on those last two words.

"I realize that we have not known each other for a great deal of time, but you have made the strongest impression on me with your beauty, your grace, and your character."

He might almost be reciting this speech to anyone, she thought angrily to herself.

"In short, I can think of no one more suited to be Lady Marwood than yourself. I have spoken with your father and he has given us his blessing."

Georgiana started to speak, but again he silenced her.

"I know that this may seem very sudden to you, my dear Georgiana, but I can only blame my own impetuous feelings."

She could restrain herself no longer. "Sir, you do me too much honor," she began, attempting to pull away from him, but he only tightened his grip on her hand.

"Please, my dear. Allow me to finish. As I said, we have known each other such a short time that I realize that my declaration may come as a surprise to you. Therefore, I will not press you for your answer now. I believe that our mutual affection may grow with time. I only ask you now to consider that possibility and also to think about the many advantages attendant upon the title of Lady Marwood. A beautiful young lady such as yourself should not spend her life shut away in the country. Why, you should be gracing the balls at Almack's, being presented at court, attending the opera and theater and the fashionable assemblies."

Georgiana could not tell him that this program did not enchant her.

"What's more, it could be of great benefit to your family also. As Lady Marwood, you could introduce your younger sisters to the *ton*. I should be happy for you to sponsor them."

Georgiana would have been glad to give him his answer there and then. These last remarks made her hesitate. Surely she did not have the right to throw away such an opportunity for her younger sisters. She looked up and met Lord Marwood's expectant gaze. "I will consider your offer, my lord."

Something flashed suddenly in his eyes. Was it surprise? Anger? It was gone in an instant and he gave her a triumphant smile.

"That is all I ask, my dear Georgiana. And please call me Bevis."

"Yes . . . Bevis."

He raised her hand to his lips and pressed them to it, then rose and offered her his arm. She took it, relieved that he expected nothing more by way of an embrace, though she disliked the proprietary way in which he tucked her hand inside the crook of his elbow. When they reached the house, however, he released her and made his farewells in a circumspectly polite manner. Only the warmth of his gaze suggested anything loverlike about him.

In all, Georgiana had to be relieved that this dreaded interview had gone as well as it had. It was most fortunate that Lord Marwood had not asked for an immediate answer. Actually, he had seemed most kindly solicitous of her feelings. She should be grateful that he was so understanding.

Deep in her heart, though, she knew that this postponement would make little difference to her dilemma. Her common sense told her that marrying Lord Marwood was the wise choice, the choice where her duty lay and also the one that would secure her a comfortable future. But could she actually go through with it when her heart belonged to another?

Letitia interrupted her musings. "My dear," she exclaimed, making no attempt to disguise her curiosity. "How was your little talk with Lord Marwood?"

Marwood himself, as he rode back toward home, also had to feel satisfied with the way the discussion had gone. He had suspected from the beginning that this marriage was more the idea of the parents than the daughter's. She had proved even more skittish than he had anticipated, however, and only clever management on his part had prevented what might have been an out-and-out refusal. That would have been fatal to his chances. No, he had done the right thing by not pressing her for an answer now. He had seen her relax visibly. The appeal to her sense of duty had had its effect also. He had to congratulate himself on reading her character so well. This little delay should prove no more than a minor setback. Between her parents' methods of persuasion and the voice of her own conscience, he had no doubts that his suit would be accepted in a short while.

True, it galled him that she was so reluctant to accept him. One would think that the chit would at least appreciate the social position he was offering her, a nonentity who had spent her life sequestered in the country. He sighed and reminded himself that it was fortunate that she had, and that her parents were so eager to entertain his suit. Under their pressure, she should come around especially quickly, since she clearly had few other options. Still, he had never wished for an unwilling bride. If she should prove difficult, there was always that younger sister, Charlotte. She seemed more malleable than the elder sister, and he had to admit that type of fair beauty appealed more to his taste. After all, it didn't matter a great deal which of the sisters he married.

When he reached the Thornbys' farm, he pulled his black up and signaled to Jem, who was toiling in the garden, to come hold the reins.

"I have a matter of business to discuss with your sister." Encountering the hostility in the boy's eyes, he smiled faintly and added, "Alone."

Georgiana had returned to her room to change back into her everyday clothing. The interview with Letitia had proved every bit as difficult as she had anticipated. Letty could not understand why she hadn't accepted Marwood's offer immediately. Georgiana was forced to explain that it was not considered seemly for a young lady to leap instantly at a proposal of marriage. It would have been a hopeless task except that Marwood himself had not asked her for an answer. Letty still could not like this arrangement, but was forced to concede that Lord Marwood was the authority on the ways of polite society.

Georgiana had realized with a sinking heart that she had won herself no more than a reprieve. How ironic it was that she had assumed that this decision would in any way be her own. She had finished changing when a knock sounded on her door. "Come in," she called.

Charlotte opened the door, her eyes fairly glowing with happiness. She rushed into the room and flung herself down on the bed. "Oh, Georgy, I've just been waiting to talk to you."

The maid, Betsey, gave her a knowing look, and Georgiana thanked her for her help and dismissed her.

"I would have come and spoken to you last night," confided Charlotte, "but I was out in the garden . . . rather late." Here she blushed becomingly.

Georgiana seated herself in an armchair. It was evident that this would take a while.

Charlotte looked at her dreamily. "Oh, Georgy, isn't he wonderful!"

"Who?" asked Georgiana, deliberately misunderstanding her.

Charlotte looked surprised. "Why William—I mean, Mr. Darley, of course. He's so handsome and has such an air about him, and such lovely manners, too—don't you think?"

Georgiana was worried. They were already on a first-name basis? She must handle Charlotte carefully. "Yes, quite the gentleman of fashion," she said, keeping her voice even.

Charlotte sat up abruptly. "But he's so much more than that. He's so kind and so understanding."

"Mmph," said Georgiana noncommittally.

"And in talking to him this morning, I found that he thinks about things so deeply and cares about them just as I do."

"You went walking with him this morning, too?"

Charlotte blushed again. "It was purely coincidence. I was reading underneath a tree and he was out taking a stroll for amusement, since Cousin Aubrey was busy sketching. He happened to see me and came over to inquire what I was reading." Her eyes grew wide. "Georgy, would you believe it? Whom do you suppose is his favorite poet?"

"Lord Byron?"

"How did you know?"

"A fortunate guess." Georgiana was becoming even more

concerned. Of course, it was possible that Darley was sincere, but from Charlotte's reports he sounded more and more like an experienced trifler.

"I know that once you come to know him, you will admire him as I do," Charlotte was saying naively when she noticed her sister's troubled little frown. "Georgy, what is it?"

"It's nothing." She glanced at her younger sister and saw from her expression that Charlotte would not be forestalled. She shrugged with an assumption of carelessness. "Lord Marwood came to visit this morning, that's all."

Charlotte was gazing intently at Georgiana's face. "Georgy, did he . . . did he?" She saw the answer there and her face crumpled. "Oh, Georgy."

Her sister crossed quickly over to her. "No, you goose, it's not as bad as all that. He did not ask me for my answer yet. He thinks we should know each other better first."

"Oh, Georgy." Charlotte took the handkerchief her sister offered and began to dab at her eyes. "What will you do?"

Georgiana tried to hide the bleak despair she felt. "Why, try to know him better, as he suggested. Then I'll make my decision."

Charlotte was weeping in earnest now.

Georgiana stroked the fair curls gently. "Come love, even if I were to accept him this moment, which I am not, would it be such an awful fate? Social position, a title, Mother would have to call me 'my lady.' "

Charlotte looked up at her sister through her tears. "Georgy," she choked, "how can you joke at a time like this? I know those things mean nothing to you."

Georgiana shook her head sadly. "In any case, it's my decision, love, and not yours. I must do as I think best." She rose. "I must go. There are some things that Mother wanted me to do." She smiled wistfully at her sister. "I wish you would not take all of this to heart. I am not actually betrothed yet, you know." She exited the room quietly, shutting the door behind her.

The one other person who would have been most intensely interested in the events of that morning had yet to be informed of them. Aubrey had spent the better part of the day closeted with three rather bored and increasingly weary girls. Every time he decided it would be appropriate to dismiss them, Letitia somehow magically appeared to check on his progress. Aside from the inconvenience of it, he had the strongest dislike of allowing anyone to view an unfinished work, particularly when he was still making preliminary sketches. More irritatingly, despite her self-professed ignorance about art, Letty was only too eager to share her opinions on the subject. It was only with the greatest difficulty that he managed to dissuade her from arranging the girls in stiff, formal poses, which she conceived to be more elegant than the more natural ones he favored. The resultant delays only served to tire the girls further. Little Amelia had been rubbing her eyes wearily for over half an hour when he finally judged it safe to end the sitting.

As soon as he had collected his supplies, he rushed upstairs to change into his riding clothes. Frustrated by the long delay, he had no intention of letting Letitia stop him again. So, when he was finished, he made his way surreptitiously down the back stairs. He was traveling with all possible haste toward the stables when he beheld a small figure flying down the end of the drive. He paused to shade his eyes against the afternoon sun and saw that it was the very person he was seeking. Jem spotted him at about the same time and veered in his direction. Aubrey began to head toward the boy as Jem, not slackening his speed, almost collided with him. Aubrey caught the gasping boy by the shoulders or he would have fallen. Jem did not have the air to speak, but the panic in his eyes was unmistakable.

"The lavender house," Aubrey said curtly. Jem managed a nod. Half-supporting the exhausted boy, Aubrey set out swiftly.

Once they reached the house, Aubrey closed the door and seated Jem, waiting for him to recover his breath. There was evidence of tears on that young, determined face, and Aubrey knew that the situation must be grave indeed.

After a few minutes, Jem had recovered sufficiently to look up at Aubrey and gasp. "You . . . you must help us!"

Aubrey halted his pacing and walked over to face Jem. He leaned on a table and looked at him questioningly.

"My sister . . . my family . . . Miss Georgiana," sputtered Jem urgently.

Aubrey held up a hand. "Slow down," he commanded. He

watched as the boy fought to reorganize his scrambled thoughts. 'Now, start at the beginning,'' he said gently.

Jem's face was flushed with more than his recent exertions. ''It's Lord Marwood,'' he said heavily. ''You see, my sister . . .'' Here he dropped his gaze. ''Lord Marwood is interested in my sister.''

A stern look crept into Aubrey's face. ''And?''

The boy bit his lip before continuing. The words were hard for him. ''After my father died, we had difficulty making a go of the farm. We fell behind on our rent, which had been increased.'' He swallowed, then continued. ''Lord Marwood spends most of his time in London. We hoped we might be able to find the funds before . . .'' His voice trailed off to silence.

''His agent is an understanding man, then?'' prodded Aubrey.

''Oh, yes. He tried in every way to help.'' Jem paused and took a deep breath. ''In any case, Lord Marwood returned here in the spring. We had no idea that he was coming. One day Mr. Higgins, the agent, came to our house and told us that Lord Marwood had ordered that we be evicted. We were to be gone within the week.'' He looked at Aubrey, pleading for understanding. ''We had nowhere to go, you see. My father's family are all dead and my mother's family . . . Well, they won't have anything to do with us.'' The young voice was not bitter, it merely recounted the facts of the matter. ''We were desperate, and since we knew nothing could worsen the situation, Susan went to ask Lord Marwood if we might have just a little more time.'' Here Jem swallowed again and his ears began to redden with anger. ''When he saw Susan, he was willing to give us more time; in fact, he was willing to give us all the time we needed, provided . . .'' Jem choked on the words and could not continue.

Aubrey's high color indicated his own growing wrath, but he merely said dryly, ''I take it that his offer to your sister did not include marriage.''

''No!'' Jem spat out the word. ''As if she'd have that . . . that—''

''Steady,'' Aubrey said quietly.

Jem fought for self-control for a moment. He pursed his lips and went on. ''She had no intention of . . . But she saw that she might win a delay by pretending to consider it. She thought that when this harvest came in we would be able to repay him and so put an end to it.'' Jem's eyes began to moisten. "We all worked so hard, while Susan kept putting him off, but he became more and more insistent.'' Jem heaved a sigh. "Finally, the last time he left, he told Susan that she would have no more time. He expected her to comply with his wishes when he returned.'' Jem fell silent.

Aubrey held his peace for a moment before speaking. "So you found out which day he was to return and, knowing that he always rode alone, waited for him in the bushes beside the road and shot him—or so you thought.''

Startled tears leapt to Jem's eyes as he lifted them to Aubrey in surprise. "I never meant to . . . You must believe me, sir, I thought that I would die when I saw that I—''

Aubrey shook his head gently, motioning for silence. "I know it was unintentional, Jem. I acquit you of homicidal designs upon my person.''

"How did you know?'' Jem breathed, still shocked.

"I wasn't sure until now. I didn't know why you would wish to kill Marwood, other than his being a disagreeable fellow.'' The ghost of a smile lit Aubrey's eyes.

Jem looked at him, a sudden question in his own.

"Don't worry, I have no intention of denouncing you to the authorities, or to Marwood,'' said Aubrey.

Jem heaved a sigh of relief before resuming his tale. "Well, anyway, when I saw you there, I realized how wrong I was.'' He looked at Aubrey squarely. "Whatever Lord Marwood had done, or was going to do, I was wrong to try to kill him for it.''

"A hard-earned lesson,'' Aubrey said softly.

"Yes. Naturally, Susan found out and I thought I should never hear the end of it. Of course, she mostly was afraid that Lord Marwood would discover the truth. She was trying to protect me. That's why she was so cold to you when you began asking questions the other day.''

"Does he suspect, do you think?'' Aubrey asked, leaning forward intently.

Jem shrugged. "Not that we've seen. There are a great many people hereabouts that dislike him, after all.''

Aubrey could well believe that the proud Marwood would be unlikely to suspect a small boy of being his would-be assassin.

"I know it seems like a lot to ask after what I've done," Jem was saying slowly. "But I thought that you should know the truth about him at least, and even if there is nothing you can do for us, perhaps you at least could prevent his marrying Miss Georgiana."

Aubrey shook his head uncomprehendingly. "What marriage? I thought I told you we need not worry yet about—"

Jem's eyes opened wide once again. He regarded Aubrey with surprise. "I thought you'd know," he breathed. "Lord Marwood rode over and told us just now. He proposed to Miss Georgiana this morning!"

9

Aubrey was quite pale. The look on his face alarmed Jem. "The devil you say," he breathed.

Jem hastened to reassure him. "She hasn't accepted him yet, but he said it was only a formality."

"She wouldn't accept him."

Jem shrugged helplessly. "That's what my sister said, but he just laughed and said that Miss Georgiana had few other choices, that pressure was being brought to bear upon her."

"Mrs. Chalford."

Jem nodded unhappily. "I fear that he is speaking the truth." He looked at Aubrey earnestly. "You could speak with her father."

Aubrey shook his head. "He obeys Mrs. Chalford's every command, and I doubt that even this information would have any influence upon her desire to be the mother of a baroness, if she were to believe me, which is not likely."

Jem's face sank with disappointment. "There is nothing that can be done?"

"I didn't say that." Aubrey's eyes were sparkling now, but not with amusement. He regarded Jem seriously. "I am in a more powerful position than I seem, and I am determined that Georgy, your sister, and your entire family will be extricated from Lord Marwood's clutches. But to do so, I must know everything. Why did Marwood wish to inform you of his marriage? Did it make some difference to his designs upon your sister?"

Jem flushed again, but he did not evade the question.

"He told Susan that there could be no question of further delay now. He said that his marriage would have no effect whatsoever upon the arrangement he had already proposed, but that since he must be circumspect for a little while after the wed-

129

ding . . . ." Jem was turning redder. He managed to choke the
words out with an effort. "He said that their arrangement must
be established before then. He said that—"

Aubrey stopped him. "Never mind, Jem," he said softly.
"I can guess the rest."

Jem looked at him, his eyes filled with tears. "He told her
how convenient it would be for him."

Aubrey was furious, but he asked quietly, "And what did
your sister tell him?"

"She said . . . she pretended she did not believe his argu-
ments. She said she was not convinced that he truly was about
to be married."

"He must have been enraged."

"Yes, but it was for the best. In the end, he stormed out,
saying that she would have no more excuses when his betrothal
was announced—and that would happen within the week."

Aubrey looked thoughtful. "That doesn't give us much time,"
he said, half to himself.

A tear escaped down Jem's cheek. He brushed it away angrily.
"But, sir, I have not told you the worst." He smothered a sob.
"My sister . . . Susan . . . she says she has no choice now,
she says she must do as he wishes."

Aubrey crossed over to the boy and put an arm about the
shaking shoulders. "It will not come to that," he promised.
"We shall contrive something, you'll see."

Aubrey's assurances managed to restore Jem to hope. He left
some fifteen minutes later with a decidedly less anxious
expression. Aubrey sighed as he watched him go. He wished
he had been able to inspire the same sort of confidence in
himself. Jem and his family would be no problem. Some
situation could be found for them in Dorset, if nothing else
occurred to him. The real problem was Georgiana. A week was
little time in which to devise and execute a plan of action. Even
worse, Herne could not be sure that marriage to Lord Marwood
wasn't what she wanted. Oh, he had no illusions that she was
in love with Marwood. He was certain that she was attracted
by himself as he was by her. He might have misjudged what
the title might mean to her, though. Else why shouldn't she have
refused him outright? Letitia was undoubtedly as angry with
a postponed acceptance as she would have been with a refusal.

Georgiana had nothing to gain by delaying tactics. Most ominous, though, was the fact that she hadn't seen fit to confide in him, not after Marwood's talk with her parents—and not today, either.

He shook his head. He could not allow an innocent girl to marry such a blackguard, whether or not she wished to be Lady Marwood. Since her heart was not involved, he could feel free to act. He hoped that she would not be too deeply disappointed.

He brushed away these thoughts. The important thing was that he must begin planning their strategy. He would need to confer with William. He began to stroll thoughtfully back to the house.

In the meantime, though Aubrey could not be aware of it, another person was busy devising a means to rescue Georgiana. After an entire afternoon spent weeping in her chamber, Charlotte had come to realize that her sister's salvation depended on her and her alone. She had nourished high hopes for Cousin Aubrey, but he had not taken any action. She must have been mistaken about his feelings for Georgiana. She supposed she had been expecting too much of such a humble creature for him to have whisked her sister off to Gretna Green. On the other hand, he should at least have spoken to Georgiana of his regard and pleaded with her not to marry Lord Marwood. It was evident from her talk with Georgiana that he had not done so, even though matters had come to such a serious pass.

She sighed deeply. She had been turning it over in her mind for some hours now, and it was clear that there was only one solution: Georgiana had to have another desirable suitor immediately.

Charlotte had seen how impressed Letitia had been by William with his handsomeness, his gracious manners, and his air of fashion, with that accompanying suggestion of wealth. He wasn't titled, but he did have aristocratic friends, which should be some compensation.

She had to restrain another little sob. Her heart tore asunder at the thought of her darling William married to someone else, but it was the only thing that could save her beloved sister. Of course, Georgiana must not know what she was doing. She would never accept such a sacrifice. It would make things much more difficult, especially given the speed at which she would have to work, but William must be made to fall in love with Georgiana without either of them suspecting that it was she, Charlotte, who had contrived it all.

She stifled a little moan of anguish and set to work thinking about ways to bring Georgiana's worth to William's notice.

Her plan went into action that very evening. With a lack of subtlety, Letitia again had seated Charlotte and William together. William, of course, was perfectly happy with this arrangement, but found to his surprise that Charlotte was singularly uncommunicative. She avoided his eyes and returned only terse answers to even the most leading of his questions. He was frankly baffled. He couldn't imagine what had happened since that morning to produce so great a change.

He was too well-bred to reveal his dismay and instead politely turned his attention to Mr. Chalford. Harry had been inclined to dismiss him as a mere man milliner, but William unwittingly raised himself several notches in that gentleman's estimation by introducing the topic of sport. Harry tested his opinions and found them sound, and when it was established that William had actually hunted with the Quorn upon occasion, it was clear that he was a most estimable fellow and that he possessed every amiable quality.

Letitia, observing this animated conversation from the other end of the table, scowled at Harry meaningfully but was unable to attract his eye. She had missed the earlier abrupt exchange between Charlotte and William and was quite willing to blame their lack of interaction entirely upon Harry's thoughtlessness. She would speak to him about it later.

Aubrey was also a little irritated by William and Harry's preoccupation with their subject. He had not been able to locate William before dinner and was attempting to communicate through a series of gestures and significant glances that he needed to speak with him urgently. William was oblivious to all these signals. Aubrey was becoming frustrated. He needed William's help in planning what to do about Lord Marwood.

As dinner concluded, Harry, in his enthusiasm, so far forgot himself as to ignore Letty's warnings about the effect of spirits on his guest and asked William if he wished for a glass of port. Fortunately for him, this danger was averted as William declined with a smile and announced his intention of taking a turn in the garden. As the company was rising from the table, he helped his dinner partner up and in his courteous way asked if she cared to join him.

Charlotte declined abruptly, saying that she had a touch of the headache. Since she refused to look at him, she missed the look of dismay that William quickly strove to conceal. It was her heart that was aching, but she knew what she owed her sister. Still unable to meet his eyes, she told him that Georgiana was a great walker and doubtless would be happy to accompany him. Having used up all her resolution, she fled the room precipitately, leaving William frowning after her.

He was frankly puzzled. He must have offended her inadvertently, but how? She certainly had shown no such coldness to him this morning.

Recollecting his manners all of a sudden, he turned to Georgiana, smiled politely, and asked if she cared to take a stroll. Out of everyone at the table, she alone had witnessed Charlotte's curtness throughout dinner and her avoidance of William's eyes. No more than he could Georgiana imagine what had inspired such standoffishness on the love-stricken Charlotte's part. Although she had been inclined to think him merely an experienced trifler, the hurt on his face when Charlotte hastily rejected his invitation convinced Georgiana that she might have been mistaken. She felt genuinely sorry for him, and in any case it seemed that the least she could do was to try to compensate for her sister's rudeness. She accepted his offer with a smile, just as Aubrey drew up to her side.

He scowled fiercely as he heard her acceptance. He had assumed when Charlotte left the table so hurriedly that William would be free to discuss strategy with him. It seemed that the fates were conspiring against him.

William, seeing his cousin's look and misinterpreting the reason for it, asked if he might like to join them. Aubrey accepted morosely, hoping that he might at least be able to cut short their promenade and still manage a talk with William this evening.

Luckily for Charlotte, Letty, who had noticed her hasty departure, was inclined to blame it all on Harry. Charlotte assuredly had taken a pet at being ignored all the way through dinner in favor of talk about dogs and horses and guns, and

who could blame her? What a thickheaded sapskull she had
married, doing his best to ruin their chance of a most eligible
connection for his second daughter. She approached her husband
with a martial light in her eyes.

Charlotte herself, who lay weeping in her chamber, might
have been comforted to know that the romantic assignation she
had engineered was not being enjoyed by any of its participants.

Georgiana was preoccupied with consoling William for
Charlotte's defection, assuring him that she was frequently
subject to headaches. "And, I must admit myself that nothing
irritates me more. I become out-of-reason-cross when I am
suffering from one myself."

She could not help but glance involuntarily at Aubrey as she
spoke. Something evidently was afflicting him, for he had hardly
spoken a word since joining them. To their attempts to politely
include him in the conversation, he had answered with mono-
syllabic grunts. She had seen him in a bad mood before this,
but never in such a sullen one.

William hardly was aware of what Georgiana was saying.
His mind was taken up entirely with the question of what he
had done to offend Charlotte. Rack his brain as he might, he
could not imagine what it had been. He did his best to respond
to Georgiana's remarks politely, but at the same time he tried
to remain somewhat distant. He was sure that Aubrey's joining
them and his subsequent churlishness sprang from an unreason-
able jealousy. It is ridiculous, he thought. None of his attempts
to draw Aubrey out or to make him cast off his mood was in
the least successful.

Aubrey was becoming more irritated with every passing
moment. Their time for planning was so limited, and here they
were, exchanging ridiculous small talk with the very person who
was in danger. Even worse, Georgiana herself seemed entirely
nonchalant about the whole affair. Didn't she think that he at
least deserved to know she was soon to be engaged? When did
she plan to tell him anyway? After the wedding? Perhaps he
had misjudged her, perhaps the thought of being a baroness held
a great deal of appeal for her. Well, it was fortunate that he
had never told her of his own title. Still, given what he knew
about Marwood, he could not simply abandon her to her fate.

Curse William! There he was making some inane remark about the beauty of the gardens in the moonlight.

The three rather disgruntled young people returned to the house a half an hour later. Georgiana would have welcomed an opportunity to speak privately with Aubrey, as they had not had the chance to do so for the past few days. It was apparent, however, that he did not intend to leave his cousin's side. Well, possibly it was better not to try to consult with him when he was in such a black humor anyway.

She bid them good night and went up to Charlotte's chamber. At least she might discover what was amiss there. She knocked softly on the door. There was no response. She tried again, with a similar lack of luck. She opened the door gingerly. All that was visible was a mound of bedclothes.

"Charlotte," she called softly. The mound did not stir.

She closed the door again and shrugged to herself. Possibly Charlotte truly had been feeling ill tonight. It was odd, though, for she would have sworn that Charlotte would have walked on a broken ankle in order to be with William.

Behind the closed door, a muffled sob escaped the heap of bedclothes.

As soon as Georgiana had departed, William took the opportunity to begin to explain to the obviously angry Aubrey that he personally had no designs upon her. He was cut off by a stifled curse, seized by the elbow, and yanked unceremoniously upstairs.

"But I'm telling you, Aubrey, I couldn't very well uninvite her when her sister had—"

"Will you be quiet," Aubrey said as he thrust William into his chamber, closing the door behind them.

"I see no cause for you to be—"

"Will you stop being so pigeon-headed and listen for a moment?"

"See here, Aubrey, you have no call to—"

Aubrey rolled his eyes in his head. "William," he said urgently, "the mystery is solved. I need your help. Now, will you be quiet while I explain?"

Startled, William closed his mouth and began to listen.

For the next twenty minutes or so he heard Aubrey's account

with ever-growing amazement. By the time his cousin had finished, William's lips were firmly compressed and his eyes sparkled with anger.

"Well, it is clear that there is only one course of action to be taken," William said.

"Which is?"

"I shall call him out."

"What!"

"Since you are living under an assumed identity, it's hardly likely that he'd agree to meet you—not being his social equal."

"What a hen-witted idea!"

William looked insulted.

Aubrey gave him a placating smile. "In the first place, since it's my quarrel, I should be the one to call him out. In the second place, I have no intention of doing so since I do not wish either to put a period to my existence or to spend the rest of my days in exile." He shook his head. "Violence won't answer. It would suit his purposes better than ours."

William frowned thoughtfully. "If the fellow is capable of this sort of thing, likely there are more incidents that might be brought to light. We could begin by asking—"

Aubrey shook his head again. "I thought of that, too. The problem is that I'm not sure that anything would sway Letitia. It's difficult to obtain proof of villainy, and finally, our time is much too limited if we have only a week."

William sighed. "This is difficult. It will require some thought."

Aubrey frowned. "My problem is that in my position here, I am at the Chalfords' beck and call. I should not be surprised that, having started, Letitia would expect me to spend every minute of my time working on the portrait."

"We do have a dilemma then, coz," said William absently.

A depressed silence reigned in the room for several minutes. William drummed his fingers thoughtfully. Aubrey gave a cough. They glanced at each other, sighed, and glanced away. Suddenly William's fingers stopped drumming. He took a deep breath and let it out slowly. Aubrey looked at him expectantly.

"Mrs. Chalford may not care what Lord Marwood has actually done," William began slowly. He looked at his cousin. "But . . . but perhaps she might care what others would think."

Aubrey's brows drew together as he waited for his cousin to explain. William was still trying to formulate his idea.

"I mean, if word were to get out among their neighbors about all this . . ." He hesitated for a moment. "At least that way there would be considerably less glory in being the mother of a baroness."

Aubrey began to pace slowly back and forth while he considered the idea. "You may have something there," he said thoughtfully. "It's true that she would . . ." He halted, shaking his head. "But we have no acquaintances in this neighborhood, and to spread the word within a week, and to be believed . . ."

William gave a little sigh. Aubrey began pacing again. "It's a pity we don't have just a little more time. I daresay that Marwood would like it no better than Letitia if . . ." He halted again, then startled William by spinning on his heel. "That's it," he exclaimed.

"What?"

Aubrey's eyes sparkled in the familiar way. "You had the right idea—just the wrong person."

"What do you mean?"

Aubrey chuckled, but there was no lightness in it. "Lord Marwood is a proud man."

"Yes?"

"He is the one who would be bothered by talk, not Letitia." He smiled, and William did not like the look upon his face. "He probably doesn't care about being thought a blackguard. Danger obviously doesn't frighten him, or he wouldn't ride alone through a countryside where he is hated."

William was becoming impatient. "So?"

Aubrey's eyes were very cold indeed. "His one vulnerable spot in his pride. There is probably nothing he would fear more than the possibility of being made the laughingstock of London."

William leaned forward eagerly. This was the Aubrey of old. "Tell me your scheme," he breathed.

Within the hour, the two cousins had managed to hammer out most of the details of the plan, Aubrey providing the rough outline and William contributing the finishing touches. They retired to bed well-satisfied with their work. It was fortunate that they had been able to accomplish what they had, for

Aubrey's predictions about Letitia were confirmed the next morning when she asked if he cared to begin her sitting. It was clear that he was expected to devote all his time to his work now.

Charlotte deliberately had absented herself from breakfast, but even this failed to disgruntle William, whose head was full of other thoughts. He had his curricle readied early, and remarking somewhat mysteriously that he had an errand to run in the village, he disappeared for the morning.

Georgiana felt a little pang of disappointment upon learning that she would not be able to speak to Aubrey this morning either. She told herself that she simply needed to confide in someone, and Charlotte was useless. Even her godmother had proved singularly unhelpful. A part of her knew that it was not wise to entrust her secret doubts to Aubrey, that the last thing she needed was to draw closer to him. At the same time, there was some small clinging hope that if she did explain matters to him, he might find a solution, or even declare his feelings for her.

She blushed at the thought. A mere drawing master. No, she could not stoop so low. It was impractical. No, things were much better the way they were.

She permitted herself the luxury of a sigh before turning her mind to other matters. She reminded herself that the intriguing fossil was still waiting. She needed to begin work on it now if she was to extract it from the rock before . . . She swallowed hastily, her eyes beginning to moisten at the thought. She read herself a lecture. There was no need for this dramatic nonsense. Hadn't Lord Marwood said everything that was reasonable and hadn't he behaved in an entirely gentlemanly fashion?

She shook her head to banish the gloomy thoughts. No, she must concentrate on her find. After all, she hadn't even been given the opportunity to examine it yet. It might be the one big discovery for which she had been searching so long.

Having comforted herself with this thought, Georgiana ran upstairs to her chamber for her tools. Wearing a tired muslin dress and with an elderly straw bonnet jammed on her head, she began to make her way downstairs, puzzling over the problem of obtaining a ladder and how to get it to the quarry. She had just reached the bottom of the stairs when the elderly butler, Wilkins, came up to her anxiously.

"Miss Georgiana," he said, "Lord Marwood is here to see you."

Georgiana froze in her tracks. The idea of escape crossed her mind, but she rejected it quickly, for she would be sure to be spotted. She saw the worried look in the old retainer's eyes and managed a small, tight smile.

"Very well, Wilkins. I will need to go upstairs and change my dress. Perhaps Lord Marwood would care to wait in the parlor."

He bowed and scurried off to do her bidding.

"Blast," she exclaimed under her breath; then, grasping her skirts, she began to run up the stairs.

On her way up she barely missed encountering Charlotte, who had decided that she finally must put in an appearance downstairs. Charlotte was feeling far from well today, having spent the greater part of the night in tears. By the wee hours of the morning she had begun to repent her generosity in bestowing her suitor upon her sister. After all, she told herself, how can I be sure that William and Georgiana will suit? A myriad objections occurred to her. William, for example, was so very fastidious in his dress. Surely he would expect his wife to be the same. And Georgiana was a darling, of course, but one had to admit that she had always shown a deplorable want of interest in such matters. It wasn't that she couldn't make herself quite presentable if she chose. It was just that, on a day-to-day basis, she seemed so careless about the way she looked.

With these and similar thoughts, Charlotte gradually made her way down to the breakfast room. She might have been too hasty. After all, Georgiana had not actually said she was going to marry Lord Marwood. Suppose all her worry was for nothing? It was a horrifying thought.

She happened to glance toward the entryway and saw a whip standing propped in the corner. Wilkins was shuffling back from the direction of the parlor, so she had to assume that there was a visitor. She motioned to the butler.

"Who is here, Wilkins?" she asked softly.

"Lord Marwood, Miss Charlotte."

Her heart sank within her. She had been right in the first place. Georgiana had merely been trying to comfort her when she said she had not given him an answer. The fellow would not come calling the next day if he really intended to allow her time to consider her decision.

No, she had done the right thing. Now she must be brave and adhere to her resolution. She unconsciously straightened herself a little.

"Thank you, Wilkins," she said gently, and proceeded on her way.

The old butler looked after her curiously. He wondered what it was that could have made the normally happy-natured Miss Charlotte look so very miserable.

Although he was unaware of Marwood's arrival, Aubrey also was very much occupied with Georgiana's problem. Despite her other faults, Letitia was a good subject, at least. He supposed it was gratified vanity at having her portrait taken that made her so cooperative. In any case, he could not but be glad that she had the ability to remain so motionless when he asked. He was free to let his hands do the work while his mind puzzled over the final details of his plan. The solution to one problem eluded him.

He glanced up at his subject to see that her smile had become fixed and that she obviously was in some discomfort. He realized with a twinge of amused remorse that he must have left her sitting frozen for forty-five minutes or so. He put down his charcoal.

"Please, take a rest," he told her kindly.

Letitia fell back in her chair with an audible sigh of relief. She glanced down at her skirt and began rearranging the folds critically. "I am still not certain that this was the wisest choice," she said. "I can't help but think that the new net gown would have been . . ."

Having belatedly discovered that he did indeed have a conscience, Aubrey had persuaded her to wear one of her least objectionable gowns in a subdued rose satin for the portrait, rather than one that bore the marks of his own creative suggestions.

"I agree that it is a pity," he remarked carelessly. "But, as I explained, since it is a group portrait, we have to worry about the harmony of the whole."

She looked at him concernedly. "I know, but you are certain

that this gown will serve to make me the focal point rather than—"

"You have my word," Aubrey said, lying unashamedly as he picked up the charcoal and added a few strokes. Glancing at Letitia and seeing that she was still not satisfied, he added placatingly, "Besides, I would hate to take the risk of anyone seeing you in it before the Eversham ball. You are certain to create a sensation."

His words brought a self-satisfied gleam to Letitia's eyes. "I am, aren't I?" she said. Her forehead puckered in a little frown. "But since the ball is Saturday next, it does not seem that we would be taking so very great a chance—"

Aubrey's charcoal halted in midair. "Saturday next?"

"Yes," said Letitia, fiddling with her skirt once again. "And the Evershams have graciously agreed to include both Mr. Darley and yourself."

The charcoal hesitated for a moment more, then it resumed its activity. "How very kind of you, Cousin Letitia."

It was the solution he had been seeking. He smiled at her. "Shall we begin again?" He hummed happily to himself as she resumed her pose.

10

Georgiana was finishing dressing when she heard the commotion coming from downstairs. Muffled at first, it suddenly increased in volume. She turned to Betsey with a startled expression, and neglecting to even run a comb through her tousled curls, she headed down the stairs at full speed.

Lion's excited barks rang through the house. She could also make out Emmy's wails among other voices. Wilkins, too, had apparently joined the fray, alternately cajoling and scolding. The sounds were issuing from the parlor, and as she came around the bottom of the staircase, she could see that its doors were opened wide. She rushed into the room, then halted, momentarily stunned.

Pandemonium confronted her eyes. In the corner of the room by the fireplace stood Lord Marwood, red with fury. Having snatched a convenient poker, he was brandishing it menacingly at Lion, who apparently had taken him in the greatest dislike. The dog was barking excitedly and making little feints toward Marwood, who only just managed to keep the great snapping jaws at bay through a dexterous use of his weapon. Little Emmy had thrown herself on the floor and was wailing inconsolably, while Augusta made vain but valiant attempts to seize Lion and drag him from the vicinity. Wilkins, clearly overwrought, was alternately reprimanding Lion, trying to console Emmy, and apologize to Lord Marwood without any effect whatsoever. Sophia looked on, primly disapproving.

Georgiana came to her senses and rushed up to Lion.

Marwood, seeing her approach called out, "Watch out! I think the animal's gone mad."

Ignoring the warning, she took hold of the hysterical dog by the collar and with Augusta's help managed to pry him back from the corner. Fortunately a footman appeared at that moment and she was able to turn the still-snarling Lion over to him, with directions that he be lodged in the stables.

Emmy, perceiving that her adored older sister had come to the rescue, ran to her. She threw her arms about Georgiana's waist, sobbing that Lord Marwood was a "wicked, wicked man."

Nonplussed, Georgiana patted her head and murmured that she mustn't say such things.

Emmy raised a tearstained face to her. "But . . . but he said he was going to shoot Lion," she protested, then collapsed afresh in a flood of tears.

Marwood still retained his defensive position, though he had lowered the poker at Lion's eviction. "I merely said that a cur that vicious should be put down," he retorted testily.

"No one's going to shoot him," Georgiana reassured Emmy. "Now, come and apologize to Lord Marwood."

Emmy's hiccuping sobs lessened at the first sentence. Her face assumed a mutinous expression at the second. She met Georgiana's eyes and saw that her sister would not brook a refusal. Accordingly, she turned to Marwood and dipped a resentful curtsy. "I'm sorry," she said sullenly.

"Very well," said Marwood, gazing at her with a dislike only slightly less than that he had reserved for Lion. He suddenly realized that he was still holding the poker and he replaced it hastily.

Judging by Marwood's expression, Georgiana decided that this was not the time to effect introductions. She turned to Augusta. "Will you take the others upstairs?"

"Yes. I'm sorry, Georgy." Augusta clearly held herself to blame for the debacle.

Georgiana laid a sympathetic hand for a moment on the girl's shoulder. Augusta straightened herself, then shepherded the two younger girls from the room.

Wilkins, meanwhile, had seen his primary duty as that of soothing their injured guest. He was busy between apologizing and trying ineffectually to brush off Lord Marwood's jacket, to the latter's intense annoyance. Georgiana interpreted Marwood's expression correctly, thanked Wilkins for his efforts, and sent him out to order refreshments for their guest.

Marwood's eyes snapped angrily. "It is not safe to let a vicious beast of that size have the run of the house. I can't imagine why you should keep such a bad-tempered cur about, anyway. He should be shot."

He had drawn himself up stiffly, like a cat whose fur had been rubbed the wrong way. Georgiana repressed a sigh. It was clear that her work was cut out for her. She murmured a few placating words as she offered him a chair.

"I am so sorry. I have never seen him act this way. He usually is so good-tempered."

Marwood refused to be mollified, though he did lower himself gingerly into the chair. "Well, I should certainly have him put down, then. Once a dog turns, you have no reassurance that he won't do it again."

"But really, he's usually so gentle," protested Georgiana. "Why we trust him with the children. You can see how devoted little Emmy is to him." She was just about to ask him if he were sure that he hadn't done something to provoke the dog, but remembered just in time to whom she was speaking.

Marwood, glaring at her, seemed to hear the unspoken question anyway. "I didn't do a thing to the brute," he said furiously. "The butler showed me in and the creature was napping in the corner. I had strolled over to the fireplace when I saw that it had risen and started growling at me. It started in my direction and—well, it was fortunate that I had the presence of mind to seize the poker."

Georgiana murmured in sympathetic agreement, though privately she had to repress a smile at the remembrance of the picture Marwood had presented upon her entrance.

There was a tap at the door and for a sickening moment she thought that the racket had been enough to bring Letty downstairs. She was relieved to see it was only the footman, bringing the tray of refreshments in accordance with her instructions.

After having a great deal more sympathy lavished upon him and after being plied with sherry and biscuits, Marwood was in a fair way to having forgotten his grievances. After all, he told himself, he mustn't forget his purpose in coming here. It was a matter of pride now that he bring this skittish girl to accept his proposal within the week. It would take all of his considerable charm to manage it.

Aubrey was beginning to wonder wearily if Letty would ever tire. He had spent most of the morning and a good part of the afternoon closeted with her, not even pausing for victuals. She apparently was so thrilled to have her likeness taken that the increasingly long periods of time for which she had to remain motionless did not appear to bother her. The noise of some disturbance downstairs did not seem to perturb her. She rejected out-of-hand Aubrey's suggestion that they discover its cause.

Therefore, he was both delighted and surprised when at length she abruptly called a halt to the proceeding, complaining of a slight ache in her neck. He half-dreaded that she would order that he spend the remainder of the afternoon working on the girls' portraits, but fortunately the thought did not occur to her.

He was free to make his escape, which he did as promptly as possible. A few minutes later, he was heading downstairs in his riding leathers, intent upon visiting the Thornbys, when Wilkins, the butler, stopped him.

Aubrey's impatience must have shown in his face, for Wilkins gave him an apologetic look as he presented him with a note. Aubrey tore it open in haste and could have cursed in frustration. Georgiana's godmother, Lady Dowles, requested that he wait upon her immediately regarding a matter of the utmost urgency. Both manners and necessity dictated that he comply. He knew that if she believed Georgiana to be in some kind of danger from Marwood, she might feel justified in doing whatever was necessary to stop the marriage, including revealing his identity. He must prevent that, at all possible cost.

When he encountered her some thirty minutes later, the implacable expression upon her countenance convinced him that he had made the right decision. He was beginning to apologize for the casual appearance he presented when she silenced him with a dismissive wave of her hand.

"I have more important matters to discuss," she said majestically. A sharp glance at the lingering butler sent that venerable gentleman scurrying out of the room hastily, shutting the door behind him. She indicated a chair opposite her, and Aubrey obediently sat.

"Now," she said coldly, "what is this that I hear about my goddaughter becoming engaged to Lord Marwood?"

Aubrey met her eyes directly. "It is true that he has offered for her. I mean to take steps, however, to ensure that it never comes to an actual engagement."

Her gaze remained steely. "And what assurance do I have that you can prevent that?"

She was startled to see a quick spark of something unreadable flash in those brown eyes. "You have my word as a Herne." He paused for a moment before continuing. "I have reason to believe that Marwood is not expecting an immediate answer to his proposal—"

She cut him off. "Then why did he call upon her again this morning?"

She was pleased by the way that lean jaw tightened with anger. "Did he, by Jove?" He snorted in disgust, then turned to her coolly. "Your ladyship seems remarkably well-informed."

She shook her head silently. "I do what I must to protect my goddaughter." There was a pleading note in her voice that he had not heard before. "This engagement must not take place."

"I agree with your ladyship that Georgy must be spared the indignity of—"

"It is more than that," she said abruptly. "Georgy must not enter into an engagement with that man."

Aubrey looked at her questioningly. Slowly she raised her eyes to meet his.

"When we first met, I told you of my concerns about Lord Marwood," she said slowly. "Even though my acquaintanceship in town has been reduced greatly in recent years, I have discovered the information I was seeking." She hesitated for a moment as if unsure how to continue. "I am persuaded that my goddaughter's reputation might be ruined by entering into an engagement with that man."

"But surely no blame could attach to Georgy."

She shook her head firmly. "To have her name associated with his in any way could . . . could jeopardize her future."

Aubrey's eyebrows ascended. "As bad as that?" he asked coolly.

She nodded heavily. "The injustice of it is that he is still received, while his unfortunate victims—"

To her surprise, a gentle hand was laid on hers. "You need not worry," said Aubrey firmly. "I have already been made aware of the man's villainy and I have a plan to stop him."

She felt a giddy sense of relief. "You mean to reveal your true identity, then? Have you decided to offer for Georgy?"

She realized that her question had been premature when she saw his scowl.

"No, my plan does not involve such a contingency. In fact, I require your ladyship's word that you will continue to conceal who I am from your goddaughter."

She stared at him, frankly perplexed. "But I know that Georgy has a decided *tendre* for you."

He gave her a wistful little smile and suddenly she understood Georgiana's attraction to this sometimes unprepossessing young gentleman.

"I suppose you will think me a hopeless romantic, rather like Charlotte," he said softly. "But I do not wish to be wed for my title." He held up a hand to prevent her protests.

"It is a situation in which I have found myself previously," he said quietly. "Although I mean to prevent Georgy's marrying a villain like Marwood, I am not certain that she is not willing to do so." He looked at her squarely. "His position must hold a certain attraction for her to have taken the possibility of an engagement this far."

Lady Dowles' jaw had dropped in astonishment. "Never tell me that you mean to see whether she would marry you if you were a common drawing master!"

He shrugged slightly. "I would have some proof of her sincere affection."

"You're mad," she said flatly.

After some artful persuasion, Aubrey managed to convince her that it was to Georgiana's benefit for her to maintain silence on the identity question. Out of a certain delicacy, he forbore to mention the details of his strategy, but he was able to offer her his assurances that her goddaughter had nothing whatsoever to fear.

By the time he was through, the hour was becoming late. He had decided that he could risk no further delay in conferring with the Thornbys, so he rode there with all possible haste.

Upon his arrival, Susan greeted him with an unencouraging mixture of embarrassment and resentment. At a pleading look from Jem, though, she rapidly shooed the younger children outside and turned to face Aubrey, her arms crossed. Her defiant expression proclaimed her belief that there was nothing that this outsider could do. It was Jem who made Aubrey comfortable in a chair and saw that he had some refreshment.

Aubrey did his best to broach the subject in his most delicate manner, but even that did not prevent a ready blush from springing to Susan's face. This naturally was a most uncomfortable experience for her and it was obvious that having a stranger discuss such matters was painful in the extreme. He had hardly begun when she stopped him.

"I . . . I am aware, sir that you have been most generous to Jem, that you have promised to keep that matter secret. We appreciate your concern, but since there is nothing that you can do, I wish you would—"

There was no help for it. He knew of only one thing that could win over this obstinate girl. He took a deep breath.

"I believe I may change your opinion on that. Before I speak, however, I must have your solemn word that you will not reveal what I am about to tell you."

Impressed by his seriousness, she and Jem quickly nodded their heads in agreement.

Aubrey gave a little sigh. "You would have discovered this shortly in any case if you agreed to my plan." He met their wondering eyes. "I am Lord Herne."

The next few days passed in deceptive calm. Aubrey was kept quite busy with his different portrait sittings. At Letty's impetus, he began work on Harry's portrait. This subject proved not only unwilling but uncomfortable with such a proceeding. Aubrey had to admonish him continually to hold still. He couldn't decide if it was the discomfort of being attired in his best suit that bothered Harry or just the fear of Letitia's frequent intrusions that made him fidget so. In any case, such a difficult subject proved a blessing in disguise for Aubrey, since Harry was only too happy to keep their sessions short, freeing Aubrey for other matters.

William also was proving an invaluable aide to Aubrey. Fortunately none of the Chalfords saw fit to question why he must make so many frequent trips to the village. Of course, the one who most noticed his absence was Charlotte, who found it a serious impediment to her own schemes. It was true that William did notice her continuing coolness toward him, but busy as he was, he had little time to ponder its cause. Having made her sacrifice, it was all the more irritating to Charlotte to feel that it might have been in vain.

It was not that Georgiana was around a great deal, either. Since Marwood had established a pattern of calling upon her every morning, her time was also limited. Each visit rendered Letty more complacent and Charlotte more miserable.

Georgiana herself was aware of the fine balance she had to maintain. Despite his previous assurances, Marwood definitely was beginning to press her for a decision. She had to evince interest and uncertainty at the same time. Her worst difficulty lay in that the better she came to know Lord Marwood, the less she liked him. Such complacent arrogance irritated her in the extreme, as did his obvious belief that she, like every other young lady of his acquaintance, must find his charm and good looks fatal. She was not sure if she could stand to be around someone who was so used to having his own way in everything. Nor was she certain that she could wed a man who was so positive that *he* was the one conferring an honor by wedding *her*.

She came out of every meeting determined to refuse him at the next opportunity. By the following morning, however, her common sense would have convinced her that accepting him was her only choice. It would be impossible to live in the same house with Letty if she refused him, to say nothing of the opportunities she would be denying her younger sisters. They certainly deserved to have their chances of contracting eligible marriages someday, and she knew that it was unlikely that Letty would ever agree to sponsoring Seasons for them, even if she were able.

At the word "eligible," she could not refrain from a little sigh. How could she have fallen in love with someone so hopelessly ineligible? A part of her yearned for him to confront her with his feelings. The more practical side of her could not help but honor him for being gentleman enough to keep his emotions to himself, since there was no possibility of his being able to offer her a future with him. It would only make her inevitable decision more difficult.

Marwood, meanwhile, was becoming impatient with her. Georgiana welcomed him cordially enough every day, and perhaps he was imagining it, but she seemed to grow more distant with each visit. He could not imagine the cause. Why, he might have his pick of a dozen of London's reigning beauties for a romantic interlude. How could a nineteen-year-old provincial chit fail to be dazzled by his appearance and manner? His lip curled angrily at the thought. He had refrained from enlisting her aid until now, but perhaps it was an opportune time to speak to Letty. This skittish girl must be brought to a decision, and quickly.

Marwood's continual presence was an irritant to Aubrey also. He needed Georgiana's cooperation if his plan was to be a success. As much as he dreaded confronting her with the news of her suitor's infamy, he knew that he could not afford to delay much longer. Between Marwood's visits and his sittings, Aubrey hardly had a chance to exchange a word with her. And then there was that barrier that had sprung up between them since Marwood's arrival on the scene.

It was clear that he would have to make his own opportunity if he wished to have a serious talk with her. Accordingly, he took the initiative one afternoon, and announced to Letitia flatly that he wished to begin Georgiana's portrait that day. Since Marwood had already departed, there were few objections she could make.

Fortunately, Letitia did not think to inquire about Georgiana's whereabouts. Aubrey had noted her absence and had a strong suspicion that she had fled the house immediately after Marwood's departure. He had a fair idea where she might be.

Accordingly, he was soon to be found, sketchbook under his arm, entering the quarry. Lion rose to greet him, tail wagging. Aubrey patted him absentmindedly, for his whole attention was occupied by the charming picture before his eyes.

Georgiana was perched on a ladder, one leg above the other,

busily chipping away at the stone's face. Frowning with concentration, she did not notice his arrival. He was free to admire the unrestricted view of a trim ankle and hint of a shapely calf that his perspective afforded him. Realizing that he was taking advantage of her preoccupation, he alerted her to his presence with a quiet cough.

She looked down, saw the wicked gleam of appreciation in his eyes, and lowered her upper leg instantly, blushing vividly as she did so.

"Wh-what?" she stammered.

He smiled politely at her, though his eyes still sparkled with mischief. "I've come to take your portrait. I've already begun on the rest of your family."

Still pink, she began to descend the ladder. "Of course. How stupid of me. I had forgot."

He looked up with interest to where she had been working. "What have you found?"

As she reached the ground, he offered her his arm by way of assistance. She shook her head shyly in reply to his question. "It's rather too early to tell, I'm afraid."

Aubrey had seen Georgiana in many moods, but never diffident. By way of relieving her tension, he pulled a sheaf of papers from his sketchbook. "I've had these ready for several days," he said gently. "I haven't had the opportunity to give them to you."

Taking the papers, she saw that they were more of the sketches of fossils that she had originally commissioned him to do. She blushed even darker with embarrassment. "Oh, dear. It had slipped my mind. Wherever did you find the time?"

"In the evenings. Are they satisfactory?"

"Oh, yes," she said inadequately. She dared to meet his eyes. "About . . . about your fee . . ."

There was an odd, unreadable expression on his face. "We can discuss that when I have completed all of them," he said gravely.

She gave a quick nod of her head and dropped her eyes once again. There was a moment of silence before she spoke.

"Well, where would you like me to pose?" she asked awkwardly.

Aubrey gave a little sigh to himself. It was going to be as

difficult as he had anticipated. She did not mean to discuss her dilemma with him. Well, he supposed he could not blame her. He was a mere drawing-master, after all, in her eyes.

He indicated a nearby boulder. "If you could sit there for a few moments, just long enough to let me begin, I could let you resume your work while I finish the sketch."

She sat obediently where he told her and followed his instructions as he posed her. He stood back and scowled in dissatisfaction. "No, no, that's wrong."

She had been unable to meet his eyes. Suddenly she felt a firm but gentle hand under her chin. Startled, she looked up into a pair of warm brown eyes. Something electric passed between them, and she trembled. Her lips parted as if to speak, then closed again. She found she was breathing with difficulty.

Abruptly, he released her and turned to walk back a few paces. "That's better," he said approvingly. "I must see your face."

She willed herself to hold her chin up and meet his eyes without flinching, but his gaze was already on his sketchbook. Aubrey himself was having trouble concealing the effect she had upon him. For a moment his heart had caught in his throat. He had been ready to reveal his love for her and his identity. He had stopped himself just in time. If Georgiana was hanging out for a title, it would be all too easy to get her to reject a baron for a viscount. No, he must stick to his original plan.

He worked in silence for some minutes as he regained his self-control and organized his scrambled thoughts. He began by broaching the subject delicately.

"Lord Marwood has become a frequent visitor," he said in his most casual way.

"Yes," she said. She could not prevent the color from rising to her cheeks.

Aubrey was silent for another moment or two. "It seems that he has made you the object of his attentions."

"Yes." There was nothing more she could say. She was uncomfortable and yet oddly eager for this discussion. He said nothing again for a minute or so. How she loved the serious expression his face assumed while he was sketching. This was the real Aubrey, strong yet sensitive, easily wounded, quite opposite to the laughing facade he chose to present to the world.

She wondered abruptly how many people knew it. That girl, Cressida, for example . . .

He interrupted her train of thought. "I know it will seem impertinent," he said slowly. "It is, after all, none of my affair, but would you tell me: are your affections seriously engaged?"

A great feeling of hope shot through her. What else could this mean? He intended to declare his own feelings for her! Heart triumphed over mind, and she threw caution to the winds.

"No. That is, I have known him just such a short time, you know," she replied modestly.

Aubrey breathed a sigh of relief. "Good," he said. "That will make what I have to say a great deal easier." He laid down his crayon and sketchbook and crossed over to where she sat. He took her hand, an earnest expression on his face.

Georgiana's heart was pounding. She trembled as he took her hand in his. This was the moment for which she had been waiting.

"Although we have known each other only a few weeks, I have a high regard for you and I believe that there is a friendship between us," he began hesitantly.

Georgiana could not even speak. She managed to nod her head to show her agreement.

"I have meant to speak to you for quite some time," he continued. "Georgy . . ." He swallowed, then his words came in a rush. "Georgy, you must not marry that man!"

Her answer was ready on her lips, both logic and duty forgotten for the moment. Her hand burned in his and she could feel the fire creeping up to flush her cheeks. Why wouldn't he come to the point?

What a sensible girl she was! Most females would have been asking all sorts of questions, but there she sat, quietly waiting for an explanation. This was a great deal easier than he had anticipated.

"I have learned that he is not an honorable man."

Her heart was racing dangerously fast. Still, she could hardly press him to be more direct.

He leaned forward nervously. "I have our scheme all worked out. I am sorry, because I know it will be hardest on you, Georgy, but we have few other options. You won't be able to tell anyone, and especially not Charlotte."

Georgiana could hardly believe her ears. Was he speaking of a runaway match? Somehow, despite his madcap antics, she had never thought he would be so impetuous regarding such a serious matter. "What?" she began.

"I need just a little time to finish taking care of the details. I have thought it all out and the ball Saturday night will provide the perfect distraction." Unconsciously, his hand tightened on hers. "Georgy, I need you to tell Marwood that you won't be able to give him an answer until after Saturday. Tell him whatever you wish . . . that you would like to enjoy one last social function before becoming affianced . . . or any excuse you can invent. After Saturday, Marwood will no longer be a problem for us—" He looked at her steadily. "That is, if you're willing."

Stupefied, she could not find the words to answer him. She simply had been daydreaming that he might reveal a tendresse for her. To discover instead that he apparently had an elopement all planned was quite a shock, though not actually an unpleasant one.

Perceiving her amazement, he twisted the corner of his mouth into a grimace. "I have burst all this upon you too suddenly, haven't I?" He gave a tiny shake of his head. "I suppose I should have spoken to you earlier, but . . ." He searched for the words for a moment. "I didn't know what Marwood's true character was like and I couldn't be sure whether or not you returned Marwood's interest."

Abruptly, everything became clear to Georgiana. Aubrey's anger when he had seen her riding with Marwood, for example. Why, all this time he head been hiding his love for her. "Oh, Aubrey," she said tremulously.

"With that uncertainty, and . . . well, I simply thought it best to speak to you after I'd everything planned. I regret the necessity for this, Georgy." He gazed into her eyes with sincerity shining out of his own. "My greatest wish is to keep you from harm, you know."

She was choked by an overpowering emotion. Instead of painting a romantic picture of their elopement, he had acknowledged the detrimental aspects of it in a most frank and manly way. She knew full well that a runaway marriage meant scandal and social ruin. He was right, though. Exigency was forcing them to take this step. What other options did they have?

"I am sorry that I cannot give you the details of my arrangements," he continued. "It is for your own safety." She remained silent and he looked at her with a slight impatience. "As I said, I am sorry to be so abrupt about all this, but I do need your answer, Georgy. Are you willing, or not?"

She didn't take a second to decide. Her choices were clear: marriage to Marwood and respectability or marriage to the man she loved. "I am," she said faintly.

"Good girl," he said enthusiastically. Pleased by her cooperativeness, he so far forgot himself as to give her a hug. He realized his mistake instantly. "I am sorry," he apologized, springing back hastily.

What a gentleman he was. Most men would feel entitled to embrace their affianced bride. She gave him a weak little smile. "That's perfectly all right," she said, her knees still trembling.

Georgiana had felt marvelous in his arms—a little too marvelous, in fact. Looking at her sitting there with that little smile upon her face, he had the greatest desire to take her in his arms again and kiss her. No. He must control himself. Just because she didn't want to marry Marwood didn't mean she loved him.

He walked over to his art supplies and packed them up. He gave her a little bow before putting on his hat. "I'd best go put things in motion," he said.

They made their good-byes and he strode off whistling. It appeared that Georgiana wasn't interested enough in a title to actually marry Marwood anyway. He must keep from getting his hopes up too high, though. He knew she was attracted to him, but it didn't follow that she would be willing to marry a common drawing master.

Georgiana watched the tall, slender figure as he made his way out of the quarry and onto the road. How wonderful he was. She was still trembling from excitement. She, who had laughed so often at Charlotte, was now involved in an adventure every bit as foolishly romantic as anything in any of Charlotte's books. She, who always had been the practical and logical one, was soon to elope!

She shivered slightly at the thought. It would mean the end

of the world as she knew it. Still, since her social life was so limited, it was not so great a sacrifice. Even if her stepmother persuaded her father to cut her off without a penny, she would still receive a large inheritance from her mother's estate when she reached twenty-one.

In any case, there was no sense in worrying about it. She had made her decision. She could never marry Lord Marwood, anyway. She knew that now just as certainly as she knew that she would have no other choice if she remained.

Still, she was a little uneasy about the precipitateness of this whole affair. Wasn't it odd that he had made his decision so suddenly? And wasn't his proposal slightly peculiar, too? It struck her abruptly that there had been no words about love, only a "high regard." Why, Marwood had said nearly the same thing. And of course it was comforting to know that he was so much the gentleman, but surely he could have been more loverlike? After all, she hardly knew a thing about his background, other than his profession and that he had been an officer in the war.

She realized that her imagination was beginning to run away with her, and she shrugged off these thoughts with a forced laugh. She was even beginning to think like Charlotte! The thought of Charlotte made her frown. It was possible that Letty might offer her to Marwood as a substitute. No. Charlotte had the perfect suitor in William already. It was true that he hadn't a title, but he obviously was wealthy. Letitia could scarcely complain, anyway, since she'd pushed the two together at every opportunity.

Georgiana frowned again as she realized that things had not been going so well with Charlotte and William. She had scarcely seen them together, and when they were, Charlotte had been decidedly cool. Could he have done something to offend her? Perhaps it was just a lover's tiff. She was certain that Charlotte had been smitten by the young man, and from what she could judge, he felt the same way. Still, perhaps it might be best to have a talk with Charlotte. Of course, she must be careful not to say a word about her own situation.

11

Georgiana's little interrogation was to try Charlotte sorely. She tried desperately to turn the subject every time Georgiana introduced William's name. Failing that, she tried to praise him in a way that indicated that, although he was a fine fellow, she certainly did not think he was the man for her. At least she did not have to bear listening to raptures from Georgiana. Really, it was almost strange. She did not describe him in the glowing terms of a young woman in love. Of course, no one could help falling in love with William, it was just that her sister had always been such an unromantic creature.

All in all, Charlotte could be proud of herself. She had held the tears back until a dissatisfied Georgiana had left the room. At that point, she naturally flung herself on the bed and had a good cry. Her sister must never suspect the great sacrifice she had made.

After half an hour or so of sobbing her heart out, Charlotte began to recover herself. Wiping her eyes, she started assessing the situation. Marwood had been most assiduous in his attentions toward Georgiana, taking up a great deal of her time. And when she thought about it, she realized that William had been absent a great deal these past few days. Although admittedly she had been trying to avoid him, she only had known him to be at the hall at dinnertime. Something must be done.

Her frown lifted as she remembered the ball Saturday. It would be the perfect opportunity to thrust William and Georgiana together and make them fall in love. Of course, it would take skillful management. There would be other young ladies there who doubtless would try to ensnare such a prize as William.

She pictured to herself Georgiana waltzing in William's arms, William laughing aloud at some remark she'd made. No, it was too much for her. She buried her face in her pillow and began weeping afresh.

Among all the inhabitants of Chalton, there was a broad spectrum of feeling about the ball as Saturday approached. Harry's feelings were perhaps the easiest to analyze, consisting entirely of irritation at being forced to forgo a day's hunting. Letitia alternated between complacency at the thought of the effect her new gown would produce on everyone, and aggravation with Georgiana and Lord Marwood for preventing her from arriving as the mother of a future baroness.

Charlotte's heart was heavy as she selected her gown for that evening with more indifference than she ever previously had exhibited. Georgiana could not help but be concerned about her, though it hardly compared to the worry she felt about her own situation.

She had not managed to see Aubrey alone since the afternoon at the quarry. Admittedly, Marwood had kept her busy every morning, but Aubrey seemed to be gone every afternoon. She was fortunate at least that Marwood had seemed to accept her explanation. He had said that he understood perfectly how she would wish to have one last ball before she became affianced, though he had asked her to reserve two of her dances.

Aubrey hadn't done that, she thought, not without irritation. Well, perhaps he thought that if he paid her marked attentions it might rouse everyone's suspicions. Still, it was uncomfortable for her, not knowing any of the arrangements. She didn't know when or how they would leave, though she supposed it was to be Saturday night. She hoped so, anyway, thinking with a shiver of how Marwood had said meaningfully that he would be certain to wait upon her Sunday afternoon. She hoped Aubrey had enough money to hire a carriage or at least procure them seats on the stage.

She had packed a bandbox, in order to be ready, though she scarcely knew what items to include. Tormented by all the questions, she had risen from bed Friday night, and putting on her wrapper and taking a candle, she had sneaked to Aubrey's room. Her tap on the door brought no response. Blushing at her own temerity but forced by necessity, she opened the door and peeked in the room. The bed was still unmade. He had excused himself hurriedly after dinner that night. Where could he have gone?

Had she investigated further, she might have discovered that the one person likely to know was also missing. In fact, William had accompanied Aubrey to the Thornbys that evening for last-minute preparations. Georgiana might have been surprised at the earnest discussion the two young gentlemen were having with Susan and Jem.

"So I told him to meet me here at eleven," Susan was saying, "just as you told me to."

"He didn't seem suspicious?" asked Aubrey.

"No. I told him that I had to send the children—" here she inclined her head in the direction of a closed bedroom door— "off to stay with Mrs. Sweeney for the evening."

"Excellent," said Aubrey, leaning back in his chair. "We have him, then."

"My lord, I mean, sir?" amended Susan hastily as he shook his head warningly at her.

"What is it?"

"Lord Marwood . . ." Her face was troubled. "He is a proud and vengeful man. Are you certain that he will not pursue us?"

Aubrey smiled at her reassuringly. "My men will be in an unmarked carriage when they pick you up tomorrow, and Marwood will be at the ball so he'll have no idea that you've gone until too late."

He saw the remaining doubt upon her face and added reassuringly, "That is why we wished you well out of the way. After all, he can hardly vent his anger on you if you're not here, and no one shall know where you've gone."

Susan's face was still far from happy. "That's what I dislike, sir—for you and your friend to intervene for us in this way. Lord Marwood will be in a towering rage and it will fall entirely upon you."

Aubrey laughed, but there was harshness in the sound. "You are quite right, of course, but our arrangements will leave him with little he can do about it, short of making himself a laughingstock in the eyes of the world. You need not fear for us, Miss Thornby."

Jem interrupted them here. "But you and Mr. William have done so much for us, sir," he said, his eyes shining with emotion. "I don't know how we can ever thank you enough."

Aubrey dismissed them with a wave. "I am merely providing transportation. You will be earning your keep, I assure you."

William directed his words to Susan. "Yes, Mrs. Blackburn has been very lonely since her only daughter died. And with her rheumatism afflicting her so sorely, you are doing her a favor by moving in with her."

"But the children—"

"She is delighted by the thought of having them there. Her house is large and she complains that it has been empty too long," William continued.

"And you," Aubrey addressed Jem. "The rector has great plans for you, and if he is not able to persuade you to follow in his calling, I mean to put you to work myself."

"Sir, I can never repay you properly for—"

Aubrey rose hastily, cutting off what Jem was going to say. "Enough of that. We must be on our way." He turned abruptly and laid a hand on the boy's shoulder. "Do me credit in your new situation, and that will be payment enough." He smiled at him. "Wish us well."

"God bless you, sir," replied Susan sincerely.

The first of Charlotte's schemes was to be frustrated Saturday evening. She had conceived a plan to thrust Georgiana into William's curricle and so give them a tête-á-tête on the way to the ball. Surely she could not help falling in love with him, given such an opportunity.

Much to her dismay, it was Aubrey who leapt into the curricle instead, while William explained in a gentlemanly fashion that he knew the ladies would not wish to be blown about in an open carriage. She was frankly dismayed, having expected him to offer to carry her. The headache she had been feigning soon became a reality. It was to worsen as the night progressed.

For her part, Georgiana was feeling little better. The enormity of the step she was taking had hit her with full force when she had awakened this morning. To make matters worse, she still had not had an opportunity to speak to Aubrey. When she had seen him this evening, he hardly had glanced at her. Surely this was taking discretion a bit too far? Her stomach was feeling decidedly queasy and the motion of the carriage did nothing to improve it.

It was a far from merry group who rode to the ball that evening. Harry sat resentful in the corner of the carriage. Charlotte was wan and Georgiana was peculiarly silent. The one occupant of the carriage whose spirits were unruffled was Letitia, though her nonstop chatter did nothing to relieve anyone else's oppression.

In fact, Letitia rarely had enjoyed a moment as triumphant as that of their arrival at the ball. The audible gasps that greeted them she accepted with equanimity, being sure that they were inspired by admiration. She was happy to let her shrinking family stand a few paces back, so that her ensemble might show to better advantage as she greeted her hostess.

Her dress was designed to catch the eye, indeed one could not help looking at it try as one might. One of the new net frocks, worn over a satin slip in a rich shade of purple, it might have been innocuous except for its ornamentation. Most striking was the green trim that was cleverly woven through the net so as to suggest a vine, while leaves of green satin dangled from it. The deep lace flounce sported the fruit of the vine; bunches of satin grapes dangled about Letty's feet, promising a serious impediment to dancing.

Probably the most original aspect of her attire, and one that clearly testified to Aubrey's contributory hand, was the head-piece she wore. Letty had forsaken her old-fashioned aigrette with ostrich plumes for a most curious structure. Reposing upon those frizzled curls lay a veritable fruit basket of wax grapes. As she had not been small-minded enough to limit herself to a single bunch, the concoction towered nearly a foot into the air. It showed a dangerous propensity to topple over whenever she gave a toss of her head, which she did frequently. Those unhappy enough to converse with her, having an understandable fear for their own safety, could not forbear watching it as it pitched about on her head. Letty, assuming these looks were inspired by fascinated envy, bloomed under their fixed gazes and called further attention to her glory with little careless pats of her head.

The smug expression upon Letty's face was the perfect

complement to the ensemble. Had it been any other night, Georgiana herself might have been hard put to avoid outright laughter. As it was, she looked about the room for Aubrey and saw him talking quietly in a corner with her godmother. All her attempts to catch his eye failed.

She might have gone across the ballroom to see if she could have a word in private with him herself, but she and Charlotte were quickly surrounded by the eligible gentlemen of the neighborhood, such as they were. As her card began to fill, she was again conscious of a feeling of irritation with Aubrey. Surely he would take the opportunity of a dance to let her know the details of his plan. No one would find anything amiss with two cousins sharing a dance. If he didn't speak to her soon, her card would be full.

She remembered herself and forced a smile at the shy sixteen-year-old who was requesting her hand in the quadrille. As she wrote down his name in her card, a shadow fell across the page. She looked up, expecting to see Aubrey. It was Lord Marwood.

He took her hand and kissed it, seeming not to notice the way her gloved fingers shrank involuntarily from his lips. He murmured the requisite compliment to her beauty and asked if she had remembered to save him his dances.

"Yes, my lord—" she was beginning when he interrupted.

"Please, my dear. Bevis."

"Very well, Bevis." For some reason she had difficulty getting the name out. It was as if it produced a bad taste in her mouth. He was still smiling at her expectantly.

"I have saved you the first and last dances, my lor—Bevis."

There was a subtle change in his expression. "Ah, well, I shall be delighted to dance the first with you, my dear, but I am afraid that I shall have to leave early this evening. A pressing matter of business."

Georgiana let out a little sigh. She had dreaded going in to dinner with him, even though she knew that Letty would expect it. She tried to hide her relief from him.

"Another dance, perhaps?"

She held out her card to him. Now she was glad that it was filled. "I'm sorry."

"Ah, well." He gave her an enigmatic smile. "Since I will have you all to myself so shortly, I can afford to be magnanimous tonight.'' He swept her a polite bow and departed while she tried to ignore the little chill caused by his words.

She looked up and a gleam of hope shot through her. Aubrey was crossing the room toward her. Nothing could be more propitious. If he partnered her in the last dance, they could speak all during supper. Without thinking, she scratched out Marwood's name with her pencil. She realized her mistake too late.

''Miss Chalford, I see that you lack a partner for the last dance.'' An elderly widower of her acquaintance had materialized at her elbow. ''May I hope that you will favor me with it?''

She could have screamed in frustration, but instead, she gritted her teeth and made herself smile politely at him. Having eliminated Marwood's name, she had no choice but to accept his offer.

As Aubrey approached, she was ready to berate him for having missed such a perfect opportunity. She was forestalled by a voice behind her.

''Oh, Cousin Chalford . . .'' Letty's voice carried across the ballroom easily. Aubrey was forced to alter his course. ''I should like you to make the acquaintance of some of our neighbors,'' said Letty before turning to her friends and remarking, in a self-satisfied way, ''This is the young gentleman of whom I was speaking. He recently did the portrait of the family of Viscount Herne and now is working on ours.''

Aubrey greeted her friends in a preoccupied way. His mind busy elsewhere, he missed the darkling glances Georgiana was throwing him from time to time. He remained unmoved when Letty mentioned his military record. He appeared oblivious when the headdress made a sudden, though arrested dip in his direction, eliciting a squeal of alarm from old Mrs. Farquhar, whose nerves were no longer good. He excused himself as soon as it was politely feasible and went to join William.

Georgiana was not the only one who was miffed by all the time the two young men were spending together. Charlotte saw in it the ruination of all her plans. As soon as William had asked her to dance, she had meant to make some excuse and suggest her sister instead. But William had never approached her!

Her card had filled rapidly and she could see that Georgiana's had, too. The sinking feeling she experienced when she saw Marwood approach her sister had lifted somewhat when she saw her scratching a name off her card afterward. Unfortunately the dance, which should have gone to William, now belonged to the elderly widower. She bit her lip in frustration. Really, what could she do? How was it possible to spark a romance when the principals involved were so uncooperative?

Her partner in the reel noted her expression and flinched. Perhaps it was best not to introduce the usual small talk tonight.

William himself was barely conscious of a feeling of disappointment at being forced to forgo dancing with the lovely Charlotte. He was caught up in the excitement of being a part of Aubrey's deviltry once more, and he had scarcely a thought for anything other than the evening's scheme. According to plan, he and Aubrey disappeared into the back as the first strains of music were beginning. They mingled for a few minutes with the gentlemen who had elected to play cards, then disappeared discreetly out a side door. As they had anticipated, their departure went unnoticed.

Georgiana meanwhile was feeling more and more desperate as the evening passed. She had survived her dance with Marwood as best she could, glad for the fact that it wasn't a waltz. Even the brief contact they had unnerved her.

She was thinking furiously about Aubrey's words. Surely if he meant for them to elope tonight, he would have told her by now. But he had said that Lord Marwood would no longer be a problem by tomorrow. Was it possible that she had misunderstood him? She certainly hoped not, since Marwood was coming to receive her positive answer then. What could Aubrey have meant?

She almost halted in the midst of the quadrille she was performing, but recovered herself quickly and regained the steps. Was it possible that Aubrey had not meant an elopement? He had said rather pointedly that she need know nothing of the details. It came to her suddenly that he had never mentioned marriage by word. She frowned at this puzzling new idea. If he hadn't meant an elopement, how else did he intend to rid her of Marwood's attentions?

Her thoughts were interrupted by Charlotte, who had sought her out at the conclusion of the dance.

"Georgy, have you seen William?" Charlotte demanded.

Georgiana scanned the room quickly. "No, I haven't, but I don't think he's stood up with any of the other girls, Charlotte."

Charlotte gave a little stamp of exasperation. "I know that," she said, betraying herself inadvertently. "I wanted to know if you'd seen him leave."

Georgiana shook her head. "No, the only one that I've seen leave is Lord Marwood." She gave a little shrug. "William's probably in the back playing cards."

Really, her indifference was most provoking. "No, he's not," said Charlotte impatiently, "and I haven't seen him for ages."

Georgiana gave a little sigh. "Well, I'm sorry. I can't help you. If I see him, I'll tell you." As her current partner came up to claim her hand, she excused herself, leaving Charlotte standing disconsolately behind.

They took their places for the dance, and as the music began, she went through the steps mechanically. Obviously Charlotte was more interested in William than she'd been pretending. It was odd that William had disappeared like that. Perhaps he'd wanted to check on his horses. He was the sort of man who would. That idea brought to mind a picture of him and Aubrey riding off in the curricle. Aubrey! She glanced about the room as best she could. No, he wasn't there. She hadn't seen him since the first part of the evening, when he and William had disappeared into the back to play cards, or so she had assumed. And William wasn't in the back. She could only guess that Aubrey was gone, too.

She knew their absence portended something, but what? Marwood had left also. That could be significant. She tried to remember Aubrey's words exactly. "After Saturday, Marwood will no longer be a problem." That could mean almost anything. What else had he said? That he couldn't give her details of the plan and it was for her own safety. That choice of words had sounded odd even then. For her own safety. Marwood will no longer be a problem. Her heart almost stopped at the realization. Oh, dear heaven, she thought, it can mean only one thing—a duel!

It was fortunate that the dance had ended, for her knees nearly buckled under her at the thought. Her dancing partner took alarm at her sudden pallor and asked if she were ill. She replied

truthfully that she was feeling very weak and he escorted her
solicitously back to Letty's side.

It was a matter of some minutes before she could convince
Letty that she really was feeling badly enough to leave the
assembly. Fortunately, Letitia saw no real point in Georgiana's
remaining since Lord Marwood had left. She reluctantly gave
permission for her to use the carriage and send it back for the
rest of the family.

Having achieved this much of her ambition, Georgiana was
left with a dilemma. Where to go? She had no idea where
gentlemen would wish to fight a duel. After puzzling over it
for a moment, she decided that the most likely place in which
she would find an answer was Marwood House. She gave the
wondering coachman her orders, and after urging him to make
haste, she settled in for an anxious ride.

While Georgiana was still dancing at the ball, happily unaware
of their absence, Aubrey and William were engaged in an
argument.

"Dash it, Aubrey, we agreed upon this beforehand. You
mustn't go changing your mind now."

"I don't like it. It's too dangerous. What if he's carrying a
pistol?"

William laughed. "It's not like you to worry." He saw that
Aubrey's concern was genuine and smiled. "Besides, you'll
be right here." He held up a nightgown. "And you're too tall
to wear it."

Aubrey shook his head. "I'm sorry I thought up this whole
idea."

William grinned. "Well, I'm not. I've never been a major
participant in one of your madcap schemes before." He
chuckled aloud. "How I shall love to see Marwood's face
when—"

"Well, if you're going to do it, you'd best get started,"
Aubrey reminded him. As William went to dress, Aubrey
checked his own pistol. He suddenly was glad he had brought
it. Marwood was known to be hot-tempered and certainly would
not regard their scheme as a laughing matter.

Soon, their preparations made, the two cousins settled down
to wait for their prey to arrive.

* * *

Lord Marwood was in an unusually jovial mood that evening. That Chalford chit was to give him her acceptance tomorrow. It had taken slightly longer than a week, but his extra patience had served him well. He could always call for an early wedding. That title-hungry mother undoubtedly would second him in that notion. Yes, Georgiana would suit his purpose admirably. Personally he preferred women with a little more flesh on them, but she was a rather appetizing morsel for all that. Of course, had he seen them first, he might have selected the other sister, however time had been of the essence.

He smiled to himself as he reined in his black at the Thornbys. He would have some consolation. The persistent pressure he had exerted here finally was to reward him. He smiled to himself at the thought. The girl was almost as skittish as the Chalford chit, for all her initial flirtatiousness. You would imagine that she considered herself a lady rather than a simple farmer's daughter. Well, she would keep their bargain now, willing or not.

He tied his horse up, then entered the cottage. A single candle was burning. The house was unusually quiet, owing, he supposed, to the absence of the children. He pulled off his gloves and then shrugged off his greatcoat, laying them on the table.

"Susan," he called.

A muffled sort of moan came from the direction of the bedroom. He smiled to himself as he stripped off his cravat.

"It is Lord Marwood," he announced.

There was another smothered sound from the bedroom. The girl must be frightened. At least her location suggested that she intended to go through with their agreement.

Taking the candle, he stepped over to the bedroom door and opened it. By its light he could see her lying with her back toward him, almost hidden by a mound of bedclothes. The golden curls lay spread upon the pillow, glistening in the candlelight. He drew in a satisfied breath. This had been worth waiting for.

He walked over to the bed and put the candle on the nightstand. The figure did not stir. He pulled off his coat and began to unbutton his waistcoat.

"You needn't be frightened, my dear. I believe that you will come to find this experience quite enjoyable, given time."

The figure whimpered slightly. It only served to whet his appetite. He unhooked his braces and rapidly unbuttoned his shirt. Yanking it off, he reached down to fondle one of those curls. The figure shivered and gathered the bedclothes about itself more tightly. Marwood gave a short laugh.

"You see, you can't help responding to me already."

He sat down on the edge of the bed and began to remove his shoes.

The figure cleared its throat. "The agreement?" Her voice was husky from fear.

"What a suspicious creature you are. You would think that my word would be adequate." Having removed his stockings, he stepped over to the nightstand, where he had thrown his coat, and extracted a paper from it.

"Shall I read it to you, my dear?" Without waiting for an answer, he began. "Susan Thornby and the members of her family are hereby absolved of the back rents owing to me in exchange for valuable services rendered." He refolded it. "I've signed and dated it today. I'll just put it on the nightstand, where it will be safe, shall I?" He was starting to unbutton his breeches hastily when he was frozen by an unexpected voice coming from behind him.

"Thank you, Marwood, that should do nicely."

He spun around and saw a tall, slender figure leaning against the door frame. "What the devil?"

He took a step forward, as if intending to dash past the intruder and into the main room. The fellow waved a pistol at him in a negligent way.

"I shouldn't attempt it, if I were you. I've already taken the liberty of removing this from your greatcoat."

He knew that face. "The Chalfords' drawing master," he said in amazement.

"You almost waited too long, Aubrey," said another distinctly masculine voice from the direction of the bed. Turning around again, Marwood saw a somewhat stockier figure in a nightgown remove a wig and throw it onto the bed in a disgusted way. "That thing was itching my head," complained the second figure. Marwood's jaw fell open as this person pulled the nightgown over its head to reveal a young gentleman in evening clothes underneath. He recognized this figure as belonging to the Chalford household also.

"And you—"

"Grab the paper, will you, William," Aubrey ordered. Marwood made a quick motion toward it, but stopped as the pistol quickly was leveled at his chest.

"It is cocked, as you will observe, and I do assure you that it is loaded."

As William snatched the paper, Marwood, who had recovered somewhat, turned to Aubrey. "What do you mean by this? Where is that jade Susan?"

"She and her family are safely out of your reach. You won't see them again."

Marwood took a menacing step forward, nearly purple with rage. "By God, I'll kill you for this!"

Aubrey straightened and his eyes were cold. "I should remember, my lord, that I am holding the pistol, not you." He gestured with the gun. "Sit down on the bed."

"You interfering puppy—"

Once again the pistol was leveled at him.

Marwood glowered at Aubrey as he sat. "If you mean to rob me, you'll have little for your pains."

"I think you've said enough. Now it's your turn to listen." He nodded at William, who had drawn up a chair and was watching Marwood in an expectant way.

"I would remind you that even should my shot miss you, which is extremely unlikely at this close range, my cousin is also ready to lend me his assistance and his pugilistic prowess is such that he's been known to take a turn with Gentleman Jackson himself."

Marwood was still furious, but he could see that his enemy was both implacable and deadly serious. "Very well, you have me," he said curtly. "What is it that you wish?"

Aubrey let out a long breath. "That's better," he said coolly. "You will immediately retract your offer for Miss Chalford's hand and cease to annoy her with your attentions."

"You're joking," Marwood said incredulously. He began to rise to his feet. "You'd hardly shoot a man in cold blood, after all. You'd swing for it."

The pistol was raised again hastily. "Not if we dragged your body down to the road. It would surprise no one anyway. The bullet I received was meant for you, after all."

Marwood sank back down on the bed. "Well, then, we may sit here until doomsday as far as I am concerned," he said fiercely. "Don't imagine that I shan't be missed. By tomorrow morning, they will be combing the estate looking for me."

Aubrey smothered an indifferent yawn. "Because you're so well-loved, you mean?" He held up a hand to forestall Marwood's furious retort. "We have no intention of remaining here that long. You've wasted enough time. Now you must listen. To begin with, you have an excellent reason for complying with our request. You see, we have the paper"—he nodded toward William, who still held it in his hand—"as proof of your villainy."

"Oh, do you mean to try me before the assizes?" asked Marwood sarcastically. He sneered at Aubrey. "What I did was hardly a crime, and that paper says nothing anyway."

"Silence! You are beginning to try my patience." Aubrey let out a little sigh of annoyance. "It would be so much easier to shoot you," he said wistfully.

Marwood scowled at him.

William interrupted. "Aubrey," he said reproachfully.

"Oh, very well," responded the viscount. He continued, "No, the paper will merely lend a note of authenticity to our story. You see, Marwood, society will be your judge and jury. Ravishing a defenseless young girl on the eve of your proposal to another is hardly considered the thing to do."

Marwood's lips curled. "What would you know of society? Do you imagine that the word of a mere drawing master would carry any weight against mine?"

Aubrey's eyebrows raised. "Dear me, I knew there was something I had forgot," he remarked. He inclined his head slightly toward his prisoner. "Permit me to introduce myself. I am Lord Herne and this is my cousin, Mr. William Darley."

Marwood was almost speechless. "You're mad," he said disbelievingly.

Aubrey blew out his breath impassively. "Show him my ring, William." As his cousin complied, he added, "I have my own reasons for this masquerade. Naturally you also will promise not to reveal my identity."

Before Marwood could speak, Aubrey cut him off. "We can also furnish you with the names of our clubs if you really feel it necessary. Needless to say, since there are two of us, and given your reputation, our account should carry a great deal of weight."

Marwood looked at him contemptuously. "Do you really suppose that anyone would care that I tried to seduce a farm wench? I doubt that you'll even find anyone that's interested in the tale."

There was a dangerous gleam in Aubrey's eye. "There you have exactly the little problem that confronted us. I think we solved it rather neatly, though, don't you?" At Marwood's expression of incomprehension, Aubrey continued. "Don't you see, then? This charade was not conducted entirely for our own amusement, though I admit it had its moments. No, the tale we will be spreading is not the simple one you seem to think, but rather a highly entertaining account of our little prank tonight. I think it should make a rather good story, don't you? Particularly how in your eagerness William nearly had to defend his virtue from you." He smiled at Marwood, but there was no laughter in it.

Silence reigned for a few moments as the full import of his words struck Marwood.

William saw fit at this point to interject, "The viscount is well-known for these types of practical jokes. No one is likely to think it in the least remarkable."

Marwood brooded for a few moments more. The fury of a trapped animal rose within him and he stood up heedlessly, fists clenched. "By God, you'll pay for this!"

"I doubt that," said Aubrey coldly. He stared into Marwood's eyes. "As I told you, you have only to cooperate with us to buy our silence."

In spite of his rage, Marwood could see that he had no choice. He did not doubt that Aubrey meant what he said. It would be bad enough to be a laughingstock, but such a tale could forever ruin his chance for a match with another lady. Georgiana Chalford was nothing to him anyway, he reminded himself.

"All right, then. What do I have to do?" he asked angrily.

"Swear that you will withdraw your offer of marriage to Miss Chalford and not annoy her further with your attentions."

"And how am I to do that? You know it's the female who always does the crying off."

Aubrey eyed him frostily. "In view of your other choice, I think you can be creative. You need not embroider the truth to convince her father that you are unworthy. In any case, Georgiana will certainly refuse you. You must simply see that the match no longer has her parents' support."

"And?"

"And as long as you keep our identities a secret, we will not reveal what occurred here tonight."

"Very well." Marwood's expression was enigmatic. "I swear that I will withdraw my offer of marriage to Miss Georgiana Chalford and will trouble her no more on the subject."

Satisfied, Aubrey put away the pistol. The corner of Marwood's lips curled in a sneer. "Got an eye on the chit yourself, have you? Not willing to make an offer of marriage, though? Think to keep her as your fancy—" Marwood's words were cut off as Aubrey's hands were clasped around his throat.

"Aubrey, no! We've accomplished what we came for." William sprang forward and was wresting his cousin away when they all heard a loud gasp. The three men turned and saw Georgiana standing in the doorway to the cottage.

"Aubrey! Are you all right?" She started into the house, but suddenly noticed that Marwood, glaring at her furiously, was in an advanced state of undress. She halted, averting her eyes.

"Georgy!" Aubrey released his intended victim and was across the main room in a second, hurrying her out of the door. "My dear, what are you doing here?"

She looked up at him, the unshed tears still glistening in her eyes. "I was frightened for you. I thought from what you said that you meant to fight a duel with Lord Marwood and I hoped I might prevent you."

"You little idiot." She looked so adorable there in the moonlight that Aubrey could not help kissing her. Unfortunately the kiss lingered a little longer than it should have. When he recovered himself, they were both breathless.

"You darling little idiot, you shouldn't have come."

"I was so worried that you might be hurt. I was on my way to Marwood House to see what had become of you when I saw Lord Marwood's horse tied up in front of the cottage and . . ." She looked about her distractedly. "Where is Jem? And what were you doing with Lord Marwood? You looked as if you meant to kill him!"

Aubrey smiled and stroked her cheek tenderly with a finger. "A momentary laspe, my dear. I assure you that Marwood is fine." He could see that her face was still full of questions. He shook his head gently at her and led her back to her carriage. "Not now, Georgy. I'll explain it all to you when we return to Chalton."

She could see that she would have to be content with that for now. She accepted a chaste kiss on the cheek and ordered the coachman to carry her home instead.

Aubrey looked after her wonderingly for a moment as she departed. Then, letting out a long breath, he turned and went to finish his work in the cottage.

12

"But I thought the game was nearly up when he touched the wig." William collapsed again in helpless laughter. He glanced at his companion and saw that Aubrey's face still wore a somber expression. "Aubrey, you must at least admit that when I stood up, the expression on his face was most amusing." There was no response. He prodded his companion. "Aubrey, stop wool-gathering."

Aubrey shook himself slightly as if to clear his thoughts. He turned to William and remarked with some asperity, "Have a care, William! At least I am not about to ditch us."

His attention recalled to his driving, William made a quick correction with the reins and rather narrowly avoided landing them in the aforementioned ditch. As soon as they were back on course, he gave Aubrey a quick, analyzing glance.

"What is it coz? Are you worried about the threats Marwood made?"

Aubrey gave a derogatory snort. "Not likely." He paused for a moment, then continued. "No, I was just thinking how . . . how odd it was that Georgiana happened to find us."

William shrugged. "I don't find it odd. She's a clever girl."

"Yes, she is, isn't she?" There was a certain dreaminess in Aubrey's tone of voice that brought a smile to William's lips. Just then Aubrey turned to him again and, seeing the expression, frowned.

"I just keep picturing to myself the look on Marwood's face when he found out," William said by way of explanation.

Aubrey permitted himself a smile. "Yes, I think he was confounded for a moment there."

When they arrived back at Chalton, the two cousins were able to treat Georgiana to a judiciously edited explanation of the facts, though it took all of Aubrey's glibness to keep from revealing

174

matters that might shock a young lady's sensibilities. As matters stood, however, Georgiana was properly enraged by Marwood's behavior and proportionately grateful to her rescuers.

As he retired to his chamber that evening, Aubrey was conscious of an odd sense of dissatisfaction. Georgiana had been effusive in her thanks to him and William both. Was he just imagining that she seemed just a little distant also? After all, this was the girl who had come racing after him to save his life, or so she thought. He had held her in his arms and kissed her, and she certainly seemed receptive then.

There had been none of that warmth in her eyes when she met them upon their return, despite all her gratitude. In fact, now that he thought of it, she had been doing her best to avoid meeting his gaze. She had greeted her returning family's interruption with something resembling relief.

He shook his head. Possibly she was merely exhausted by this night's adventure. Her actions had proved how important he was to her. He smiled. It appeared that there was every likelihood that Georgiana would be willing to marry a mere drawing master.

Meanwhile, she had been busy in self-recrimination. After the warm glow from Aubrey's kiss had faded during the carriage ride home, she realized abruptly what a fool she had been. First of all, she had been idiotic enough to imagine that he wished her to elope with him. The thought made her cheeks burn. He had never spoken even one word of love to her, and yet she had dreamt up this entire foolish fantasy. She had no room to criticize Charlotte; it was much worse than anything Charlotte had ever done. What a mercy it was that she hadn't told her about it.

Having abandoned the elopement idea, she had come up with another notion just as hen-witted. How could she have decided that he wanted to fight a duel over her? It was simply too preposterous. It was clear that he'd never regarded her in that light. How absolutely ridiculous she must have looked to him, rushing into the house in that harebrained way.

She covered her face for a minute with her hands. And what a shameless hussy he must have thought her, with the way she pursued him and nearly threw herself at him. It was no wonder he had kissed her. She blushed again. Why, she might very well have put the idea of marriage into his head. It was clear that he, as an ordinary drawing master, would never have aspired to such heights. No, she had encouraged him.

She felt like crying, but drew herself up quite erect and attempted to compose her face and thoughts. There was only one course open to her. She must demonstrate to him that it was simply a lapse on her part, that she ordinarily wasn't given to that kind of behavior. She must behave as if nothing had occurred and treat him with a remote civility. She must remember that, after all, he was her employee.

Her resolution made, she was able to greet the two young men with a smile when they arrived and evince the proper amount of interest in their account. She felt that she handled herself with exactly the correct mixture of gratitude and distance. She was pleased with herself, but later, when she was ready to go to bed, the awful truth assailed her. The memory of his kiss still burned on her lips. She was still in love with him, every bit as much as when she thought he wanted to marry her. What was the matter with her? Had she no pride at all?

"I'm in love with a drawing master, without his even being interested in more than friendship with me."

It probably would have shocked Charlotte to see the profoundly practical Georgiana, weeping into her pillow over a hopeless love.

The next morning, before the rest of the family had risen to dress for church, Marwood sought out Harry Chalford and withdrew his offer for Georgiana's hand. A rather bemused Harry waylaid his daughter on her way to the breakfast table to inform her of this development. When she took the news complacently, he became suspicious.

"See here, did you have anything to do with this, my lass?"

Georgiana opened her eyes wide in offended innocence. "I? What should I have to do with this?"

Harry was not appeased. "That's what I'd like to know. Marwood said you meant to refuse him anyway."

"That's right, Father, so it's all for the best."

"Your stepmother will be in a rare taking, I can tell you, but there's little she can do about it." He stroked his chin reflectively. A close observer might have spotted an unusual gleam in Harry's eye, but Georgiana was too preoccupied with her own thoughts to notice.

"I wish I knew what you had to do with this, my girl."

"Really, Father, you're being absurd." She shrugged to show her indifference. "What could I have done to compel him to withdraw his offer?"

"That's what I'd like to know," said Harry meaningfully. Georgiana merely looked at him with an expression of boredom.

"Very well, minx, get along with you," said Harry, accepting defeat. "I'd best go tell your stepmother."

Harry's prediction about Letty's reaction was to prove an understatement. Though he did his best to break the news to her gently, the full force of her fury descended upon his unfortunate head. She rang a peal over him for the whole household to hear. She catalogued her opinions of his mental capabilities and many other deficiencies before he was able to interrupt and relate to her Marwood's exact words. An awe-inspiring hush followed.

The one benefit of Letty's tirade was that it allowed the entire household to share in the joyous news. As might be expected, Letitia's chagrin was exceeded only by Charlotte's elation.

Charlotte ran to Georgiana's room as soon as church was over, eager to confer with her about this wonderful development. She hugged her sister effusively and began to express her delight.

"My dear Georgy, nothing could have made me happier. I knew it was true when I saw Mother's face. Did you notice her expression during the sermon today? I thought it was too perfect that Reverend Davies should have chosen the text on worshiping false idols."

Letty's visage had suggested that of someone who had eaten a great many sour grapes, and she had been unable to look at Georgiana during church. Ordinarily, Georgiana might have found some amusement in it, but her heart was too heavy for such levity at that moment. She managed a weak little smile for her sister.

Charlotte, caught up by her own raptures, didn't noticed her sister's lack of enthusiasm. "You must be so relieved. I am myself. But who could have imagined it? Lord Marwood withdrawing his offer and Mother not objecting! I wonder what he could have told them?'' She paused for the moment, a new thought striking her. "And why would he have done it? That's what puzzles me most of all. He was most assiduous in his attentions, seemed most determined—''

Georgiana had been sworn to silence by Aubrey and William, but there would have been little point in confiding in Charlotte anyway. "Perhaps he changed his mind?'' she suggested faintly.

Charlotte snorted. "I can't believe that. It seems so odd.'' Another idea claimed her and she abandoned the question, to Georgiana's relief.

"Georgy, I know you will think me ridiculous—''

"No, Charlotte, I will never think you silly in any way whatsoever again.''

Charlotte was so intent upon what she was saying that she missed the oddness of her sister's tone. "I know it probably seems foolish, but I was so worried that Mother meant to force you to marry Lord Marwood.'' Her eyes lowered, she was now blushing with embarrassment. "You see''—she toyed aimlessly with a fold of her skirt—"I thought that if William proposed to you—''

Georgiana cut her off. "So that was what you were trying to do!'' She hugged her sister. "It was very dear of you, but I'm afraid that William never gave me a second thought. It seems that all our time together he spent talking of you.''

"Really?'' Charlotte's face lit up like a candle. "I thought that neither of you acted as if you were in love with the other, but . . .'' Her eyes strayed involuntarily to the door.

Georgiana read her thoughts. "Go on and find him now then, you goose,'' she said, giving her sister an encouraging little push. "I daresay you can mend matters easily enough.'' Charlotte's glowing face recalled her own situation painfully to her. "Just don't let him guess that you're doing the looking.''

Charlotte drew herself up haughtily. "Really, Georgy, I'm not a child. Do you imagine that I have no *savoir-faire*?'' She swept from the room.

Georgiana smiled after her, but with sadness in her face. Charlotte would always be as transparent as glass. How like her it was to try a solution that had all the earmarks of having been borrowed from one of her favorite romances. Charlotte secretly must have relished playing such a self-sacrificing part and many must have been the tears she shed. Knowing Charlotte as she did, Georgiana suspected that if William had ever paid her the kind of attentions Charlotte had envisioned, her sister would have been the first to be dismayed. She frowned at the direction her thoughts were taking. After all, she had no room to criticize Charlotte. At least her impractical sister was in love with an eligible gentleman.

By the time the family sat down for dinner that afternoon, it was evident that Charlotte and William had encountered little difficulty in regaining their former understanding. Each had eyes for no one but the other: they were quite oblivious of everything and everyone else.

The sight of these two lovebirds had the happy effect of lifting Letitia's spirits somewhat. Nothing could reconcile her to Marwood's loss, but she was cheered by the prospect of this good match for Charlotte. She came out of the sullens long enough to remark again to Aubrey what a beautiful couple his friend and her daughter made.

Aubrey agreed with her politely, his mind on something else entirely. Despite a certain resolution he had made last night, he had not been able to have a moment alone with Georgiana today. He might be imagining it, but it seemed to him that she had been avoiding him. He had been trying to catch her eye at the dinner table, but she appeared to be totally engrossed in her father's discourse upon the selection of a good hound. He was surprised, for he had assumed it would be a topic in which Georgiana had very little interest.

Most of the parties at the table hardly paused in their conversation as the main door was opened. So, many of them missed the sound of heavy boots stamping in the hall and Wilkins' gasp of astonishment. However, no one could ignore the rich bass voice that boomed out through the house.

"No need to stand on ceremony, Wilkins. I'll just announce myself."

Every eye automatically fell upon the figure that appeared in the doorway and stood there, surveying their astonished faces appreciatively. He stood well over six feet tall, burly of figure and shrewd of eye. His age, which must have been somewhat over forty, was suggested only by a slight paunch of the belly and the lines that crinkled good-humoredly at the corners of his eyes. His muscular build implied an active life, while the rather leathery skin revealed that it had been spent in a southern clime.

Most arresting, though, were the sparkling blue eyes, which together with the rest of his physiognomy strongly suggested a familial resemblance. Half-rising, Harry was the first to speak.

"Thomas," he exclaimed in an unwontedly faint voice.

It's all over now, Aubrey was thinking to himself with a sinking feeling in the pit of his stomach as he encountered Georgiana's despairing gaze. Fortunately, Letty provided a diversion by giving a shriek of fright and slumping over in a faint. As Charlotte sprang to offer her succor, Aubrey began busily inventing and discarding possible explanations for his behavior.

Meanwhile, Thomas seemed not even to have noticed this slight diversion. His gaze traveled over their pale and shrinking countenances. The lines about his eyes deepened suddenly as he smiled.

"And which," he asked, "of these two promising lads is my son and heir?"

Aubrey rose magnificently to the occasion. He stood up somewhat unsteadily and in his most emotional voice exclaimed, "Father, we thought you were dead!"

Thomas' bushy eyebrows raised a fraction, whether from surprise or amusement no one could say. In a half-second, he had embraced Aubrey in a crushing bear hug.

"Son, I can't tell you what this means to me."

"I can't tell you what it means to me either," choked out Aubrey truthfully.

Thomas released him abruptly and stood back to survey him at arm's length. "Ah, I should have known you immediately," he said with a trace of mournfulness. "You're the very image of your dear mother."

Letty, who with the aid of Charlotte's ministrations had been coming around gradually, gave another shriek at these words and subsided again into insensibility.

Aubrey fancied he saw a gleam of appreciative humor in Thomas' eye before the latter turned abruptly to regard Letty with some disfavor. "I suppose this vaporish female's your wife, then, Harry?"

Harry, who had stood as if frozen, now sprang forward to clap Thomas on the shoulder awkwardly. "That's right, she, uh, that is . . ." Catching sight of the elderly butler peeping into the room, he barked, "Wilkins, have another place laid for Tom." He led his brother to a chair and the latter sat thankfully.

"I'm much obliged to you; I must admit I'm famished. Traveling always serves to whet my appetite"—here he patted his paunch regretfully—"which is a bit too keen as it is."

Georgiana was watching him with fascination. "Tell me, Uncle Thomas, did you just return from India?"

He looked up abruptly at her. "So this lovely young lady is my niece? Georgiana, is it? And the other, too?" His gaze flickered over to Charlotte and back again. "A pretty pair, Harry, I congratulate you." The edge of his mouth curled upward as he met Georgiana's eager eyes.

"Yes, lass, I've just returned from India. Naturally, my first wish was to be reunited with my family after all these years." He glanced at Aubrey. "And what a happy coincidence it was to find my son here with you," he added artlessly.

"Happy indeed," murmured Aubrey.

At this moment, Letty's eyes focused upon the intruder. "That . . . that," she began before her eyes fell shut again.

"I think we'd better get her upstairs," said Charlotte. "The shock . . ."

"I'll be happy to help," said William, springing up quickly.

"My second daughter, Charlotte, and your son's friend, Mr. William Darley," Harry observed.

"Happy to make your acquaintance. Can you manage by yourself?" asked Thomas.

With a struggle, William had managed to lift Letitia from her chair. "Yes, thank you," he puffed. "We're all right."

In spite of Letitia's absence, the remainder of the dinner could hardly have been said to be peaceful. Aubrey was on tenterhooks lest he inadvertently make a gaff that would reveal his imposture. Georgiana did her best to aid him by plying her uncle continually with questions. While saying a great deal, however, Thomas managed to reveal little, giving Aubrey few leads on which to draw. Charlotte, aware of Georgiana's deception, followed the conversation with a strained, anxious face. So taut were her nerves that she upset a water glass upon herself and had to be excused, much to her sister's relief. William, without Aubrey's lead to follow, found himself resourceless and therefore kept his mouth clamped firmly shut for the duration of the meal.

The one individual delighted by Thomas' appearance was his brother Harry. The fondness between the two was evidenced by their volubility, which at length managed to exclude everyone else at the table, to their relief. Both Georgiana and Aubrey might have been struck by how the brothers' discourse centered around events of the past few weeks only, but the two conspirators were concerned too much with their own nerves to notice this suspicious circumstance.

To Aubrey, the dinner seemed to last an interminable amount of time. He needed to speak to Thomas privately, but it appeared that Harry was not going to give him the chance. Letitia once again intervened in his behalf, by sending Betsey down with the message that she needed to speak to Harry on an urgent matter. Aubrey was certain that it concerned their unexpected visitor and felt a stab of pity for Harry. He was therefore surprised by the grim look of determination upon Harry's face as he rose from the table. This was evidently one matter in which Letty would have no say.

The ladies already having left them, just William and Aubrey remained with Thomas. At a look from Aubrey, William excused himself, with perhaps just a shade too much eagerness than might be considered polite. Thomas was rising also when Aubrey addressed him.

"If I may have a word with you, sir?"

The eyebrows rose a fraction, and though the rest of the face did not alter, Aubrey had the decided impression that Thomas was deriving some secret amusement from the situation.

"Would you mind joining me outside?" Thomas asked courteously. "Just one of my many bad habits, I'm afraid."

Aubrey followed him outside readily, but as the other lit his cigar, he found that he was at a loss as to how to begin.

Thomas smoked for a moment or two in silence before turning his eye upon his squirming companion. "You said you had something to say to me?" he asked mildly.

Aubrey swallowed. He might as well get it over and done. "Yes, sir. I . . . that is, I'm not really your son."

The moonlight revealed no look of shock upon Thomas' face. "Is that so?" he remarked pleasantly.

Aubrey's words now came in a rush. "Yes. You see, I was in a position where we thought it best to conceal my identity, and Georgy suggested that I pretend to be your son since no one had heard from you for years—" He broke off in the middle of what he was saying. "I must say, sir, you don't seem very surprised by all this," he ventured.

"Ah, well, you should have seen me when old Peavey told me my son was staying here. I *was* surprised then." He caught Aubrey's mystified expression and explained. "Outside—when he took my horses. Told me how pleased he was to have me back after all these years and then told me how much everyone around here liked my son. Could have knocked me over with a feather." He paused and took another puff on his cigar. "You see, I haven't one," he added apologetically.

It was Aubrey's turn to register astonishment. "You mean to say that you knew all the time?" In the darkness, Aubrey could almost swear he saw Thomas' eyes twinkling.

"I'm afraid I have what you might call a frivolous nature," Thomas replied. "It seemed such a lark I couldn't help but join in for a bit." He smiled to himself. "Besides, I was interested to see what you'd do when your long-lost father suddenly appeared." He chuckled to himself. "I might have known Georgiana was in on this. The way she kept questioning me. That's a minx after my own heart."

Aubrey could scarcely believe his good fortune. "Then you don't mind my pretending to be your son? You'll go on acting as if I am?"

A certain grimness set in about Thomas' mouth and the corners of his eyes. "I don't mind a lark," he said, "but as to the rest, I'll make you no promises until I hear how you happened into this masquerade and why."

"That's certainly fair enough, sir." Aubrey thereupon launched into the tale of how he had landed at Chalton Hall, beginning with the shooting.

Thomas' cigar had long been extinguished by the time Aubrey

concluded his account. He had thoroughly enjoying many portions of the story, in particular Aubrey's depictions of Georgiana's ingenuity and Marwood's recent discomfiture.

"Well," said Thomas, wiping his eyes and chuckling, "I can see that you're just such a young rapscallion as I was at your age."

Hopefully, Aubrey asked, "Does that mean that you'll keep my secret, sir?"

Thomas' face retained its smile, but his eyes were serious. "That all depends. First I should have to know who you really are."

Aubrey frowned in puzzlement.

"A nineteen-year-old chit who's never been away from home might take you for a drawing master, but I'm not so easily gammoned."

Aubrey's mouth was set. "I have my own reasons for not wishing my identity known."

"And when I know them, perhaps I'll agree with them," said Thomas pleasantly. "Come, now, you can't imagine that I would agree to deceiving my brother's family in their own house without at least knowing why."

Aubrey nodded reluctantly. "I can see that you're right. Very well. I must ask you please to keep my identity a secret, for reasons I will make known. I am Viscount Herne." He took a deep breath and began. "You see, when Georgy took me for a drawing master, I thought it would be a lark to pretend to be one for a while. She had need of my artistic abilities"— here he shrugged—"such as they are, and I thought it would do no harm to continue the masquerade."

He caught Thomas' knowing eye upon him and gave a little nod of the head. "And I did have some responsibilities I wished to avoid for the time being." He looked Thomas squarely in the eye. "The longer I stayed, the fonder I grew of Georgy."

"I suspected the wind blew in that quarter," commented Thomas wisely.

"I told you about Marwood," continued Aubrey, "and I would have found myself in the same position regarding Georgy. Letitia would have attempted to marry us off, whether or not Georgy was willing."

"And you're not sure you wished to marry her, is that it?"

"It was." Aubrey dropped his eyes. "You see, I mean to ask her shortly. I want to know if Georgy would marry me if I actually were just a drawing master."

"Romantic nonsense." The words exploded from Thomas' mouth, but his tone was indulgent. He regarded Aubrey steadily for a few moments in silence. Finally, he came to a decision. "Very well. Your reasons seem foolish to me, but I can see no harm in them. I'll do as you ask, for now." His eyes narrowed warningly. "I may be an idiot to trust you, but I'll be close at hand to make sure that you take no unfair advantage of your position."

"Thank you, sir," said Aubrey in a heartfelt way.

Thomas shrugged. "Well, if I'm to be your father, we might as well be familiar. Call me Tom."

That Letitia was reconciled badly to having the family black sheep as a guest was evident the next morning at breakfast. Harry had made a major concession and had remained at home for the repast instead of hunting. Apparently Letty had been informed that her presence would be required also, for she too graced the table, though obviously sullen at having to be downstairs at such an unaccustomed hour. Aubrey was able to reassure Georgiana with a speaking look, so for the rest of the family, the meal passed pleasantly enough. As for Thomas himself, he disappeared as soon as the meal was finished, but soon returned downstairs carrying a load of exotic-looking parcels.

Despite her prejudices, Letty could not help but be delighted with the beautiful Kasmir shawl she received as well as the length of delicate muslin. Georgiana and Charlotte had been remembered in similar fashion and he even had brought toys for the younger girls.

Letty unbent so far as to thank him graciously for his gifts and even invited him to entertain them all with the tales of his travels. He declined and, to everyone's surprise, asked to be excused on a matter of some urgency, though he did promise to recount his stories later. Somewhat miffed, Letty turned to Harry in surprise as soon as his brother had left.

"Whatever do you suppose he meant? Surely he could have no urgent business here after being absent for twenty years."

Harry, who had been lost in his own ruminations, mumbled something that might have been taken for some form of assent and made good his chance to escape. William and Charlotte, who hardly had taken their eyes off each other during the meal, rather blushingly excused themselves also.

Aubrey saw his opportunity before him at last. He was feeling both excited and unexpectedly nervous. No one could object to his having time alone with Georgiana under the guise of portrait-sitting. Before he could speak, however, Letty forestalled him.

"I think my new shawl would look well in our portrait, don't you?" she asked Aubrey.

"Yes, of course," he murmured, his eyes on Georgiana, who was rising from the table.

Letty sniffed. "Although your father's arrival has upset my schedule somewhat, I believe that I have time this morning to sit for you."

No! Aubrey wanted to exclaim, but it was too late.

"I'll go speak to Cook about dinner then, Mother," said Georgiana, her eyes avoiding his.

Letty waved her away and, as Georgiana was disappearing through the door, turned to Aubrey with a slightly reproving look. "I should think that the portrait would be nearing completion by now."

Aubrey could not repress a sigh. Argument was useless. Well, he might find time to be alone with Georgiana this afternoon. He knew where to find her.

13

Lady Dowles was seated in the parlor working on her needlework when she heard the sounds of a carriage approaching. It seemed rather early for anyone to be paying a social call. She laid down her sewing and addressed the maid.

"Molly, will you go see who that is? I am really not dressed to receive company."

Molly obediently went to the window. "I don't recognize the carriage, my lady."

Lady Dowles frowned slightly. "I wonder who it could be?"

"There's a gentleman getting out."

"Is he alone?"

"Yes, milady." She anticipated the next question. "I've never seen him before."

"How curious. Perhaps you'd better help me up, Molly. I should put on another dress."

Molly was helping her up when the butler appeared.

"You have a visitor, milady."

"Yes, I know."

"A Mr. Thomas Chalford."

Despite the maid's hold upon her, her legs suddenly gave way and she sank abruptly back into her chair. Her eyes were closed as if in pain. She did not move or speak for a moment. The butler hovered nearer, anxiously.

"Milady?"

Still not opening her eyes, she asked, "Mr. Thomas Chalford, did you say?"

"Yes, milady."

Opening her eyes, she turned to the butler with an effort. "Show him in, then." She inclined her head toward the door. "Leave me, Molly."

The maid started to obey her, but she was stopped by her mistress's voice. "Wait! Help me to my feet first."

Molly had accomplished this and was about to leave when the visitor appeared in the doorway.

"Thomas," said Lady Dowles faintly.

"Nell," growled the bass voice in a tone so redolent of tenderness that ready tears sprang to the warmhearted Molly's eyes. She whisked through the door as quickly as she could, but not before she had seen him cross the room to crush her mistress in a fervent embrace.

The two stood like that, silently, without moving, for several minutes, as if they feared that in doing so, they might break the spell. At last, Thomas released her, only to cup her face in his hands.

"Nell, you're as beautiful as ever," he said softly.

Tears were streaming down Lady Dowles' face. "Thomas, I . . . I . . ."

He shook his head gently, still retaining his hold on her. "I've burst in upon you like a thundercloud, haven't I? Ah, my der, it was always my way."

"Thomas, I . . ."

He understood her unspoken wish. He smiled gently and dropped his hands down to take one of hers. She wiped her tears away with her free hand in a most unladylike fashion. He pulled a handkerchief from his pocket and gave it to her before lowering her delicately into the chair. He stepped back to take hold of another chair and pull it up to hers. He sank into it, immediately regaining possession of her hand and fixing his eyes on her face lovingly. She dabbed at her eyes liberally with her handkerchief.

"Thomas, why couldn't you have told me?" she asked in a trembling voice.

He smiled an odd little smile. "I was afraid, Nell, and that's the truth."

"Afraid," she said, managing to convey an expression of scorn despite her pinkened nose and shaking hands.

His mouth twisted into a rueful grimace. "You might not have wished to see me, you know."

"Don't be ridiculous," she snapped, almost forgetting her situation.

He gave a faint chuckle. "That's my Nell," he said appreciatively.

She blew her nose emphatically.

"So shall we set the date, then?" he asked softly, a wheedling note in his voice.

Her eyes filled again. "Thomas, how dare you tease . . ?" she began to ask, chokingly.

His smile vanished instantly. "I'm not joking, my love," he said in a low voice filled with affection.

She dabbed at her eyes again. "Well, just to march in after twenty years and expect me to behave like some silly school-girl—"

"I don't want a schoolgirl." His expression was serious. "It's you I want, my own love."

She shook her head frantically. "Don't say that," she ordered. She extracted her hand from his and transferred handkerchief operations to it. "What are you doing here?"

"I'm here to marry you," he said innocently.

"I told you to stop saying that," she demanded. "You know very well what I mean. What are you doing in England?"

"I came back to see you."

"Be serious!"

"I am," he replied, hurt. Seeing that she wasn't satisfied, he continued. "My, uh, position there terminated and I thought it was time to return home, now that I've made my fortune and all. Shall it bother you to marry a nabob, Nell?"

"Won't you act sensibly for a moment?"

"I am acting sensibly." He met her eyes with a pleading expression. "Must you know everything that I've done for the past twenty years right now? We'll have the rest of our lives, you know, and we've lost a great deal of time already."

Her face was adamant.

"Very well." He gave a small sigh. "Well, let me see. On the morning that my father evicted me, I believe that I had eggs and a slice of gammon for breakfast. I was wearing . . . let me think—"

"You can't ever be serious for a moment, can you?" Her voice was accusing and tearful.

He saw her real distress and unobtrusively regained his hold of her hand. "I'm sorry, my love. I think I am giddy with the joy of seeing you after all these years. I've dreamt of this moment so often." His smile held a share of sadness. "What is it you need to know, then? Were there other women? Yes, you more than anyone should know that I've never been a saint, Nell."

He paused for a moment, then continued softly. "I wouldn't think you'd expect it of me, any more than I'd expect you to say that you never loved Sir Roger."

Quite overcome, she could not repress a little sob. Still sitting, he folded his arms about her awkwardly.

"He was an honorable man and a kind one. It was only natural that you, as his wife, should love him. I would be disappointed in you, had you not."

She raised her tear-streaked face to his. "How can you understand so much?"

He tightened his hold upon her. "I told you there were other women, Nell. I didn't marry any of them, and none of them ever made me forget you."

A shadow passed across her face. She straightened herself, unconsciously withdrawing from his arms. She looked at him levelly.

"Why didn't you tell me when you left?" Her eyes were seeing into the past. "I became worried when several days passed without hearing from you. I finally rode over to Chalton and your father told me you were gone." She turned her gaze back to him. "Not even a note for me, Thomas? Not even a word?"

"Oh, my dear." His distress was evident. He grimaced unhappily. "What a young fool I was." He paused, then continued. "You remember what a fierce temper my father had—"

"I remember yours, too," she said softly.

He sighed. "Well, there you have it. We always rubbed each other the wrong way. It seemed we could never be together without brangling. We had a final, terrible argument and he told me I must leave." He shook his head. "What a young hothead I was. I packed my bags and was gone within the hour."

He frowned at the memory. "At first I thought to go take my leave of you, but then I realized that your father would hardly welcome me with open arms. As for a note to you, my father was just as opposed to the match as yours—probably more so, given his opinion of me. I knew it was no use leaving a note with him. And Harry, well, he already had landed in enough trouble on my account. I thought I'd write you when I got to London.''

The corner of his mouth curled up ruefully. ''You don't know how many letters I wrote and then tore to shreds. Oh, I lived like a prince for a few weeks, but as the money ran out, I gradually realized that our fathers had been right all along. I was nothing more than a rakehelly young good-for-nothing. What could I offer you? I myself had nothing to live on.'' He shook his head again. ''I hadn't even the wherewithal to buy a pair of colors for myself. I was so desperate, I even thought of enlisting as a common soldier.''

He leaned back in his chair. ''A friend took pity on me. Through his father's influence, he managed to procure a position for me. I shipped out to India, determined to make my fortune so that I could return to claim you for my own. Everything seems so simple to you when you're young.''

He drew in a deep breath and exhaled with a sigh. ''Well, of course, things didn't happen quite as I had foreseen. By the time I had earned enough to support us, quite a bit of time had passed.'' He dropped his eyes. ''I was planning to return when I heard of your marriage.'' He shrugged. ''There was no point in my returning then.''

''I see.''

There was an awkward silence in the room for a few moments. Thomas was the first to break it. ''In any case, those years were not entirely wasted. I spent them accumulating a fortune so you can live like a queen once we are married.'' He brightened suddenly. ''I know that you must have been a grand political hostess. What do you say? Shall I buy a seat in Parliament?''

She gave him a little push with her hand. ''Great idiot,'' she remarked.

He looked at her expectantly. ''Well, what's my answer, then? Is it yes? I shall have to order a new suit of clothes if it is.''

She put a hand to her forehead. ''You're confusing me. You've given me too much to think about—''

''I don't want you to think. I want you to say yes.''

"I can't."

The boldness of the statement startled both of them. She saw the surprise and hurt in his eyes and amended her words. "I can't tell you anything today. You've worn me out. I'm not a young chit of a girl, you know."

His eyes smiled at her. "Very well, grandmother." He rose and kissed her on the forehead. "I'll be back tomorrow like a proper suitor with flowers and a ring. After twenty years, I suppose I can bear to wait one more day, my love."

She gave him a tremulous little smile. Her eyes watched the tall figure as he strode from the room. She lifted the handkerchief to wipe her eyes once again and saw his initial upon it. Clutching the hand that held it into a fist, she dropped her head in despair.

At Chalton, meanwhile, at least two of the lovers were enjoying a measure of unalloyed bliss. Charlotte and William were able to spend a rapturous morning in each other's company. She at last had been able to confess her former scheme for thrusting Georgiana at him and if he did call her a little goose, the adjective "dear" did precede it. Moreover the epithet was delivered with such affection that it quite made her blush. She also had the satisfaction of hearing from his own lips that while he thought Georgiana was a nice-enough girl for all that, in his eyes she couldn't hold a candle to her sister. Many other compliments of the same sort followed. It was clear that nothing remained to mar their happiness.

The only tiny cloud on the horizon appeared when William announced that he must leave that afternoon for a short outing. It had been some days since he had mailed a letter of progress to Aubrey's mother, Lady Herne, and he was well aware that this omission might very well bring her swooping down upon their heads. It was a great pity, for he would have liked to confide in Charlotte, but then it was not his secret. He did permit himself to say that he needed to run an errand on behalf of his friend and that he would return in time for dinner. The grays needed a bit of exercise at any rate.

Charlotte endeavored to hide her disappointment and her curiosity. She managed to secure a short ride in the curricle by claiming that there were some late-blooming wildflowers on the main road that she wished to gather for an arrangement. Even though a short drive, it was quite a thrill for Charlotte, who had never ridden in a fashionable sporting vehicle before. She secretly admired William's mastery of his well-matched team and found the precariousness of her perch thrilling. As he set her down upon reaching the main road, William promised that she should have a demonstration of the grays' paces on her next ride. Charlotte watched dreamily as the dashing vehicle sped away, then with a sigh turned to the side of the road to begin to try to discover it there actually were any sorts of late-blooming wildflowers growing.

A short distance away, William encountered Marwood, who had dismounted and was beginning to examine his horse's leg. Though loath to intervene, mere decency compelled William to pull up and ask whether he might be of assistance.

"No." Marwood's reply was both succinct and frosty and the look that he gave William was withering.

Happy to depart, William gave the ribbons a shake and was on his way once more.

Marwood meanwhile turned the horse's right front hoof up and found a stone lodged in it. He muttered a little curse and, extracting a knife from his pocket, managed to work the stone free. He led the black a few steps, but evidently there was some residual tenderness, for the horse continued to favor the hoof.

The prospect of a long, dusty walk was enough to put Marwood in a black mood, and seeing William flash by in his curricle had done nothing to improve it. It had been galling to let a pair of young pups dictate his actions, and worse still was the humiliating way in which they had chosen to tie his hands. Although they could not have known it, the timing of their actions had proven particularly unfortunate for him, and he was nearing the point of desperation. A desire for revenge burned within him, but no coherent plan had presented itself to him.

There had been a short gleam of hope during his trip to the village. He had stopped at the local inn for a brief dalliance with the chambermaid. He had scarcely closed the door behind the willing girl and pulled her into his arms when he was startled by a suspicious noise outside the door. He opened it abruptly

to discover a large ruffianly fellow lurking in the hall. Though
unprepared for Marwood's attack, the fellow managed to give
a good account of himself, and with a blow sent Marwood stag-
gering back into the room. It proved an unfortunate move, for
Marwood almost fell onto the table that held his pistol. Faced
with the weapon, the fellow had no choice but to yield. Upon
Marwood's order, he reluctantly entered the room as Marwood
thrust the frightened girl outside and shut the door. Marwood's
demands produced the information that the fellow was looking
for another gentleman altogether, and he apologized for having
disturbed his lordship. The last two words brought the first
glimmerings of an idea to Marwood's mind, and lowering the
pistol, he asked the man if he were looking for a titled gentleman. The fellow looked alarmed to have revealed so much, but
upon further questioning, Marwood could have no doubts.

Marwood had been involved with enough shady dealings to
recognize a Bow Street runner when he saw one, and it definitely
was Viscount Herne that the man was seeking. The hopes that
had been raised evaporated when he learned that the viscount
was not wanted for murder or any other such matter, but that
it was a simple case of disappearance. Marwood could not
decide how best to make use of the interesting new development, and so mysteriously promised the runner that he could
supply some information if the man would call upon him at
Marwood House.

As long as they did not meet in a public place, where his name
might be connected with the runner, Marwood saw no reason
not to reveal Aubrey's hiding place. Although he assumed that
discovery would thrust some sort of spoke in the viscount's
plans, Marwood could not rely upon its being the major debacle
he hoped for.

Such were the thoughts that occupied his mind as he continued
on his walk. As he came around a bend, he saw Charlotte's
artless figure bent over in the grass to gather her posies. The
sight made him even angrier. If only he'd had the good sense
to pursue that one first, convention be damned. She was much
more to his taste than the older, and if what Letty had said was
true, she had just as large a portion. This one was not the type
to put up any resistance. Though during his time with the Chal-

fords he had concentrated on Georgiana, he also had spent enough time in conversation with Charlotte to be able to read her character. He knew that he might have managed this romantic miss with ease. She wouldn't have involved a pair of perfect strangers in the affair.

Unaware of his approach, Charlotte continued happily with her task. Marwood stared dispiritedly at her. His chance for this one was gone, too. Letty had as good as told him that Charlotte was now intended for William. Marwood's anger rose again as he gazed upon her. How convenient it would be for the two young men with him out of the way. He had not missed the intimacy between Georgiana and Aubrey the other night. Yes, there were no obstacles to hinder the young lovers now.

Hearing the hoofbeats at last, Charlotte spun around and was startled to see Marwood approaching. Though she did not know the details of why the engagement had been called off, she still felt awkward at seeing him. It always seemed as if he could read her very thoughts. She gave him a tentative smile. "Good afternoon, my lord."

The sight of the beauty standing before him served only to fuel Marwood's rage at what he had lost. He concealed his emotion, however, and instead gave her his most charming smile. "Good afternoon, Miss Charlotte."

She had not had time to assimilate his situation before, but she did so now. "Is something the matter with your horse, my lord?"

He waved his hand carelessly. "A trifle, though I have rather a long walk ahead of me, I'm afraid." His eyes widened in concern. "But surely you are not out here by yourself, my dear? A young girl is so vulnerable . . ."

I could abduct her now, he thought, and Chalford would have no choice but to put a good face on the match. A tug at the reins in his hands reminded him of his predicament and he discarded the idea wistfully.

"Well, it's so close to home. I wished to gather these flowers." Here she blushed. "And Will—Mr. Darley was kind enough to give me a ride."

"He abandoned you out here alone?" Marwood's face was expressive of shock.

"Well, I had asked him to, you see," began Charlotte, frowning slightly, realizing that she might have taken a rash action. She shrugged off the thought and smiled brightly at Marwood, lifting her basket. "I'm through now, though, so I'll return home."

"My dear, I could not possibly let you travel this road alone. Had you forgotten about the shooting?"

She frowned again and he had to smile to himself. The seeds he was planting were finding fertile ground, indeed.

He inclined his head slightly in a graceful and self-deprecating way. "I am afraid that I cannot accompany you all the way to Chalton, but I will be happy to escort you to the drive."

Charlotte could see no polite way to refuse his offer so she assented. As they walked, the notion that had come to Marwood began to take definite shape.

"I saw Mr. Darley on the road just now," he commented. The little information he had gleaned from the runner was proving useful, after all. "A trip to the village, I suppose? He travels there quite frequently, or so I'm told."

Charlotte was determined not to betray her own curiosity upon that point, so she merely smiled at Marwood instead. "I'm afraid I don't know the reason for any of Mr. Darley's comings and goings, my lord."

Without realizing it, his eyes had narrowed thoughtfully. His idea was beginning to take on flesh. Obviously, the two young men were still maintaining their imposture. They would find it to their disadvantage. Now he had a way to make use of that runner. Why, the fellow's very presence would lend some credence to his tale. He could have laughed aloud at the thought. Instead, he turned to Charlotte with a serious expression.

"Miss Charlotte, I can't tell you how glad I am to have the chance to speak with you alone. I hope you will forgive me for saying so, but you have always struck me as one who would not take the notion of family honor lightly. I have a pressing need to meet with you about a most urgent and secret matter that directly involves your family."

By dinnertime, Aubrey was thoroughly irritated. Not only had Letty insisted that he spend his morning painting her portrait, she had commanded that he spend the afternoon finishing up with the three youngest girls. It had seemed a very simple thing to manage a few moments alone with Georgiana, to tell her his feelings and wait for her answer. It seemed that fate was against him. He did his best to catch her eyes, but her gaze always happened to be elsewhere. It almost seemed as if she were avoiding him. Surely he must be imagining it. The kiss had been real enough. He had felt her response. There could be no mistake about it. Probably she was only feeling shy. After all, she had led a secluded, sheltered life.

He shook his head. The fossil sketches were nearly completed, as was the portrait, and he was weary of this masquerade. It was time to return to the world in which he belonged. Spurred by these thoughts, he broke into the one-way conversation Letty was conducting.

"Since I've finished with the younger girls, I mean to ask Georgy to pose for me tomorrow. As you yourself pointed out, there is no purpose in delaying its completion."

Caught off-guard by this sudden forcefulness, Letty could think of no objections to make, so the matter was settled.

Though apparently oblivious, Georgiana heard this exchange of words with a sinking heart. Ordinarily she should have been in a good mood, for after working all day in the quarry, she had revealed enough of the specimen to be certain that it was a unique find. In its significance, it would overshadow anything she or Dr. Browne had found. Previously, she should have been ecstatic, particularly knowing that her work would not be interrupted now. Instead, she was miserable. She longed to say that she would not be able to pose tomorrow, but what excuse could she make? No, she had been the one foolish enough to arrange for Aubrey's stay here and now she must pay the price. She longed for him to go and put an end to her suffering, and yet a part of her shrank from the thought of his leaving. Hadn't she been terrified lest Uncle Thomas expose him, and relieved when she saw that it was not to happen?

She rubbed her forehead in an unconscious gesture. All order and logic had vanished from her thoughts. She might as well get it over with and sit for him tomorrow. She hadn't been alone with him since the kiss. She could act coldly dignified. No, then he would be puzzled and wonder what was wrong. It wasn't his fault that she had thrown herself at him. No, she must treat him with friendliness, but maintain a slight degree of reserve so that he would know that the kiss was purely an accident. She groaned inwardly. How did one manufacture ease? What's more, how in the world was she to keep her love for him from shining through her eyes?

Charlotte should have been perfectly happy, but a worrisome thought kept returning to her mind. She wondered if she were wise in agreeing to meet Lord Marwood. Clandestine meetings were all very fine when you read about them in a novel, but in reality . . . She wondered what William would think if he knew. Really, she shouldn't have agreed, but Marwood had seemed so earnest. As she mulled it over, the thing seemed even more odd. What on earth could he possibly have to tell her?

William noticed a slight abstraction on the part of his beloved, but ascribed it to the tumultuous events of the past few days. It was getting to be rather too much. He was willing to wait a certain length of time for Aubrey to drop the masquerade, but this patience was wearing thin. Well, he intended to offer for Charlotte soon, and if Aubrey was still dragging his feet, it would be just too bad. Dash it, a man couldn't propose to his love while he was practicing a deception upon her. He was going to confess the whole, with or without Aubrey's consent, but he'd give him a few more days yet.

Although the next morning dawned cold and misty, it seemed a beautiful day to Thomas. He breakfasted in the sunniest of moods, charming even Letitia with his good spirits. Although impatient to depart, he dawdled long enough to ensure that he would land at the correct hour for a morning call. Having carefully attired himself in his best suit of clothing, he was pleased upon his arrival to observe that his lady-love had taken similar care with her dress. Although he was not conversant with all the niceties of female costume, he could see that it was much less severe than the one she had worn the day before, being of a most flattering shade of peach. She also seemed more imposing than when he had seen her yesterday in her well-worn morning dress. It was clear that this was a strong, shrewd, and capable woman, used to running an estate all on her own.

She lifted her chin slightly to smile at him. "Good morning, Thomas."

The formality of the greeting and her obvious self-possession caused the first shadow of doubt to fall across his heart. He did not betray his feelings, however, and instead gave her a peck on the forehead. She indicated a chair and he pulled it up beside her. She shook her head smilingly at him.

"I can't tell you what a shock you gave me yesterday. I was quite nonplussed to have you suddenly appear after all these years."

Relying upon his instincts, he contributed nothing to the conversation. The fixed smile remained upon her face.

"Not that I wasn't glad to see you. I often had wondered whatever became of you. It's good to have the mystery solved at last."

His heart was slowly falling, but Thomas endeavored to keep his face expressionless.

She continued, still smiling at him in a brittle fashion. "I can't tell you how pleased I am to know that you've done so well for yourself. It's a great satisfaction to me—"

Thomas could stand no more of it. "Don't toy with me like this, Nell."

She assumed an expression of puzzlement, but he slowly shook his head at her. "You should know me better than that, Nell. I've come for my answer and I mean to have it. All this chitchat won't deter me."

He looked at her gravely. She could not help but drop her eyes.

"If it's to be no, I must hear it from your own lips, my love."

She lifted her eyes to meet his. "It is no," she said softly.

"Do you care to tell me why?" he asked.

Her mouth trembled slightly. "I'm not sure that I can explain it so that you would understand." She drew in a little breath. "It's just that I have become accustomed to an independent life. I run this estate by myself and I do a good job of it, too." Her gaze flickered downwards again. "I suppose I've been my own mistress too long now." She shook her head. "I've simply no desire to marry again."

Thomas was not about to take this lying down. "Dash it all, Nell, I've no desire to take over the estate from you. Why, I'd be a helpless child as far as running it is concerned. By thunder, if you're so fond of doing it, I'll buy you fifty more estates to run."

"No, please, Thomas—"

"But that's why I wish to marry you, to make sure that you do exactly as you want for the rest of your life."

She was shaking her head in some distress. "It's the very fact of marriage that—"

His eyes opened in amazement. "It's the fact of marriage that's bothering you? Well, my dear, I do not mean to disparage poor Sir Roger, but—"

"Please, Thomas, don't—"

"I'm only saying that there has been something between us since we were scarcely more than children." He looked at her incredulously. "It's there even as we speak. You can't tell me that you don't feel it, Nell."

She lifted her eyes, brimming over with tears, to his. "I wish you wouldn't, Thomas," she said with deceptive calm. "There's nothing you can say that will make me change my mind."

He leaned forward, gripping her hard by the shoulders. "You mustn't throw it away, Nell."

Her eyes met is, but she said not a word.

Slowly his grip relaxed and his hands fell from her. "Nell." The one word expressed lingering hope, hurt, shock, and a sense of betrayal.

In spite of herself, a tear slipped down one cheek. "If I were to marry anyone, it would be you."

It took him several moments to compose himself. He opened his mouth to speak, then paused as he encountered her inflexible gaze. Slowly he rose from his chair. The words came torturously from him.

"I don't know why you are doing this, Nell. I suppose that if you will not listen to me, there is no point in my remaining here." He looked at her with burning eyes. "There is one thing I do know. I told you I was no saint. Well, my dear girl, neither are you. You'll regret this decision every night as you lie alone in your cold bed.''

She dropped her eyes, but vouchsafed no response.

''Good-bye Nell.'' He nodded at her curtly, turned on his heel, and left the room.

She watched the door close behind him with a hopeless expression. ''Good-bye, my own dear love,'' she whispered.

14

It certainly was odd, Aubrey thought as he painted. He had engineered this entire situation to his liking. With the inclement weather, it was obvious that Georgiana must pose for him inside the house today. He had given strict orders that they were not to be disturbed, so he had no need to fear an untimely interruption. Without her work to divert her, Georgiana's full attention had to be focused on himself. He had carefully rehearsed exactly what he was going to say.

Georgiana herself sat before him, in the lovely green frock that became her so well. He had opened his mouth a half-dozen times to speak, and yet each time his nerve had failed.

He drew in a deep breath and tried once more. "Uh, um, Georgy?"

"Yes?" Her response was politeness itself.

Blast! He could feel his courage slipping away again. "Um, would you lift your chin just a little, please?"

She obediently raised it a quarter of an inch.

It was not that she had been rude or even cold, he thought. She had displayed the most perfect manners. That was it, he realized. When had he and Georgiana ever had anything to do with manners? Their relationship had begun on a more intimate footing than that. No, she was treating him as if he were a mere acquaintance, as if these past few weeks had never happened, as if she had never kissed him.

His brush halted momentarily as the thought struck him. Was that it? She had seemed to alter after that point. Had it brought the realities of her situation home to her? Did she feel that he, a mere drawing master, had taken liberties and now must be firmly put in his place? He ground his teeth for an instant. So, she was no different than any other young lady of his acquaintance. One simply did not marry beneath oneself.

What a fool he'd been! When he thought of all the trouble he'd been to, bringing her the carefully executed drawings, following along with all her schemes. And Lord Marwood! He should have let her marry the miserable rogue. His hand trembled and he had to withdraw it from the canvas to steady it for a moment.

She looked at him quizzically. "Are you through for now?"

He laid down his brush. With a snort of disgust he replied, "Yes, I think you could say that I'm finished."

It was a somber little group that partook of dinner that evening. Charlotte was acting quite distracted and hardly responded to half of William's conversational gambits. Remembering her previous attempts to thrust him at Georgiana, he determined to waylay her after their meal and force her to tell him what was troubling her. Unfortunately, she managed to evade him by excusing herself when dinner was only half over, pleading a terrible megrim. William ate the rest of the meal sunk in gloomy silence.

Aubrey, meanwhile, was full of bitterness. He could not prevent a slightly sarcastic tone from creeping into his speech. Fortunately, Letty, as usual, was blithely delivering a monologue on one of her favorite subjects and so noticed nothing. He should have been cheered by merely gazing upon her, for she had chosen to wear one of his particular creations, which boasted a bold color scheme of scarlet and primrose. The ostrich plumes, which bobbed ridiculously above her nose as she spoke, ordinarily would have been enough to entertain him for the entire repast. He took no joy in them or anything else tonight. He had been tempted to pack his bag and go this afternoon. Two considerations prevented him. The first was William, who probably needed to be rescued from this socially ambitious family. In any case, William would have no excuse to remain if his "friend" departed and probably would not look kindly upon Aubrey's doing so. Aubrey's shoulders sagged unhappily. He would need at least one ally in order to face his mother's inevitable wrath. He sighed to himself. He had acted too impetuously as usual and now must pay the price. He supposed he should be comforted by the thought of Georgiana's chagrin when she learned what a rich prize she had let escape, but somehow it afforded him no satisfaction.

Second, there was also the portrait to be finished. Though his heart was no longer in the project, he had promised to execute it and so felt an obligation to stand by his word, false identity or not. Well, he thought glumly, at least I've always been a fast worker. With no further reason to deliberately dawdle, he could probably have it finished in a few days.

Georgiana herself, while far from animated, was doing an admirable job of concealing the fact that she had spent the entire afternoon in tears. At least she could still hold her head high. After all, the portrait was nearly done and she expected to extract the fossil within a day or two. Once he had sketched it, there would be no reason for her and Aubrey to be thrown together. Somehow, these thoughts, which should have reassured her, sank her spirits lower than ever. With an effort, she dismissed them from her mind and joined her father in trying to rally an inexplicably listless Thomas.

To his credit, Thomas was aware of these efforts on his behalf and did his best to respond. He came out with a droll story or two for their benefit, but even an appreciative audience could not quite restore the sparkle to his eyes. He excused himself quietly after dinner and disappeared outside for the solace of his cigar. Harry found him there a few minutes later. He vouchsafed no greeting, but seated himself on a nearby bench. They spent a few moments in companionable silence, until Harry spoke.

"Saw Eleanor today, did you?" he asked with mild interest.

Thomas took a puff on the cigar and exhaled slowly. "You've always seen right through me, haven't you, Harry?"

"You're about as transparent as glass," his elder brother agreed amiably. He waited for a moment or two, but still Thomas did not speak. "I take it that the news is not good," Harry said softly.

Thomas shook his head. He spoke slowly, making an effort to mask the pain he felt. "It seems that the lady will not have me. I feel a bit of a fool, rushing back here." He shook his head again. "I don't know why I was so certain she could wish to marry an aging nabob with a thickening waist and a dubious reputation.''

"Tom.'' The word protested at him.

Thomas shrugged. "No, she made it clear that, for whatever reason, she has not the slightest desire to become leg-shackled to me.''

"I can't believe that. Why, all these years she's asked me for news of you. I can't tell you how it grated on me to have to lie to her.''

Thomas took a deep breath and exhaled with a sigh. "There wasn't much point, Harry. The news wasn't good for such a long period of time and then . . .'' He extinguished the remains of his cigar. "Well, Eleanor was entitled to have at least one happy marriage, wasn't she?''

Harry returned to more pressing concerns. "Didn't she give you some sort of reason?''

Thomas shrugged again. "Said she didn't wish to be married again. Female independence and all that rot.'' Unconsciously, a hopeless tone crept into his voice. "No, if she'd wanted to marry me, none of that would have hindered her for a moment.'' His brows contracted painfully. "And I was so certain after that first visit . . .''

Harry was frowning himself, but with a different thought. "It sounds a havey-cavey excuse to me, and that sounds most unlike Eleanor.'' He pondered over it for a minute. "I know who can be of help to you.''

Thomas looked at his brother with the air of one who was not expecting much.

"Georgy. Eleanor's her godmother and the two of them have always been thick as thieves. Georgy can get to the bottom of this if anyone can.''

Thomas lifted his eyebrows skeptically.

Harry rose and waved a hand at him. "Well, come on man. At least it's worth a try.''

One person in the house who remained largely unaffected by all the undercurrents of tension was Augusta. It was true, however, that since the young men's arrival Georgiana had been busy elsewhere, so that the burden of caring for the younger children fell more heavily than usual upon Augusta's shoulders. She was not one to complain or fancy herself ill-used, but this morning she was conscious of a desire to escape the nursery clamor for a few moments of peace.

Accordingly, she had risen early and despite the chill of the day had strolled to the arbor, Horace in hand. She intended to spend a few blissful moments lost in another world. As she began to make her way to her favorite bench, she was halted suddenly by the sound of voices. She frowned for a moment to herself. Who could it possibly be at this hour of the morning?

She would have turned on her heel to seek privacy elsewhere, but she realized that the masculine of the two voices was unfamiliar. It was certainly her sister Charlotte speaking to him in that agitated fashion, but Augusta was positive that the man was not a resident of Chalton. She was able to catch a few words here and there, but not enough to be entirely clear on what they were discussing.

Feeling that duty to her sister called her forward, she gave a little sigh of resignation and walked up to peep in the arbor entrance.

In the grayish morning light that filtered through the canopy of trees, she could see Lord Marwood standing, apparently facing Charlotte, who was seated on a bench and thus obscured by the foliage. Augusta could hear their words more plainly now and she strained forward to catch them.

It was obvious that Charlotte was upset, but she seemed to be in agreement with whatever it was that Marwood had to say. The focus of their discussion was still unclear to Augusta. She unconsciously took a step forward, inadvertently snapping a wayward twig.

The noise caught Marwood's attention. He swiveled, saw her, and took a few frowning steps in her direction, causing Augusta to back away involuntarily. Charlotte had also noticed the sound and risen, coming into view as she followed Marwood. When she saw Augusta, she gave a sigh, of either relief or disappointment. She caught at Marwood's sleeve. "It's all right," she said. "It's only my younger sister Augusta."

Marwood bent a malevolent look upon her before turning back to Charlotte. "Well, at least she hasn't that vicious hound with her, in any case. Are you certain that she won't present a—"

There was mute appeal in Charlotte's face. "I can take care of this, my lord." He hesitated for a moment. "You'd best go before someone else sees you here," she added warningly.

Her last words convinced him. "Very well." He looked meaningfully at her. "It is settled, then?"

She waved a hand distractedly at him as Augusta began to approach. "Yes, yes. Now you must be off." She was too worried to notice the passing look of satisfaction that crossed Marwood's face.

"Then, *au revoir,* my dear."

He would have kissed her hand, but Charlotte was too busy shooing him away. In compliance with her wishes, he departed. As he strode past Augusta, he fixed her with a hard look, but said nothing.

Augusta walked up to Charlotte slowly, a questioning expression upon her face.

Charlotte caught her sister's hands in her own. "Gussie," she said, using the family nickname that Augusta despised, "you must say nothing—*nothing* of this."

Augusta was not to be put off so easily. "Why are you meeting with him, Charlotte? You don't even like him."

Charlotte dropped Augusta's hands to wring her own. "It's not that I don't like him, dear. It's just that I . . . well, I misjudged him in the past."

"I don't think Father or even Mother would approve of these clandestine meetings," Augusta said reprovingly. "I may not be aware of all the social conventions, but I know that a young lady is never supposed to meet with a young man unchaperoned. It would be bad enough even with the maid here."

Charlotte twisted her hands together again. "How can I make you understand? This is more important than a set of silly rules. It's a matter of life and death!"

Augusta was used to Charlotte's dramatics. She cocked a wary eye at her sister. "Whose life and death?" she asked suspiciously.

Charlotte was becoming more frantic by the minute. "I can't explain it all to you. I would be breaking my word if I told you. All I can say is that the welfare of our entire family is at stake."

Augusta had a high opinion of her sister's veracity, but a rather lower one of her judgment. She was still aware of

Charlotte's tendency to romanticize any situation and hence made her decision. "I won't lie for you, Charlotte," she said quite calmly.

"I am not asking you to lie for me," Charlotte said desperately. "All I ask is that you don't mention my meeting with Lord Marwood to anyone."

Augusta was reluctant to be persuaded. Charlotte grabbed her by the shoulders. "Augusta, if you tell someone it could ruin everything."

"Not even Georgy?"

"Especially not Georgy." Charlotte could see refusal in Augusta's eyes and sighed. "Look, I promise you that my plans with Lord Marwood involve no one but myself and that they are for the good of everyone at Chalton." She looked anxiously into her sister's face. "Please, Augusta."

It was Augusta's turn to sigh. Clearly Charlotte did not intend to let her escape from this spot without extracting a promise. She was obviously beside herself with worry. Besides, how important could this matter be? With Charlotte's love of theatrics, it could be any number of minor concerns. Augusta surrendered. "Very well, Charlotte. I promise not to mention it."

Tears, undoubtedly of relief, shone in her sister's eyes as she hugged her. "Thank you, Augusta. You . . . you won't regret it." She released her sister and hurried away.

Augusta watched her with some speculation as she disappeared from view. Possibly she had not done the right thing in promising Charlotte, but it could always be remedied. She had said she wouldn't tell anyone unless they asked; she hadn't sworn not to provoke them into asking her.

Her nerves quite strained from the morning's encounter, Charlotte returned to the house intent upon seeking the solace of her room. It was a severe trial to her when she collided with Aubrey in the hall instead and was told that she was the very person he was seeking. She tried to mumble some excuse and escape, but he was determined.

"You see, Charlotte, I've finished everyone's portrait but yours and your father's. He and Thomas have already left in search of game this morning, so . . ."

"I have a bit of a headache. Couldn't it wait until tomorrow?" she pleaded.

He was firm. "I'm determined to finish the portrait. I've delayed much too long as it is."

Had she been in another frame of mind, she might have noticed the bleakness that came into his voice as he spoke, but Charlotte was mindful of nothing but her own secret worries. She could think of no other pretext, so she reluctantly consented.

"I promise you it won't take long," said Aubrey, with an assumption of cheer. "I have everything ready in the parlor."

Charlotte unhappily dragged herself upstairs to change into her most becoming blue frock. Within fifteen minutes, she had joined Aubrey in the parlor. He went to work in a most businesslike manner and hardly noticed his model's listlessness. His mind numbed by pain, he scarcely was aware of what he was doing as he painted. Charlotte's mind was also elsewhere. Neither of them noticed William until he was actually standing in the room. Charlotte could not prevent giving a little start.

Aubrey raised his eyebrows inquiringly.

William looked at his cousin apologetically. "I'm sorry to disturb you. I know you hate interruptions, but I heard Charlotte was here and I had to see her." He stepped forward, proffering a neatly wrapped parcel. "I picked this up on my last expedition. I've been meaning to give it to you, but somehow I haven't had the opportunity to see you privately and I hated to give it to you in front of everyone."

Charlotte accepted it mechanically. "Thank you," she said, making no move to open it.

William looked at her expectantly. "I know how you enjoy music," he said eagerly. "It's a book of songs."

"You're very kind," said Charlotte in a dead voice, still not moving.

He could not quite hide his disappointment. "There's one I marked particularly . . ."

She did not respond. Aubrey tapped his brush impatiently.

"Well, I suppose I should leave you to your work." Neither of the two disagreed with him. He retreated, somewhat crestfallen. "Well, *au revoir*, then."

Charlotte started in her chair and looked after him, but he

had already closed the door. She glanced nervously at Aubrey, but he did not seem to act as if anything were amiss. She chided herself for her nerves. It was coincidence that William had chosen the same parting words as Lord Marwood. He could know nothing of her plans.

Georgiana's activities for the morning, meanwhile, had been curtailed by a somewhat startling request from her uncle. As much as she wished to finish extracting the fossil, she willingly agreed to help him by visiting her godmother instead. Privately she considered that she was an unlikely sort to repair anyone else's troubled love affairs, but she felt she must at least make the attempt. She had noticed Thomas' low spirits the previous night and felt genuinely sorry for him. It would be good to take her mind away from her own problems for part of the day, anyway.

She had found Lady Dowles in a state of preternatural calm. She greeted her goddaughter with the most unruffled air imaginable and proceeded to discuss trivialities as if nothing untoward had occurred during the past few days. Georgiana pursued her subject as delicately as possible, but found Lady Dowles evasive. She neatly sidestepped every question Georgiana asked, until the latter was forced to put it to her baldly.

"And all she would say, Uncle Thomas, was that she did not wish to marry again," Georgiana explained to him that afternoon.

Thomas heaved a despondent sigh. "Then I'm no better off than before. That's exactly what she told me." He gave his niece a bleak smile. "That's not to say that I'm not greatly obliged to you, Georgiana. I appreciate your trouble."

Georgiana shook her curls at him. "Wait, I have something more to tell you." When she saw she had his attention, she continued. "It seemed to me that Lady Dowles was acting almost too calm, as if she were trying to convince me—or herself—that nothing was wrong. Even when we were discussing the simple everyday things like the weather, I noticed that her mind would slip and she would speak without thinking. I told her that I thought it was a beautiful day and she agreed with me."

Thomas lifted an eyebrow. The day had dawned gray and cold and had gradually progressed to miserable, being marked by occasional but pelting rains.

Georgiana went on with her account. "I could see that she was playing a role then, which persuaded me that she does wish to marry you."

"How so?"

"The very fact that she deemed it important that even I should think she was indifferent to the matter shows how very much it means to her."

Thomas' brows contracted in a puzzled way. He turned to his brother as if asking for an explanation. Harry shook his head.

"Female logic. Takes one to understand it."

Georgiana looked at them seriously. "I'm sure I'm right. The rest of the time that I was there I kept searching for the reason that would keep her from marrying you."

"Well?"

She heaved a sigh. "I kept looking for a possible explanation. There is only one."

Irritated, Harry snorted, "Don't keep us on tenterhooks, girl. Out with it!"

She turned to Thomas with a sympathetic gaze. "Uncle, when you were there did she rise, or try to?"

Thomas' face reddened. "Blast! Are you talking about her physical condition?"

Georgiana let out her breath in relief. "Then, while you were there, she did explain—"

Thomas was apoplectic. "No, she didn't, nor did she stand, or walk, or anything like it. Do you mean that the agony she has put me through is simply because she was too proud to tell me about the blasted accident?"

It was Georgiana's turn to look surprised. "Then how did you know?"

Thomas had sprung to his feet and begun striding back and forth across the room to control the excesses of his rage. Still shaking with anger, he said, "Well, you didn't imagine that I would wish to be cut off from my brother, too? Harry and

I have had a regular correspondence from the beginning.''

Georgiana interrupted as the light slowly dawned. She turned to her father accusingly. ''You knew about Aubrey all the time, and yet you let us believe—''

''*I* said nothing,'' replied Harry pointedly. ''The purpose, I assumed, was to fool your stepmama, which it did.'' He shrugged.

Thomas wheeled suddenly as he came to a decision. ''Well, this can be remedied speedily, at any rate. I'll go to her this instant and tell her that she's put us through this misery for nothing because—''

Harry had leapt up and put a restraining hand on his brother's arm just as he was about to head out the door. ''Wait, Thomas,'' he said softly. ''I fancy Georgy has something more to say.''

She had risen to her feet, but now sank back into her chair as his brother led Thomas back to his. When they were all seated, she looked at her uncle sorrowfully.

''Father's right. You see, Uncle Thomas, I suspect that there isn't anything you could say that would change her mind. I think your awareness would make no difference to her.'' Georgiana shrugged helplessly. ''She is a very proud woman and she simply believes that you should not be saddled with a crippled wife.''

''Saddled with . . '' Thomas started to jump to his feet again, but when he saw the pity on his niece's face, he melted down into his chair. ''It's funny,'' he mused painfully, ''that's what she said to me, that nothing I could say would make her change her mind.''

He lifted his eyes to his niece's. ''Then what am I to do?'' he asked simply.

Georgiana shook her head as her eyes slowly filled. ''I don't know. Perhaps, given time, she would—''

''Time's what we have wasted so much of already,'' he said in flat despair.

Harry rose and put a comforting hand on his brother's shoulder. ''We shall contrive something, Thomas. Between you and my minx we'll formulate some plan.''

Georgiana sensed that her presence was superfluous and quietly exited the room, leaving Harry to offer his brother what comfort he could.

She felt drained and for a moment was at a loss as to what to do. The chiming of the clock reminded her that at least a portion of the day was left. If she hurried, she might have an hour or so to work on extracting the fossil.

She made her way upstairs quickly, intending to change into one of her older dresses. She had a hand on the door to her room when a sob stopped her. She looked about her. The noise was coming from the direction of Charlotte's room. She hesitated a moment. "You have dealt with enough problems today already," she told herself severely. A heartrending wail reached her ears. She sighed, turned, and crossed the hall to knock softly on Charlotte's door.

"Who is it?" The voice was tear-muffled.

"It's Georgy. May I come in?"

The reply was muted, but Georgiana took it for an assent and entered. She found Charlotte half-lying across her bed, surrounded by sodden handkerchiefs. She clutched what appeared to be some sort of book to her breast.

"Charlotte?"

She lifted tearstained eyes to meet her sister's. She tried to wipe her face with the driest of the handkerchiefs. "Hello, Georgy," she choked.

"Whatever is the matter?" Georgiana crossed the room swiftly to sit beside her sister. She stroked the golden curls.

Charlotte pushed herself up to a sitting position and blew her nose. "Nothing, really," she said in a quiet small voice.

"I'm afraid that is a taradiddle if I ever heard one," Georgiana said with a half-smile. "What is that you're holding?"

Sniffling, Charlotte extended the book. Georgiana read the title aloud, *"Scots Musical Museum."* She turned the pages slowly. "Why, this looks as if it's the sort of music book you would particularly enjoy," she said somewhat puzzledly. Her sharp eyes had not failed to notice the brown wrapping paper. "A gift from William?" she hazarded.

Still sniffling, Charlotte nodded. "That's not all," she told her sister tearfully. "He's marked one song especially," she said, reaching over to turn to it.

Georgiana read it through quickly. Privately, she thought that hardly anyone was less like a "red, red rose," than the fair Charlotte, but she supposed the sentiment was considered more

important than the accuracy of the description. The song
contained many pretty protestations of everlasting affection,
which she assumed was the main point of the thing. She closed
the book slowly.

"It looks as if he means to declare himself, then," she
remarked matter-of-factly. She laid the book down carefully,
then broke the mood by giving her sister a quick, enthusiastic
hug. "You goose! You shouldn't cry like that just because
you're happy."

"Happy?" Charlotte exclaimed with a sob. She fell into a
fresh fit of weeping. "Yes, I'm very happy."

Georgiana scolded her playfully. "What a bride you will make
if you cry like this before he even asks you."

Charlotte wiped her eyes. "It's just that it seems so odd that
he sent a Scottish . . . Why would he choose Burns?" she asked,
as if to herself.

Georgiana shook her head. Really, Charlotte was hopeless
sometimes. "He probably just divined that he was one of your
favorites," she contributed.

"What? Oh, yes," said Charlotte distractedly. "But look
here," she said abruptly, stabbing at the last verse, "what does
he mean by that?"

Georgiana could see that it said something about "fare thee
well," and coming back "Tho' it ware ten thousand mile," but
she could see nothing that should upset Charlotte so.

"I scarcely think he means it literally, my dear," she said.
"I doubt that he intends going anywhere. It's probably just that
the rest of the song fits his sentiments well."

Charlotte dabbed at her eyes again. "No, you're right. He
could not possibly intend . . ." She bit her lip but could not
quite restrain a moan.

Georgiana saw that there was something else troubling her
sister. "Is that what's worrying you?" she asked Charlotte
concernedly. She gave her sister a little hug. "You have always
fretted about the rest of us so much." She looked her sister in
the eye. "You know, my dear, we must all marry and move
away sometime. It's the nature of being female." She closed
the book with an emphatic thump. "And I'm sure that he did
not mean he wishes to emigrate. He is a London denizen if I've
ever seen one." She gave her sister a reassuring smile. "It's

so very close, after all. And think, as a married lady in London, how easy it will be for you to find suitable prospects for the rest of us."

"Oh, Georgy." The hug that accompanied these words was so fierce that it took Georgiana by surprise. Charlotte leaned back and wiped her eyes again. "I shall miss you."

Georgiana smiled at her again. "And I'll miss you, too. But as I said, we'll be very close. We'll see each other often."

"Yes, often." The words held no conviction.

Georgiana took her hands. "Come, now, you must smile at me. You can hardly expect William to declare himself to a female with a red nose and running eyes."

Making the supreme effort, Charlotte had managed a tremulous smile.

"That's better." Georgiana released her hands and rose. She heaved an almost imperceptible sigh. "It's almost time for dinner, so I'd best leave you so that we can both make ourselves presentable."

"Very well, Georgy." Charlotte bit her lip again as she watched her sister go. She must not cry anymore. How very nearly she had given the game away. But William . . . Her eyes filled again at the thought of him. How well he had expressed what was in her heart. But he could not know: it must be coincidence. She shook her head resolutely. She must dismiss him from her mind. She could not dwell on what might have been. After all, it was as much for his sake as anyone else's that she was taking this step.

15

Though she could not know it, Georgiana was quite correct in her assessment of the state of William's affections. He was aware that Charlotte gradually was becoming estranged from him, but all his attempts to confront her proved as ineffectual as before. He thought it more than likely that she had begun to despair of ever receiving a proposal from him and so he had hit upon the scheme of sending her the song as a subtle way of apprising her of his intentions. That plan had not elicited the desired response. She seemed to shy away from him even more at dinner that evening and excused herself as before with the plea of a sick headache.

William had taken enough. He had gone along with Aubrey and his madcap ideas long enough. Hadn't they effectively spiked Marwood's guns already? Wasn't Georgiana now available for Aubrey's courtship? He snorted in disgust. From the way Aubrey was acting at the moment, you'd think he was entirely indifferent to Georgiana, rather than an ardent suitor. Well, William had fulfilled his obligations to his cousin. These boyish pranks were all very fine, but certainly not worth costing him the woman he loved. The truth must out, and Aubrey would simply have to deal with it when it happened. He had no intention of confiding in his cousin, knowing how persuasive Aubrey could be. He was going to ask Charlotte for her hand and hang the consequences.

Accordingly, he rose unaccustomedly early the next morning and dressed with extreme care. Far from being nervous, he managed to tie his cravat in the difficult waterfall style on the very first attempt, eliciting an exclamation of admiration from his valet. He made his way downstairs and partook of a hearty breakfast, then retired to a corner to await the descent of his beloved.

The minutes ticked by and Charlotte did not appear. Georgiana made an early breakfast and bestowed several encouraging smiles on William before escaping to work on her fossils. Aubrey drifted into the room, a sour expression on his face. Harry had departed the house before Aubrey could catch him, thus delaying the completion of the portrait by another day. He ate rather morosely, only venturing to remark bitterly that William was quite a swell that morning. When his taunt met with no response, he meandered off into the parlor to put some finishing touches on the background of the painting.

William waited uncomplainingly as time rolled past. When at last the clock struck half-past-ten and she still had not appeared, he decided to investigate. Smith was dispatched to take it up with the maid, Betsey, from whom it was learned that Miss Charlotte was feeling extremely poorly today and would not be coming down for breakfast at any rate. Feeling bedeviled by fate, William changed into his driving clothes, feeling that his irritation might be relieved by a brisk workout of his grays. He wheeled away from Chalton at a smart pace, consoling himself with the reflection that at least this would be the last letter he had to post on Aubrey's behalf.

Aubrey, meanwhile, worked gloomily on the painting for the better part of the morning, sunk in his own unhappy thoughts. He was painting in fine detail the delicate tassels of fringe upon the curtain when his attention was suddenly claimed by a familiar voice calling his name.

"Cousin Aubrey. Cousin Aubrey, where are you? Cousin? My new book of fashion plates has arrived and I need to consult with you."

He winced as the unmelodious voice assailed his ears. There was a time when such an occupation might have afforded him some amusement; now it seemed an unendurable bore. Ungallantly, he dropped his brush and palette, streaked across the room, and dropped silently out of the open window. As he landed softly, he could hear his pursuer opening the door behind him.

"Cousin Aubrey, I need to ask you . . . Well!" The exclamation of surprise was followed by a few moments of silence as if it were taking the speaker some time to digest the fact that Aubrey was not present.

"Where could he be?" Letty resumed fretfully. "Wilkins said he was here. Hmph. Cousin Aubrey!" Her voice faded away as she exited the room.

Aubrey stood up, brushing the dirt from his jacket. He was startled by a low chuckle nearby. He spun around to see Thomas a few feet away, an amused expression on his face.

"That was quite a leap. Do you know, for all the times I've wished to avoid meeting certain ladies, I've never hit upon a method so direct as that."

Aubrey grinned at him as he finished freeing the last bits of grass and leaves from his clothing. "I know it looks rather bad," he said, "but somehow I just couldn't face being bored by . . ." A shadow passed across his features. He shrugged. "Not today at any rate."

Thomas looked at him keenly. "Crossed in love, are you?" He waved a hand to silence Aubrey's protests. "I know that look, lad. As a matter of fact, I find myself in the same situation."

Aubrey raised his eyebrows in astonishment.

Thomas gave him a bitter smile. "Yes, even such antiques as I are prey to Cupid's dart."

"Sir, I—"

"Oh, don't bother. I was young once, too. Do you care to join me? I thought I'd take a stroll about the grounds and see if anything became clearer to me."

Aubrey agreed immediately, thinking that outside at least he'd be safe from Letty's clutches. The two men walked in silence for several minutes. Thomas was the first to speak.

"Why a woman has to take such an idiotic notion into her head, I'll never know," he said ruminatively. "One thing for certain, there'll be no budging it, not if I know Nell."

Aubrey picked up quickly on the name. "Lady Dowles?"

Thomas nodded sadly. "Yes, stubborn as a . . . Well, she can be quite determined once she gets a notion into her head. But I don't mean to bore you with my troubles. It looks as if you've plenty of your own."

Despite this disclaimer, it took very little on Aubrey's part to get Thomas to unburden himself of his sad story. By the time Thomas was finished, Aubrey had to agree that things had come to a pretty pass.

"But there must be something you can do."

Thomas sighed. "Yes, that's what I keep telling myself." He shook his head as if to clear it. "But come, that's enough about me. So, tell me, did that young minx Georgy refuse your offer, then?"

Sunk in gloom, Aubrey replied, "No. I haven't asked her yet."

Astounded, Thomas stopped in his tracks. "You haven't asked her yet?"

"No, you see—"

"You're wearing that Friday face and you haven't asked her yet?"

"Well, she has been acting in a very remote manner, which seemed to indicate that she would not be amenable to—"

"Balderdash," exploded Thomas.

"Sir, her manner toward me has certainly changed over the past few—" began Aubrey stiffly.

"Young idiot! Haven't you been listening to what I told you? Life's too short to stand on points, as it were."

"I do not see the purpose in asking her when she has made it clear that—"

Thomas growled in exasperation. "What a thickheaded young fellow you are! Georgy is a female, isn't she? Well, then she might have a hundred reasons for being so contrary. Maybe she thinks you're in love with Charlotte. Maybe she's decided that *your* feelings have changed."

"Georgy is not that sort of girl," said Aubrey hotly. "She's not given to these whimsical starts, she—"

Thomas shook his head. "It's the nature of their sex. Take my Nell, for example. You know her. How does she impress you?"

Aubrey was rather taken aback. "Well—" he began tentatively.

Thomas chuckled aloud. "She's hardheaded, and I love her for it. A more practical, reasonable, shrewd, clear-thinking female you won't find. And yet, here she is making a martyr of herself for the most hen-witted reasons." He sighed in frustration. "I'll get 'round her yet," he said, half to himself.

His logic, such as it was, was beginning to make an impact

on Aubrey. "Do you really think it possible that Georgy could be playacting?"

Thomas snorted. "I have eyes in my head. I've seen how she looks at you. Besides, even if she hated you, you'd be no worse off than you are now. Hanging about like a . . . It depresses my spirits just to look at you."

Hope was beginning to gleam again in Aubrey's eyes. "Maybe I should—"

"If you take my advice you'll go, tell her you're a viscount, ask her, marry her, and be done with the thing." Thomas waved a hand in dismissal.

"I'll do it!" Aubrey turned awkwardly to Thomas. "I don't know how to thank you, sir."

"Be off with you, then. When you have things settled, maybe you and that niece of mine may bring your minds to bear on my problem. You've both a talent for devising schemes, it seems."

"Thank you." The words were scarcely out of Aubrey's mouth before he was in motion, traveling back to the house with long, eager strides. He intended to follow Thomas' advice to the letter, except that Georgiana would learn of his rank after she accepted him. He knew where he could find her. He ran whistling up the stairs to change into riding clothes.

As for Georgiana, all of her troubles were temporarily forgotten. After a day of patient, careful work, she had managed to finally free the fossil she had been seeking. Excitement rose within her as she examined it. It confirmed what she had been thinking. It was the find for which she had always hoped. Even Dr. Browne had found nothing to rival this. She looked up again at the space it had occupied. Yes, the strata in that area were different than any she had seen in the county. There could be no mistake. She hugged it to her, gathered her skirts, and set off for home, nearly bursting with the news. Lion, infected by the excitement, let out a series of hearty barks as he ran to catch up with her.

The afternoon shadows were beginning to lengthen as William came tooling his curricle up the drive to Chalton. The grays had been badly in need of exercise and the concentration and energy required to handle them had sapped him of his irritability. He was feeling quite chipper as he drove, having spent much of the return trip imagining the look of delighted astonishment on Charlotte's face when he informed her of their true identities. By tonight I shall be the most fortunate of men, he thought.

When he reached the house, he went inside with the intention of changing out of his dirt as soon as possible. A cheerful Aubrey saluted him as they passed in the hall. William did not take time to wonder at his cousin's exuberance; it all seemed a reflection of his own happy mood. He entered his chamber, throwing down his gloves and hat with unaccustomed carelessness.

His valet, Smith, rose to meet him with a troubled expression on his face.

"Hello, Smith. I'd like to have a bath before dinner, so—"

"Sir . . ." The valet's tone was respectful, but it brought William to an abrupt halt. It was most unlike Smith to interrupt him.

"I have a letter for you, sir."

William took it from the outstretched hand, noting for the first time the worried look on Smith's face.

"The young lady, Miss Charlotte, gave it to me the latter part of this morning, sir, with instructions to give it to you tomorrow. It struck me that there was something odd about the business, so . . ."

William glanced at the handwriting, which was indeed feminine. He opened the missive carelessly. "I'm sure that you did rightly, Smith. After all, there can be nothing that would matter—"

His words stopped abruptly as he saw the rather shaky, tear-stained writing.

> My Dearest William,
> By the time that you read this, I will be the wife of Lord Marwood. I have not taken this step lightly, nor is he forcing me into marriage against my will. I cannot tell you more than this now, except that as Lady Marwood I will be able to promise you and

your friend safety as I could not before. I hope that you will be able to understand and forgive me. Though I seem fickle, my heart was ever true.

> Yrs,
> Charlotte

William lowered the letter with a look of horror upon his face. "Good God, Smith, we must find her!"

Aubrey was preparing to mount Sligo when he saw a familiar figure scurrying up the drive. He handed the reins back to the groom and strode forward eagerly to meet her. "Georgy," he exclaimed delightedly.

"Aubrey," she gasped, out of breath, "wait until you see—"

"I was just coming to see you."

"Look at what I have to show you."

"I have to talk with you right away."

"I've finally done it after all this time."

They had reached a midpoint in front of the house, in their eagerness to communicate, neither hearing what the other was saying.

"I have to tell you that I want to—"

"Look at it. Do you see the teeth? That's how I first knew."

Rather impatiently, Aubrey caught one of her hands. "That's fine, but I'm trying to tell you—"

"You should have seen how nervous I was. The chisel almost slipped and—"

"Georgy! I have to talk to you."

They were interrupted by a shriek from the direction of the house. They turned and saw William in the doorway, waving a paper at them in an excitable manner. He rushed toward them, yelling out the news, "It's Charlotte—she's gone!"

Georgiana and Aubrey looked at him, nonplussed.

"She's run off," he said, remembering to lower his voice more discreetly when he reached them. "Smith and I checked and she's nowhere in the house. No one has seen her since this morning."

Georgiana was shaking her head. "She's probably on the grounds somewhere."

"No." He held out the letter to her. "I wasn't supposed to receive this until tomorrow."

She read it, her eyes widening in shock. She turned to Aubrey. "She's run off with Lord Marwood."

Aubrey snatched the letter from her hand and read it in a glance. "Our 'safety'—what does she mean by that?"

"I don't know," said William hopelessly. He caught sight of Sligo, standing bridled and saddled. His face hardened and he took a step forward. "I'll ride over there and teach him a lesson he'll—"

Aubrey caught his arm. "Wait, let us see if we can find out where they've gone first." Both he and William turned to Georgiana.

"Perhaps she's left me a note, too." Galvanized into action, she spun and fled into the house, both young men following her closely.

When they reached her room, they met with a disappointment. Despite a quick search, there was no note to be found. Georgiana shook her head as William felt under a chair cushion.

"If she had left me a note, I'm sure she would have set it in plain sight for me to find." She sat down on the edge of the bed, helplessly.

"Where else can we look?" asked Aubrey.

"I . . ." she was beginning when she saw Betsey walk by.

They questioned her closely, but to no avail. All she could tell them was that she hadn't seen Miss Charlotte since that morning, when Miss Charlotte had said she was feeling ill and did not wish to be disturbed today.

The three were beginning to feel more than a little desperate. William stated that he would ride over to Marwood House and shake the truth out of the servants.

"They might not know, old fellow," put in Aubrey gently. "And if he's taken her in another direction, you might be wasting valuable time."

"Well, what else do you suggest?" demanded William. "I will not sit here and do nothing."

Georgiana snapped her fingers as an idea came to her. "Of course," she said. "If Charlotte had left a letter here, I would

have found it today. The only place she could have left it would
be her room."

The three dashed over to Charlotte's room. The bed was
rumpled, as though she had spent a sleepless night, tossing and
turning upon her pillow. The letter sat upon the nightstand.
Georgiana seized it with an exclamation and tore it open.

The other two crowded around her eagerly to peer over her
shoulder as she scanned the missive. When she had finished,
she would have dropped it in disgust, but Aubrey took it out
of her hand and reread it.

"I can't make head nor tail of that," said Georgiana. "It's
all a jumble of nonsense. What's all that about our family's
safety? And why does she feel it necessary to forgive Father
and me? Who are the Society of Spencean Philanthropists
anyway?"

Aubrey finished perusing the letter and handed it to William
with a sigh. He addressed her last question first. "They are or
were a rather infamous radical group, bent on assassinating those
in power to set up their own government. One of their number
was executed two years ago when they attempted to assault the
Tower. It appears that Marwood managed to convince Charlotte
somehow that we were of their number." He turned to William
sorrowfully. "I'm sorry, William. I'm afraid we played right
into his hands with this masquerade."

"But I don't understand," said Georgiana irritably. "What
has that to do with anything?"

Aubrey sighed. "Well, reading between the lines, my dear,
I should say that Marwood apparently told her that the Bow
Street runners were after us and that the family might be
convicted of treason for hiding us. I suppose he told her that
with his influence he could protect your family."

Georgiana snorted. "But that's preposterous."

Aubrey shook his head. "Somehow he convinced her that
you and your father knew that we were radicals all along. I
daresay he found some way to make it sound plausible, after
all," he said, glancing at William as he spoke.

"How ridiculous. You have only to look at Father to know
he's a Tory."

William crumpled the letter into a ball and hurled it across the room. "You can sit here and discuss this until doomsday. We're no farther along than we were before." He glared at both of them. "I don't know how you can sit there when . . . when she . . ." He choked on the words. "Anyway, I do not intend to."

"Wait, William." Aubrey leapt after him to stop him, but both were halted by the small figure standing just outside the door.

"Augusta! What is it?" asked Georgiana.

"Is it Charlotte?" asked Augusta apprehensively.

Georgiana looked eloquently at the two young men before replying. "Yes, my dear. How did you guess?"

Augusta came forward hesitantly. "Well, I could hear you down the hall, for one thing. And for another . . . Well, I can't tell you, but I might know something of use."

"You'd better tell us," growled William, stepping toward her and causing her to shrink involuntarily toward Georgiana.

"What is it, Augusta?" asked her sister gently.

"I saw her meeting someone yesterday," said Augusta.

"Lord Marwood?"

Augusta smiled. "Thank you. I promised not to tell unless someone asked."

"Go on," Willliam said impatiently.

"Well, I saw them yesterday morning in the arbor. He saw me before I was able to hear too much, but I did catch a few words."

"What did he say?" Georgiana asked.

Augusta frowned with concentration. "He said something about not having the time to get a special license, and then he said something more about meeting her at the end of our drive at eleven."

"Did he say anything else, dear?" asked Georgiana despairingly.

"There was just one thing," Augusta said haltingly. "I didn't really understand it."

"Can you remember it now?"

"I think so. He said something about . . . that you're just as married when you're married over an anvil as you are in church. Does that make any sense?"

"It's Gretna Green," Aubrey said.

Georgiana's face turned white. "But that's three days away. She'll be ruined before . . ."

"I'm off, then," said William, heading for the door.

Aubrey hurried after him. "Take Sligo, he's ready," he said. "I'll follow you in the curricle."

"Very well," William said curtly. He disappeared into his room to get his gloves and hat. As a precaution, he slipped a pistol into his coat before heading downstairs.

Georgiana had come trailing after Aubrey. He explained their plans briefly. "I'm coming, too. Just let me get my bonnet and my pelisse."

Aubrey held her at arm's length. "You mustn't," he told her. "We don't know what the fellow will do."

"I have to go," she said simply. "She is my sister and she will need me when it is all over."

Aubrey started to argue with her, but the slow steady look she gave him made him hold his tongue. He sighed. "Very well," he said. "It won't be a picnic, though. Lord only knows how far they've gotten by now. Go get your things. I'm going to try to find your father, to explain matters to him."

When Georgiana appeared downstairs a few minutes later, she saw that Aubrey was attired appropriately for the drive and that he had found her father in the library. He had apparently just finished explaining matters to them.

"So you see, sir, since I am greatly responsible, I feel that I must be the one to go. You shall have a great deal to do to keep this matter from the rest of the family and the servants."

"Especially Letty," Harry said under his breath. He saw his daughter dressed for travel. "And what of Georgy, then?"

"I am going, Father," she said firmly. "This mess is at least partly my fault."

Aubrey looked at Harry apologetically. "I'm afraid she is determined, sir. But I do think she is right. Charlotte will be glad of the company on the way home."

"But what of the—"

No one noticed the gleam that had leapt suddenly to Thomas' eyes. "I'll take care of it, Harry," he said. "I'll be along with an appropriate chaperone as soon as they can hitch up the coach.''

"That reminds me, we'll need to borrow a team, sir," said Aubrey. "I'm afraid William's grays aren't fresh.''

"What chaperone?" Harry asked suspiciously.

"Will Nell do?" Thomas asked. He winked at his brother. "Don't worry. Everything will be taken care of.''

Aubrey coughed politely. Harry turned back to him. "Take whatever blasted horses you want," he said irascibly. "I don't like all this, though.''

Thomas gave Aubrey a knowing look. "Don't worry. I'll explain it all to him.''

Although it seemed like hours later, it was actually only fifteen minutes or so before Georgiana and Aubrey went racing away in the curricle. Like Charlotte, she had never ridden in a sporting vehicle before, and the openness and speed of it made her a bit nervous. Still, she did not complain, but merely gripped the seat tightly as the vehicle swayed alarmingly when Aubrey bowled through a corner. She absentmindedly noticed that he was a dab hand with the ribbons, though it did not occur to her to wonder how a drawing master would be so expert at driving blood cattle.

She was to be grateful for his expertise, because the day soon gave way to darkness, aided by a rapidly growing fog.

Aubrey continued on at speed as long as he could, but at length was forced to check the horses. "Blast," he said. "I hope William is faring better with Sligo.''

William indeed was doing his best to cover ground in a hurry, pushing the big horse as much as he dared. Although he had passed a few shabby-looking inns, he had not stopped to make inquiries, reasoning that Lord Marwood himself was not likely to stop before nightfall. He scarcely noticed the first few tendrils of fog beginning to creep over the road, concentrating on his objective instead. If only he could get there in time! He urged Sligo into an even harder gallop.

* * *

Ignorant of all the excitement, Lady Dowles sat quietly picking at a light supper.

Her old butler glanced at her plate and addressed her reprovingly. "You must eat, my lady."

Lady Dowles put her fork down wearily. "I know. I just don't seem to be hungry tonight." Her attention was attracted by a sudden commotion. As she looked up, the door at the end of the room was flung open and Thomas burst into the room.

"I'm sorry, Nell." He reached her side with two or three long strides and held out a hand commandingly. "Help us, Nell."

She stared at him in puzzlement. "Thomas, what is it?"

"It's Georgy," he said quietly, and glanced meaningfully at the butler.

She dismissed the old retainer and turned to Thomas fearfully. "Is she hurt?"

He shook his head. "No, it's a runaway match—not Georgy, the other chit and Lord Marwood, but Georgy's gone with the drawing master to find her. If you don't come with me, Nell, both their reputations could be ruined."

Laying aside her napkin, she gripped the table tightly and rose to her feet. "What about their stepmother?"

He grimaced. "She doesn't know. We thought it best."

It took only a moment for her to see the good sense of what he was saying. "I understand," she said quietly, and rang the bell beside her. A footman appeared almost instantly. "Ask Molly to bring my bonnet and cloak," she ordered. She turned her attention back to Thomas. "How long have they been gone?"

"Georgy and the drawing master, about an hour. The other chit left sometime in the morning."

"Do we have any hope of catching them?"

His face was grim. "The other boy rode on ahead, so I should think . . ." He stopped speaking as her maid entered the room and draped the cloak carefully across her mistress's shoulders. The maid's own cloak was tucked under her arm. Thomas saw it and frowned. Lady Dowles, catching his expression, followed his gaze.

"The fewer that know, the better," he said in his low voice.

"Molly, I will not require your services tonight," said Lady Dowles.

The surprised maidservant would have protested were it not for the stubborn set of her mistress's jaw. "Yes, milady," she sighed.

Thomas, who had not missed their exchange, gave the girl an engaging half-smile. "Don't worry, Molly. She is in good hands."

Eleanor had just put her bonnet on her head and was beginning to tie it when Thomas swept her off her feet. She gasped in surprise. "Thomas!"

He held her with great strength and great delicacy as he headed for the door. "I know of your injury, my love," he said bluntly. "It's best if there's no pretense between us."

She had to fight to resist the temptation to bury her face in that broad shoulder. She knew she must keep a clear head for tonight's work. Instead, she held her head proudly erect as he lifted her gently into the traveling chariot, trying not to notice that he handled her as if she were made of porcelain. He gave the coachman his directions and crowded in beside her, seeming to fill the carriage with his presence.

"I'm afraid we may be in for a rough ride, my dear," he said.

"It doesn't matter," she said simply.

When they had set off, she found that Thomas had not been exaggerating. Despite the fact that this was one of the most luxurious and modern conveyances she had ever ridden in, the rate at which they traveled made the ride most uncomfortable. She found herself bobbing painfully among the velvet squabs and was glad when Thomas put his arm about her, steadying her. She couldn't help clinging to him for support as they rocketed onward.

"Are you all right?" he asked quietly.

"I shall do," she said with a determined nod of the head. "You should be thankful that I am not subject to motion sickness."

He gave a low chuckle and pressed her to him a little more

tightly. "Ah, you always were susceptible to very few frailties, Nell."

How odd it was, she thought. She could almost have sworn that he was enjoying himself.

16

William was becoming more desperate as he rode. It had been miles since he passed the last inn, and he wondered if he'd been right not to stop. At the rate of speed he was traveling he should have overtaken them if they had halted for the night. It was possible, of course, that Marwood meant to continue on, but William thought it unlikely. For one thing, he'd need a change of horses and none of the establishments William had seen seemed likely to provide them. Well, he had no choice but to push on now. If he continued on without encountering anything, he could always turn back.

Reluctantly admitting the necessity for it, William had breathed the horse a few miles back. It had proven a wise move, for Sligo was maintaining his pace well, hardly showing the strain of the passing miles. Still, it had meant several precious minutes lost, and William was aware that every moment could make a difference. He urged the horse on heedlessly, ignoring the fog, which had become thick. He was leaning over Sligo's neck, trying to make out the road ahead as best he could when Sligo suddenly stumbled, tripped, and pulled up short, sending William flying over his head.

The shock of the landing knocked the wind out of him and he lay gasping for a minute, trying to breathe. When he regained that power, he rose and walked over to the blowing horse. He grabbed the trailing reins and the horse hobbled over to him. Sligo was favoring his right front leg. William leaned over and ran an experienced hand down its length. Sligo gave a whicker of distress.

"A strained fetlock," William muttered. "Must have hit a hole somewhere back on the road. Blast!"

Sligo tugged at the reins at the angry exclamation.

William gave him a reassuring pat on the nose. "Not your fault, old fellow. I guess we'll have to walk it for now. Hope we haven't far to go."

He set off blindly along the road, leading the limping horse behind him.

Some distance back, Georgiana was trying to control her impatience. She twisted a handkerchief nervously in her hands.

"I wish we could go faster," she murmured aloud.

"We can't," Aubrey said curtly, "not unless you want to see us ditched."

She sighed and tried to keep her mind from imagining Charlotte in various horrible predicaments. Her thoughts turned to the man beside her. She glanced at his hands. So sensitive and gentle, and yet so strong right now as he held back the restless horses. If he had not been here . . . She shuddered to think about it.

"Aubrey," she said timidly, "thank you for helping us."

A sound like a sigh escaped him. "I'm at least partly to blame for all this."

"Still," she said, "I don't know what I would have done without you. Mother would have been in hysterics. Father would have had his hands full taking care of her. I could hardly ride off on my own."

Perhaps it was the darkness or the fog that swirled about them. Perhaps it was the desperateness of their situation or the fact that he had to concentrate almost entirely upon his driving. Whatever it was, Aubrey suddenly said quite calmly, "I love you, Georgy, don't you know?"

She could hardly believe she was hearing the words. It was with a sense of detachment that she heard herself reply, "I love you too, Aubrey."

How odd it was. She should either be ecstatically happy over his declaration or profoundly worried over the prospect of marriage to a drawing master. Her thoughts remained instead on the present calamity, though she was conscious of a warm feeling that had spread over her and that was impervious to the chill and damp. No more words passed between them. None were needed.

*   *   *

In their carriage, Eleanor tried to conceal her relief when the fog caused their carriage to slow. Despite Thomas' support, the jouncing had proved most painful to her injured limbs.

"Blast," she said in an unladylike manner. "I hope we don't lose them."

Thomas hid a smile as he observed this stoic front. "I shouldn't think we would," he replied. "Lord Herne seemed almost certain that Marwood would stop for the night."

Her eyes widened as she took in his words. "Lord Herne—so you know, too."

His abrupt bark of laughter surprised her. "I should have known he couldn't bubble you, Nell. No, I haven't any offspring—that I know of at least," he added wickedly.

She sniffed. "The most ridiculous story. Imagine a viscount pretending to be a drawing master."

Thomas smiled to himself. "Well, your goddaughter has rather a vivid imagination, it seems—as does the viscount."

Plodding along in the darkness, William was left to curse his own stupidity. If he had only slowed Sligo when the fog became so treacherous, he might be reaching Charlotte by now. He was so sunk in gloom that he scarcely noticed a light shining through the mist. At length it was borne in upon him that this must be some sort of dwelling. His heart lightened at the realization.

"Come on, Sligo. Maybe I can get a fresh mount there."

Some fifteen minutes later, Aubrey and Georgiana found themselves tooling along the same stretch of road. She peered about them fruitlessly.

"Do you think they would have come this far?" she asked Aubrey.

"I don't know. I hoped we might have met William by now, or that he would have sent us word. I think we should stop at the next inn we see to make inquiries at any rate."

Georgiana was the first to spot the light. "There's something up ahead."

As they approached, they could see that it was a good-sized, prosperous-looking inn. The ostler was leading a limping horse into the stables. They could hear the chatter of voices as they neared it.

"We'll stop here," Aubrey decided, slowing the horses. They pulled up in front of the inn, leaving the team in the hands of the ostler, and Aubrey helped Georgiana alight from the curricle. He escorted her inside.

The innkeeper's wife greeted them. "I'm sorry, sir, but we're full tonight." Her cordial look changed to suspicion as she saw that Aubrey and Georgiana were alone.

"We are not staying," Aubrey assured her, "although if you could manage it, we might like a bite to eat."

"Yes, sir. I have a game pie or a nice leg of mutton if you'd care—"

Aubrey interrupted her, slipping her a guinea. "We are looking for information also. Have you happened to see a young girl, very fair, traveling with an older man, tall, dark—"

The innkeeper, hearing this exchange, had come to investigate. "Aye, they're here. It's queer, young sir, for you're not the first one to come asking for—"

A shot and a scream rang out from upstairs. Georgiana paled.

"Murther!" screamed a rather tipsy plump lady in the public room, fainting unceremoniously upon her disreputable-looking companion.

Aubrey was already running up the stairs two at a time. "William," he called.

Gathering her skirts and wits, Georgiana dashed after him.

"Here I am," William said quietly, stepping from an open doorway, the pistol still smoking in his hand.

"William, you didn't," said Aubrey desperately, grabbing him by the arm.

Georgiana was around him and into the room in a second. A scene of horror confronted her.

They had evidently been interrupted in the middle of dinner, for a half-eaten meal rested upon the table. Charlotte lay insensible in a heap upon the floor. Marwood had fallen in a corner, pale as death, with blood streaming across his chest.

"Good heavens," gasped Georgiana. "You *have* murdered him!"

For the first time in her life, she felt that she was about to faint. She caught herself, leaning on the door frame for support.

Aubrey had crossed the room in a few strides to examine Marwood, catching him by the wrist to feel for a pulse.

"Nothing of the sort," said William rather crossly. "Not that he didn't deserve it." He looked menacingly over at his fallen enemy.

"He's alive," Aubrey said with some relief. "You winged him in the shoulder."

"Told you so," growled William.

Aubrey stripped off his cravat hastily to form a pad, pressing it into the wound to stanch the flow of blood. "Here, give me yours," he ordered William.

William laid down his pistol on the table and complied reluctantly. "There you are," he said begrudingly, handing it to Aubrey. "Fellow's lucky I didn't kill him."

"Tear up one of those sheets, will you?" commanded Aubrey. "I'll need to fashion some sort of tourniquet."

Georgiana, meanwhile, was ministering to the unconscious Charlotte. She chafed her sister's hands helplessly. "Oh, dear," she said. "I wish I had thought to bring my vinaigrette."

The innkeeper also had appeared in the doorway. "What's to do, then, sir?" he said, addressing himself to Aubrey.

"Spoken like a sensible chap. The gentleman here was somewhat injured, though not fatally, by an accidental discharge of my friend's pistol. We shall need a surgeon in to remove the ball."

"I'll send one of my lads straightaway." He pushed aside his wife, who was staring curiously at the group in the room. Shutting the door behind him, he called downstairs, " 'Twas an accident, that's all, ladies and gentlemen. Please to calm yourselves."

"It was no accident," William said in a vicious whisper.

"Quiet," Aubrey replied. "Do you wish them to know?"

Marwood's eyes slowly opened. He took in the sight of Aubrey with some confusion. "Herne," he said painfully. "Thought it was your cousin trying to murder me . . . missed . . . pity . . ." He winced with a fresh pain.

"Quiet," said Aubrey again. "If he'd wished to murder you, he might have done so easily. He's been known to hit the wafer nineteen times out of twenty at Manton's."

"Congratulations," Marwood said at his most sardonic. He yelped as Aubrey tightened his makeshift bandage. "Have a care."

"I'm saving your life," said Aubrey cheerfully as he tightened the bandage another notch, producing another groan of pain. "No, you needn't thank me now, although it is much more than you deserve. Of course, if you have harmed one hair on that girl's head, your life is forfeit."

As if on cue, Charlotte gave a low moan.

"I think she may be coming around," said Georgiana concernedly.

Marwood looked at the recumbent figure bitterly. "Didn't touch the girl . . . most uncooperative . . . threatened hysterics . . ." He looked accusingly at William. "Was trying to calm her when your cousin stepped in and shot me."

"All I could see was Charlotte trying to push him away," William said defensively. "She seemed to be repulsing his advances."

"He's as bad as she is," said Marwood, regarding William through baleful eyes. "Would I want a row in a public inn? Thought the gel might be willing—I meant to marry her, after all."

William had stepped forward, his fists clenched menacingly.

Aubrey gave him a distracted glance. "William, perhaps it's best if you see to Charlotte. It might be that the innkeeper has a private parlor to which you can take her."

"William . . ." Charlotte's soft cry could not have been better-timed. He abandoned his enemy immediately to cross over to her. "My dear, it's all over now."

"Oh, William." Her eyes were full of tears and questions.

"It was a pack of lies he told you. I'll explain it to you presently."

She made no resistance, but clung to him in a becomingly feminine way as he lifted her and carried her out of the room.

Marwood watched them go with a cynical expression on his face. "Every bit as bad as she is. Do you know the silly chit actually accused me of drugging her wine—as if I ever needed to resort to such measures? Reads too many novels, I should say."

"That worked to your advantage," Aubrey reminded him,

"when you concocted that fable about our being members of the radical group."

Marwood had to smile at his own ingenuity. "So, found that out, did you?" He gave a sardonic laugh. "Couldn't have made anyone else believe the tale, but she . . ." He looked Aubrey in the eye. "You helped a great deal with your little masquerade. Even she could see that you weren't a drawing master."

Georgiana's eyes widened as he spoke, but Aubrey's attention was focused on Marwood.

"You told her I was a member of the radical group."

Marwood sneered at him. "A member! I gave you a higher honor. I said that you were the leader of the group, wanted for treason. Your cousin was just an amiable young man that you'd led astray."

"So you threatened to expose us if she didn't marry you."

Marwood lifted his eyebrows slightly. "Threatened? Oh, no. I didn't wish for an unwilling bride. No, I told her that I had just learned that the runners were hot on your trail and that you'd be captured within days, implicating the family that hid you as well." He noticed Georgiana for the first time. "Said it was obvious that the sister was sheltering you, lying for you, with her father's consent. Said she spurned the protection of my name—"

"Which she could only have if she married you," said Aubrey slowly.

Marwood's face twisted into a grimace. "Meant to take care of you as well. Told her that I could have you and your cousin sent abroad."

"Blackguard!"

"No wonder that song upset her so," Georgiana said thoughtfully. Her words went unnoticed by her auditors.

Marwood's thoughts had turned inward. "All I needed was the marriage. Came so close to—" He looked up at Aubrey suddenly. "How did you find us?"

Aubrey did his best to repress his anger, rising and crossing over to the washbasin to dampen a rag in water and hand it to Marwood.

"Well, there won't be any marriage now. No self-respecting lady will have you, we'll see to that."

"Needn't bother." For the first time, Marwood looked

defeated rather than defiant. "The word was out in London—had to find a bride in the country before the bailiffs caught up with me."

"Gambling debts?" Aubrey asked.

Marwood nodded. "The estate was already encumbered when I inherited it. All we Marwoods have a passion for gambling," he added with a trace of perverse pride.

"But you might have married an heiress in London," suggested Aubrey.

Marwood shook his head. "No bran-faced cit as a bride for me," he said. "I always did have taste in women. Besides, even the most ambitious mamas shunned me when word leaked out about my debts and—" He glanced at Georgiana and amended his words quickly. "I was too dearly priced for a bridegroom."

She stared at him. "But then our fortunes would not have sufficed," she said, entering the conversation for the first time.

"It would have been enough to hold the creditors at bay for a time, at least," he said indifferently.

There was silence for several minutes. In an act of humanity, Aubrey walked over to the table to pour the defeated man a glass of wine. He handed it to Marwood, who accepted it without thanks.

"What do you intend to do, then?" Aubrey asked him quietly.

Marwood stared straight ahead with lifeless eyes. "I don't know. Go to Calais, I suppose . . . if I can raise the blunt. Brummell's over there now, and Byron's abroad as well."

Downstairs, the innkeeper, who was becoming rather inured to all the excitement by now, hardly blinked when a tall, broad man entered, a middle-aged lady draped over his arms. He apparently recognized that the innkeeper was a person in authority, for he stepped up to him and asked, "We're looking for a young girl and—"

The innkeeper silently jerked his thumb in the direction of a half-open door.

"Thank you," said Thomas, and carrying his burden, proceeded into the room indicated. He and Eleanor halted on the threshold, startled by the sight that confronted them. It was a very pretty picture. William was down on one knee in front of Charlotte, clasping her hands in his. The two sets of fair curls were almost touching. There was no mistaking the rapt expressions on their faces.

"Harump," Thomas cleared his throat loudly, crossed the room, and deposited Eleanor gently in an armchair. The lovers looked up guiltily.

"It looks as if we arrived here not a moment too soon," Thomas told Eleanor dryly.

"Sir," William sprang to his feet. "Your niece has just consented to make me the happiest of men."

"Hm," said Thomas, cocking an eyebrow at them. "It would appear that everyone has escaped this night's escapade unharmed."

Charlotte blushed.

William dropped his eyes. "Well, I did shoot Marwood," he admitted with endearing honesty, "but Aubrey says that he'll recover."

Eleanor could not repress a gasp, but Thomas took the news in stride. "And where would they be?" he asked quietly.

"Upstairs—with Georgy."

Thomas waggled an eyebrow at Eleanor. "I'll leave you to chaperone these two," he said. He saw the anxiety in her eyes and winked. "Don't worry," he added. "We shall make everything right."

He was halfway up the stairs when he met Aubrey and Georgiana coming down. They were both disheveled from all the activity, and Aubrey's clothing was stained liberally with Marwood's blood.

"A pretty night's work," Thomas observed. He glanced over their shoulders meaningfully. "And Marwood?"

"It was a superficial wound," Aubrey told him as they met and continued down the stairs. "He was hit in the shoulder."

"Just as you were," said Georgy, much struck by the thought.

"The doctor is with him now. He says he should be up and about in a few days."

Thomas quirked an eyebrow at him as they rejoined the others in the parlor.

Aubrey understood his unspoken question. "He won't present a problem to us anymore," he said quietly.

Georgiana flew to Eleanor's side. "Godmama," she said.

Eleanor stroked her hair reassuringly. "So you are safe and well also." She leaned over to kiss Georgiana on the forehead before looking up at Thomas. "Well, if this adventure is over, I suppose we should return home now."

Thomas returned her look with a suspicious twinkle in his eye. "There is just one small matter," he said. He leaned over and lifted her out of the chair. "You see, I'm abducting you."

"You're what?" Eleanor's jaw dropped open in shock. The others looked on in stupefaction.

"Lord Marwood's plan inspired me. I'm abducting you," Thomas explained patiently.

"You're doing no such thing," she said resolutely, wriggling in his arms.

He tightened his hold on her. "I'm afraid that I am," he said apologetically. "You needn't worry. I intend to make an honest woman of you as soon as we've crossed the border."

The blood surged to Eleanor's face. "Georgy," she commanded, "help me."

"Godmama," Georgiana began hesitantly.

"I warn you, I'm a desperate fellow," Thomas advised her.

"Godmama, I think he's right," said Georgiana.

"What!" Eleanor could hardly believe her ears. She began to beat on the broad chest with her fists in an undignified manner. "Release me at once!"

"You wouldn't wish to cause a scene in a public inn," suggested Thomas.

"Oh, wouldn't I?" she asked, goaded. She raised her voice. "Help! Help me, please!"

The innkeeper appeared in the doorway. "Is something the matter?"

"Georgy, take my purse here and hand that honest fellow a couple of guineas, good girl," said Thomas. He winked at the innkeeper. "A little too much wine—you know how it is."

"How dare you?" said Eleanor.

The innkeeper bowed respectfully. "Yes, sir." He hesitated on the threshold for a secondd. "Sir, if you could see your way clear to continuing on your journey, I'd be much obliged. My regular patrons, well, they aren't used to this much excitement.''

Thomas nodded gravely. "An excellent suggestion. I will act upon it immediately."

As the innkeeper left, Eleanor's face crumpled. "Thomas," she said brokenly, "don't you even care what I wish?"

He looked at her with great tenderness. "More than anything else in the world, my love," he said softly. "I think you wish to marry me, and abducting you was the only way I could see to accomplish it."

She buried her face in his shoulder. "Thomas, you can't marry me."

"I fear that you have no choice, my love. I've already compromised you. All the time we spent together in a closed carriage . . ."

She looked up at him, her face softening. "Must you always talk such nonsense?"

"As a gentleman, I should feel myself honor-bound to do the right thing, and there's no doubt that after three days and nights on the road that you'll—"

"All right," said Eleanor, almost inaudibly.

"What?"

"I said all right. You win."

There was a sudden vulnerability in his expression. "My darling, you know I love you more than life and that all I desire is your happiness. My love, do you wish to marry me?"

She smiled up at him, her eyes brimming over with tears. "You great idiot," she said affectionately, "I've never wanted anything more."

Their lips met in the moment that for so long had been postponed. The sweetness of it quite made Eleanor forget herself. When at last she remembered where she was, she looked around with a gasp. "Thomas!"

He smiled at her and set her down gently in a chair. "They left at the beginning of our discussion, my love, though I suppose you didn't notice. Showed an excellent sense of tact on their parts, I thought."

Eleanor put her hands to her pinkened face. "But we are supposed to be chaperoning them."

Thomas looked at her with a roguish expression. "I don't think either of them will be needing us to chaperone them. Wedding bells all around, I should say."

"Well," said Eleanor, "that settles that."

He looked at her questioningly.

"You will have to give up this Scotland nonsense—as if I wished to elope without so much as a bandbox! No, I do not intend to miss any of the excitement." She saw the dubious expression upon his face and added hastily, "Nor do I mean to be cheated out of a proper wedding myself. Blacksmiths indeed!"

He could not quite hide his relief. He leaned over to pick her up again. "Just when I thought to have a bit of rest," he grumbled. "Where to, my lady?"

"To find the children outside, of course."

The glow of happiness upon their faces left no doubt in the others' minds that things had been brought to a satisfactory conclusion. They crowded around Thomas and Eleanor to congratulate them.

"We thank you," Thomas said, "but I am afraid that these ancient arms of mine cannot hold out much longer. Who means to ride with us in my carriage?"

"William and Charlotte may," put in Aubrey, a little too eagerly. "Georgy and I will bring the curricle back."

Eleanor privately thought that the more correct arrangement would be for the two young ladies to accompany them, but at a speaking look from Thomas, she held her tongue. William was holding on to Charlotte's hand so tightly in any case that Eleanor feared it would be impossible to separate them.

They all made their adieus and set off immediately, Eleanor wisely pointing out that the hour had grown late. Although the fog had melted off, Aubrey showed no desire to urge his horses, and instead he and Georgiana rambled homeward at a comfortable pace.

She found that after the excitement of the evening she was exhausted. Somehow it seemed only natural to lay her head on

Aubrey's shoulder as he drove. The tired horses presented no real challenge to him now. The events of the evening swirled through her mind. They seemed unreal, rather as if she had been to see a play. She gave a little yawn.

"Aubrey?"

"Yes?"

"It's funny. I hated him so much, but I just feel sorry for him now."

"Nothing could excuse what he did, but I felt pity for him, too."

"I know," she said, yawning again. "I saw you slip your purse into his jacket when he was busy with the doctor."

"Oh."

They drove in silence for a few minutes.

"Aubrey?"

"Yes?"

"What was the name he called you? And why did he think that William was your cousin?"

Aubrey let out a great sigh. "That's something I've been meaning to tell you, but first I must ask you, Georgy, will you marry me?"

"Of course." It must have been the fatigue, but it suddenly seemed odd that he even should have to ask. "But what was he talking about?"

"Well, you see, I gave you my real name, but I omitted my title. I'm actually Viscount Herne, and William *is* my cousin."

"Oh," she said, her tired brain digesting this with some difficulty. "So Charlotte was right, after all. Why didn't you tell me?"

"It amused me to be taken for a drawing master at first. Then, forgive me, when I came to know your mother and how she felt about titles—"

"You thought she'd thrust us together."

"I thought we should have the opportunity to make up our own minds," he said simply.

She yawned once more. "Well, that's a great relief. I wasn't at all sure that I would have liked living on a drawing master's

salary." She gave one more great yawn. "Remind me in the
morning," she said sleepily, "to ask you about Cressida . . ."

He glanced down at her quickly, but she was already
unconscious. He gave the reins a little shake and clucked to the
horses encouragingly.

17

With all that they had been through, it was not too surprising that most of the participants in the evening's events slept through the next morning and into the first part of the afternoon. It was also only to be expected that the first concern of each upon rising was to seek out his or her beloved immediately. Georgiana and Aubrey met in the dining room, where she persuaded a grumbling cook to serve them a light luncheon. Georgiana was glowing with happiness, and to Aubrey's eyes she had never appeared more lovely.

They exchanged the usual commonplaces, which suddenly seemed to have taken on new meaning. She was the first to bring up the more serious topic.

"I suppose we'll have to tell Mother and Father first of all," she said, the words bringing a becoming blush to her cheeks.

"I think your father may already have a fair idea," said Aubrey, "if Thomas did his job properly. It is rather a shame, isn't it, though," he added idly, "to fulfill all your mother's greatest ambitions at one snap like that."

"I know," she agreed, "but there's no help for it, I guess. We'd have to—" She looked up suddenly, her eyes sparkling with mischief as they met his. "We could . . ." she said.

"For just a little while . . ." Aubrey added, his eyes beginning to dance, also.

They were interrupted at that juncture by Letitia herself. She entered the room and stopped, glaring at them with disapproval. She sniffed. "And just what were you up to last night, I should like to know? Your father thought to put me off with some story about an outing, but the servants told me that you did not return until the wee hours of the morning. They also told me that the two of you returned in a carriage alone." She looked at them as if daring them to deny it.

Aubrey rose gracefully. "All you say is quite true, Cousin Letitia, but I wish to let you know that I mean to make things right. I am going to marry Georgy."

"*Marry* her," exclaimed Letitia in dismay.

"Yes, isn't it wonderful, Mother?" gushed Georgiana.

The enormity of the disaster that was facing her almost overwhelmed Letty. She rallied, though, and launched into her objection.

"It isn't that I'm not fond of you, Cousin Aubrey," she said, "but I hardly think that Mr. Chalford would countenance his daughter's marrying a mere drawing master."

"But, as you pointed out, since I have compromised her, the only thing for me to do is to marry her," Aubrey said ingenuously.

"Now I didn't say that—"

Aubrey took Georgiana's hand affectionately. "It's only natural for you to be concerned, but you needn't worry about Georgy. Why, I'm sure that my mother will look upon her as her own child."

"Your mother," gasped Letitia as she began to change to a purplish hue.

Aubrey looked at her innocently. "Yes, why, hadn't I mentioned to you that she lives with me?"

Letty did not have the opportunity to reply to this shocking piece of news, for Charlotte and William came barreling into the room, hand in hand.

"Aubrey, it's your mama. We saw her carriage coming up the drive," William gasped.

"Blast! Is it really?" replied Aubrey.

"Oh, Aubrey, your mama. Perhaps I should go change my dress," cried Georgiana.

"She will love you just as you are, my darling," replied Aubrey reassuringly, though his words did little to soothe the nervous Georgiana.

Letitia had recovered sufficiently to make her feelings known. "That opera dancer—in my house! I think I have been more than forebearing, but surely I can not be expected to receive that sort of woman here." She turned to Aubrey, whose eyes were twinkling with amusement. "And I shall tell her so to her face, if need be!"

"I'd pay a great deal to see that," muttered Aubrey under his breath to Georgiana.

Attracted by the raised voices, Thomas entered the room nonchalantly.

It took Letty only a second to round on this new enemy. "Well, I hope you're satisfied."

He lifted his eyebrows questioningly at her.

"Your wife, the opera dancer, is at our door waiting to be received, and after I've striven all my life to keep my children from being exposed to that element—"

Thomas interrupted her politely. "My dear sister, you are laboring under a misapprehension."

"Not only that, but your son wants to marry Georgiana," riposted Letitia.

"Quite sensible of him. Don't blame him a bit. But you are mistaken as to—"

Letty put a handkerchief to her forehead dramatically. "Has no one any concern for my feelings? I don't think that my nerves can take the strain of this."

"You see," continued Thomas, his eyes sparkling wickedly, "I've never been married."

The butler entered just as Letty gave a shriek that shook the rafters. She looked at him desperately. "Wilkins, you must prevent—"

He was already announcing the visitor. "The Right Honorable the Viscountess Herne," Wilkins said formally.

"Mama," exclaimed Aubrey.

Letty gave a final scream and fainted into her brother-in-law's arms.

Georgiana, who had been expecting an aging dragon, was surprised by the petite, youthful, and decidedly beautiful viscountess. Appearances were somewhat deceiving, though, for the little woman managed to freeze the entire company in their tracks with a single look.

"Well, Aubrey," she said, addressing her son first, "what sort of imbroglio have you involved yourself in now?" Without pausing, she turned the attack to William. "Whatever it is, I hold you in great measure responsible, William. You promised to inform me of his whereabouts as soon as you found him. Did you really imagine that you could deceive me with those silly letters? Why, I might have worried myself half to death if I'd believed them.'' She regarded the two culprits sternly. "It is clear that you have been indulging in your usual pranks. I may say that I do not take kindly to being—"

The unconscious Letitia, still in Thomas' arms, let out a low moan.

"It may be none of my business," Lady Herne added acidly, "but I should think that lady would be better off on a sofa." As Thomas fairly leapt to obey her, she directed her attention once again to her son. "I suppose I must despair of your ever developing any sort of sense of responsibility. What sort of explanation can you possibly offer me for—"

Aubrey cut her off smoothly. "Mama, I should like for you to meet my future wife."

He led the trembling Georgiana forward.

"Well, this is sudden, isn't it?" Lady Herne asked in the same tone of voice. Only Aubrey could see the softening light in her eyes. She took Georgiana by the hand.

"It is a pretty child. What is your name, dear?"

"Georgiana Chalford."

"One of the family, then." She turned to Aubrey with a sniff. "I suppose I should be surprised that you did not affiance yourself to a serving wench."

She directed her attention to Georgiana once again, but the harshness in her voice was gone. "And how old are you, my child?"

"Nineteen, your ladyship."

She considered the matter for a moment, then gave a short nod. "It will do, Aubrey. You might have looked a great deal higher, but according to my investigations the family is quite an old and respectable one in these parts."

Aubrey's eyes narrowed. "Just how did you come by your information, Mother?"

"Well, after the report I received from Bow Street, I naturally thought it best to make inquiries—"

"I told you so," said William explosively.

Aubrey bent to kiss his mother's porcelain cheek. "Well, you have your wish, Mother. I shall be a settled, respectable land-owner. I expect that Georgy will wish to spend most of our time at Herne, for she'll be busy investigating the cliffs for fossils."

"Aubrey," said Georgiana, embarrassed.

The viscountess gazed at them with a bemused expression. "Well, whatever you wish," she said with a sigh of resignation. "Now at least the *comte* and I may feel free to travel on the continent." She looked about her sharply. "Now, does anyone mean to offer me tea—or a chair, at least?" She looked at her son sternly. "You still have quite a bit of explaining to do."

Epilogue

Aubrey was hard at work in his study at Herne. He put down the account book he had been studying with a sigh. Really, the business of running an estate was so much harder than he had ever imagined. His estate manager had insisted that he look over the figures before his departure, to see if he approved the expenditures. All he had been able to accomplish so far was to give himself the beginnings of a throbbing headache. He picked up the book again, wearily.

Suddenly the door opened and a small figure dashed in, accompanied by a large hound. Emmy ran up to his desk and surveyed him with some desperation.

" 'Gusta says we can't take Lion with us to London,'' she told him.

He laid the book aside with well-concealed relief. "Augusta in this instance is correct,'' he told her with mock sternness.

Emmy's lower lip trembled tragically. "But *why*?'' she asked. "He won't be any trouble and I'll take care of him myself.''

Aubrey looked at her with a skepticism inspired by experience. "I, for one, do not intend to share my carriage with this large flea-ridden animal.''

Emmy's eyes were becoming moist. "He could ride in the other carriage,'' she offered.

He shook his head. "I do not intend for my valet to give me notice. He has enough difficulties with me as an employer.''

A large tear slipped down Emmy's cheek. "If Lion can't go, then I don't want to go!''

Aubrey pulled in a corner of his mouth. "That would be perfectly acceptable to me, but I doubt you'll be able to persuade Georgy so easily.''

A little sob escaped Emmy's lips. "I want to stay here with Lion!''

Alarmed, Aubrey tried another tack. "He can stay with Jem and his family. They promised they'd take good care of him."

Emmy's volume was increasing. "I don't want to go," she wailed.

Aubrey had leapt up, handkerchief in hand, but fortunately Georgiana appeared in the doorway.

"Emmy!"

"She doesn't want to leave the dog when we go to London," explained Aubrey.

Georgiana leaned down to give her little sister a hug. "It was very naughty of you to disturb Lord Herne in his study."

Emmy's lower lip was still pushed out obstinately. "But I won't leave Lion."

"Well, we'll see," said Georgiana conciliatingly. She shooed her youngest sister out the door and turned to her husband.

"Georgy, I am not riding all the way to London in the same carriage with that mongrel," said Aubrey warningly.

"Of course not, dear," she replied, as if incensed that he should think such a thing. "Of course, we may have to listen to Emmy howling the whole way."

The viscount gave a little sigh of defeat. The matter undoubtedly was settled already.

"I heard from Charlotte and William today," offered Georgiana by way of a distraction.

The viscount gave a rueful little smile. "Well, I must admit that we got the better of that bargain. How is your mother anyway?"

"They've persuaded her to remain at Chalton for a while. Charlotte says she enjoys peacocking her new London fashions in front of the neighbors." Georgiana gave a mischievous little smile. "It seems that some of them are almost as bad as the ones you helped her select."

Offended, Aubrey raised his eyebrows. "I did nothing more than encourage her natural taste," he said in his own defense.

"Well," said Georgiana. "Judging from their letters, I think William is heartily sick of Mother's company. It seems he's encouraging her to go abroad."

"Not a bad idea," he said, "if there is enough room in France for her and my mother both."

"I should think so," she said. She sat down in a chair beside him, her eyes suddenly troubled. "Aubrey, you . . . you don't really mind having my sisters here, do you?"

"You mean, I don't really mind having my home turned upside down," he began, but his face softened abruptly. "My world turned upside down when we met, my dear. I have become accustomed to it. Besides," he added, closing his account book with a sneaking sense of guilt, "what other man can boast of having a wife whose work is being presented to the Royal Society?"

Georgiana blushed. "It's Dr. Browne who will make the presentation."

"Ah, but the chief exhibit will be a mammalian jaw found in Oxfordshire by the Viscountess Herne."

"Oh, there's another thing I forgot to tell you," said Georgiana. "It appears that Godmama has persuaded Uncle Thomas to stand for Parliament."

"Respectable at last," murmured Aubrey.

"Speaking of respectability, my lord . . ."

He regarded her warily.

"Charlotte wrote that there is a certain wager being laid in the clubs in connection with you, but that William won't tell her what it is."

He looked at her with an aspect of innocence.

"Aubrey . . ." she said warningly.

"My dear," he protested, "how should I conjecture what it is? You know yourself that I haven't been in town for three weeks."

"Aubrey, I know you're up to something again."

"Convicted without a trial, I vow," he said, injured, though the wicked sparkle in his eyes gave him away.

"Aubrey," she said, rising up to advance toward him, her little smile at odds with her menacing tone.

He rose, his smile matching hers.

"I'll not be put off," she threatened.

Without warning, he pounced, his arms encircling her waist.

"My lord—"

He silenced her with a kiss. Her arms crept about his neck slowly to play with the tendrils of hair in back. She gazed into his eyes dreamily, then came awake suddenly.

"It won't work this time," she advised him.

"What?" he asked softly as his lips met hers again.

"This," she said in an abstracted way as his lips gently traveled down her neck. He nibbled delicately on her shoulder. She gave a shudder of pleasure.

"Aubrey," she breathed.

"What, my love?" he said, his voice husky.

"Aubrey . . ."

"Yes, my love?"

"Aubrey."

He smiled to himself for a moment before answering. "Yes, my love," he said obediently as he swept her off her feet and crossed the room to lock the study door.